Manhattan Grace

Grace to you!
Clarice G. James
Jer 29:11

Endorsements

As expected, Clarice G. James brings her signature wit and endearing characters to *Manhattan Grace*. Then she yanks the illusory rug out from under you with sentimentality, mystery, and a surprise twist. You'll be so glad you picked up this book!

—**Terrie Todd**, award-winning author of *The Silver Suitcase, Maggie's War,* and *Bleak Landing*

Manhattan Grace by Clarice G. James kept me up at night—laughing. James's wit with heart simply shines! Prepare to fall head-over-heels in love with the characters. They're quirky and loveable, exasperating and heartwarming. I can see this story play out on a movie screen.

—**Linda Brooks Davis**, award-winning author of *The Calling of Ella McFarland, A Christmas to Remember,* and *A Christmas Measure of Love*

James's mastery immediately draws you into the story through delightful, diverse, and colorful characters who portray simple but strong faith in everyday circumstances. Then, a sudden twist occurs, totally unexpected, making *Manhattan Grace* clever, surprising, and entertaining.

—**Rachel Britton**, author and speaker, co-director of reNEW Retreat for New England Writing

Clarice James skillfully navigates the complex worlds of acting, Jewish circumcision, and colorful relationships, with a bit of jewel thievery thrown in ... all with delicious wit and humor. Well crafted, well researched, *Manhattan Grace* serves up a feast that is sure to entertain.

—**Eleanor Gustafson**, author of *The Stones: A Novel of the Life of King David, Dynamo,* and *An Unpresentable Glory*

Manhattan Grace is packed with charming characters and a quota of questionable ones. Add to that a measure of mystery, a dose of drama, a helping of humor, words of wisdom, and the reward of romance, and you've got a rewarding read.

—**Janet Palmer Grunst**, award-winning author of *A Heart Set Free* and *A Heart for Freedom*

Manhattan Grace is filled with quirky and likable characters you'll fall in love with. The plot has that element of mystery that will keep you guessing until the very end. I guarantee if you begin reading *Manhattan Grace,* you won't put it down until you're done. And when you finish, you'll say, "That was a great read!"

—**Jeremiah Peters**, author of *A Message to Deliver*

Manhattan Grace is a delightfully fun and clever read, weaving an engaging story intertwining the lives of an aspiring actress, a mohel, and a thief. The plot grabs the reader from the very beginning and through those three lives ends in a series of twists and turns that brought a smile to my face and a tear to my eyes. *Manhattan Grace* is a win!

—**Kathy Collard Miller**, award-winning author of over fifty books including *Pure-Hearted: The Blessings of Living Out God's Glory*

A heartwarming story about delightful characters I enjoyed getting to know. Sprinkled with wit, encouragement, and intrigue, *Manhattan Grace* is Clarice James's best book yet!

—**Linda Shenton Matchett**, author of *Love's Harvest and Under Fire*

God is constantly working behind the scenes, refining us, in order to transform us to be more like His graceful and grace-filled image. Unmerited favor was a consistent theme throughout *Manhattan Grace* by Clarice G. James. A must read for anyone who wants to recount the times God has orchestrated the delicate details of their life together for good, and for His glory.

—**Stacey Thureen**, speaker and author of *Daily Wisdom for the Mommy-to-Be*

In *Manhattan Grace*, Clarice James brings readers a story about unexpected friendships and impossible dreams. With her trademark humor and sensitivity, she explores what it means to pursue our goals beneath a gracious God. Multiple points-of-view and an antagonist whose identity keeps readers guessing combine for a satisfying inspirational story.

—**Heidi Chiavaroli**, award-winning author of *The Hidden Side* and *Freedom's Ring*

With one-of-a-kind characters and a singular story, *Manhattan Grace* both delights and surprises with a Big Apple-sized twist.

—**Christy Brunke**, award-winning author of *Snow Out of Season*

Clarice G. James continues to create delightfully humorous worlds for the rest of us to play in. Her characters, quirks and all, are the tour guides who help us explore our own insecurities by revealing theirs. First baseball and family tensions in *Double Header*, then suddenly single with *Party of One*. Now, in *Manhattan Grace*, acting and international jewel thievery? Best not to ask what James will think of next. Just grab and go!

—**Michael Ehret**, freelance editor and author of "Big Love," a novella in *Coming Home: A Tiny House Collection*

Manhattan Grace

Clarice G. James

Elk Lake
PUBLISHING, INC.
PLYMOUTH, MASSACHUSETTS

Copyright Notice

Manhattan Grace

Cover Design: Jeff Gifford

Cover Photo of Model: Malcolm L. Tully of MT Photography, Savannah, GA
Model: Alyssa Skarin, Savannah, GA
Make-up Artist: Sheena Holmes, Savannah, GA
Stylist: Jessie Michelle, Savannah, GA
Interior Design: Cheryl L. Childers
Editors: Judy Hagey, Deb Haggerty

PUBLISHED BY: Elk Lake Publishing, Inc., 35 Dogwood Dr., Plymouth, MA 02360

Library Cataloging Data

Library Cataloging Data
Names: James, Clarice G. (Clarice G. James)
Manhattan Grace, Clarice G. James
406 p. 23cm × 15cm (9in × 6 in.)
Description: When a door opens for Gracie Camden to leave Cape Cod and move to Manhattan as a nanny for a Juilliard drama instructor, she fully expects God to use her acting talent and launch her to stardom. She'd been in New York for six months. What was taking God so long?
Identifiers: ISBN-13: 978-1-948888-12-7 (trade) | 978-1-948888-13-4(POD) | 978-1-948888-14-1 (e-book.)
Key Words: New York City, aspiring actress, God's plan for your life, Messianic Jewish mohel, surrender, Lincoln Center, jewel thief
LCCN: 2018944002 Fiction

Dedication

With love to my amazing daughter Erin C. Hennessey: You get me and encourage me, even when you think I'm crazy. What a priceless gift you are to me!

Acknowledgments

"Gracie Camden," my main character, was inspired by my young friend, Shannon Grace Loud Jovan. In fact, my writing a story where she plays the lead was mostly her idea. As a child, Shannon loved playing dress-up, being on stage or on the ice, and primping for her audience or any camera. Now, she's a wife and mother who's training her own daughter in the art of the selfie. Thanks, Shannon, for being such a great source of material.

Whenever I create a confident, tenacious, and delightful female character like "Gracie," my oldest granddaughter, Jessica Surro, is at the core of her being. Jessica's personality brings me such joy. I hope the readers find that in "Gracie."

The personalities of my characters "Miles" and "Leighton" were inspired by my two youngest grandchildren, Max and Margaux MacEacheron. For those readers who wonder if "Miles" is too advanced for his age, you have not met Max. "Leighton" gets all her sweetness from Margaux.

Much appreciation to my fellow writers and beta readers who made this book better for their comments and critiques: Michael Anderson, Ralph D. James, Cricket Lomicka, Susan W. Loud, Jeremiah Peters, and Terrie Todd.

Thanks to Konnie Viner who lent me her name for one of my characters. In real life, Konnie is as kind as my "Konnie" is not.

Thanks to a wellspring of talent in Savannah, GA: Malcolm L. Tully, of M.T. Photography who took the cover shot of lovely model, Alyssa Skarin. Thanks also to make-up artist, Sheena Holmes, and stylist, Jessie Michelle, for their services. Great job!

Working with talented graphic designer, Jeff Gifford, for another great cover was a pleasure.

Once again, many thanks to Deb Ogle Haggerty, Elk Lake Publishing Inc's dedicated, hardworking publisher. Thanks, Deb, for connecting me with skilled editor, Judy Hagey.

Every single day, I'm grateful to my husband David who blesses me with his wit, kindness, patience, and love.

Above all, thanks to God the Father through Jesus Christ his Son. *And whatever you do in word or deed, do all in the name of the Lord Jesus, giving thanks to God the Father through Him.* ~ Col 3:17 (NKJV)

Chapter One

February, Cape Cod

Gracie Camden shuddered as flames the color of a New Hampshire autumn lit up the black February sky, reducing the Barnstable Community Playhouse to gray ash and scorched stone. The raw evening sleet did nothing to cool its fervor—only intensified the stench of smoke.

With fellow cast and crew members, Gracie huddled across the street from where the oldest playhouse on Cape Cod had stood for nearly a century. A few were in tears, some in shock, but all were safe. Thankfully, the fire broke out a few hours before opening curtain, so no audience was present.

She was five when her grandmother, Temperance Camden—everyone, including Gracie, called her "Tempie"—introduced her to acting. She studied her craft and proved herself in bit parts for years. Her first major role at the BCP was young Helen Keller in *The Miracle Worker*. Season after season of solid performances in this landmark playhouse convinced Gracie she'd be discovered on that very stage.

Today could have been that day.

She'd lost count of the times people told her the role of Kat Hamilton in Bennett Noble's cult classic *Love and Waffles* must have been written with her in mind. Two weeks of standing ovations convinced her she'd nailed the part. Even Tempie agreed. And, after a half century working with the BCP, her eighty-two-year-old grandmother's opinion carried weight and not just with Gracie.

If that wasn't enough, Tempie had heard *a word* from God.

Then, one of the stagehands mentioned that his second cousin's husband's sister, a drama instructor at The Juilliard School in New York City, was in town and might attend a performance. That's when Gracie's hopes went up.

Right. Up in a cliché of smoke.

Being discovered wasn't the only thing that mattered to her. Working at the BCP was what gave her grandmother purpose. Apart from Tempie's two grown sons and her three grandchildren, the BCP players were family, the playhouse her second home.

In a way, this fire would leave them both homeless.

Ian Quinn showed up with Tempie twenty minutes after Gracie called him. In the three years they'd worked together at the Cranberry Fare restaurant, she and this black-haired, blue-eyed Irishman had become best friends. They'd bonded over their different career dreams—even on the nights they'd talked more about themselves than listened to each other.

Her grandmother wrapped her arms around her. "Are you all right, dear?"

"I'm not hurt if that's what you mean."

Staring at the smoking ruins, Tempie said, "I never thought I'd see this day. I expected to be gone long before this playhouse."

"If you'd been working upstairs in wardrobe, you might have—"

"But I wasn't, and no one else was hurt either." She kissed Gracie's cheek. "Let's thank the Lord for that."

"You're shivering." Ian draped Gracie's shoulders with the woolen blanket he kept in the trunk of his car. "This'll warm you."

Chin trembling, she pushed the cold and musty blanket off, uncovering a waitress costume, one of her few wardrobe changes in the play. "Thanks, but I prefer the scent of sopping cotton over wet wool."

Tempie turned Gracie around, "Come. You need to get out of these clothes."

"Why? Not like anyone will need them now." She didn't mean to be unreasonable, but this whole event had been unreasonable.

Ian steered her toward his car. "You've given your statement to the fire investigator. They'll call if they have any questions."

Her eyes flamed between tears. "Questions? I have a question. What am I supposed to do now?"

Tempie rubbed her back. "We can't do anything tonight. You're in no state to drive. I'll call your parents to let them know you're spending the night with me. We'll get your car in the morning."

At the mention of her parents, Gracie groaned. She could feel the pressure already. With the playhouse gone and her free time restored, her bachelor's degree wouldn't be enough. Her mother, a nurse practitioner, and her father, a financial planner with a dozen letters after his name, were all about security and benefits. Her grandmother was her only ally.

"Why, Tempie, why?" She stomped her foot like a child. "I thought you got a word from God? This can't be from him, it just can't!"

Three days later, Gracie stood in front of her bedroom closet, choosing an outfit for her first hostess shift at the Cranberry Fare since the fire. This was school vacation week, which made going back to work almost fun. She loved seeing the kids' reactions when she showed up in character. Today, she'd be Jessie from *Toy Story 2.*

She put on her jeans and cowhide chaps, then pulled on her boots. Her yellow-trimmed blouse was a near perfect match to Jessie's. Once she added her braided red wig and cowgirl hat—click!—she took a selfie and posted the pix.

Costumes at the Cranberry Fare hadn't always been the norm. The idea began innocently enough one Halloween when she showed up for her shift dressed as Lucy van Pelt from *It's the Great Pumpkin, Charlie Brown*. Playing dress-up naturally progressed to other holiday roles for kids, like Priscilla Alden at Thanksgiving and the Grinch at Christmas. One Easter, Gracie came as Moses from *The Ten Commandments* and told the kids the true story behind the movie.

When grown-ups began submitting requests and showing up to catch her mini-performances, the owner saw the value in Gracie's quirky sideline. He gave her a raise *and* a small clothing allowance. Now her closets and drawers overflowed into her grandmother's guest bedroom.

She checked herself in the mirror one last time. "The show must go on, Jessie." She tipped her hat. "Even if I have to perform in a restaurant instead of a theater."

After chatting with a few of her regulars, Gracie greeted a family of four. "Howdy, pardners!" She recited a few of Jessie's lines from the movie while showing them to their table.

The sandy-haired boy and his tow-headed sister were wide-eyed and giggling.

"You're Jessie!" the little girl said.

She hung her thumbs on her belt. "Sure am. The rootin'-est, tootin'-est cowgirl in the wild, wild west, missy."

"I'm not missy. My name is Weighton." She held up four fingers. "I'm this many."

Her older brother corrected her. "She means *Leighton.* My name is Miles. I'm seven." He studied her face. "And you're not Jessie."

The father tapped his index finger on the table. "Son, remember what we've told you about respecting adults?" Except for a dusting of gray at his temples, the man's hair was the same shade as his son's.

Miles's mother, a petite woman with an easy smile, didn't seem much older than Gracie. "Why do you say that, Miles?" The woman pushed her shiny black-brown hair behind her ears. "You know this young woman is playing a role, right?"

"Yeah, but I liked her better as Kat Hamilton."

The father glanced from his son to his wife. "Who's Kat Hamilton?"

Gracie stooped, eye level with the boy. "How do you know Kat Hamilton?"

"Mom and I saw you in *Love and Waffles* the other day. We clapped so much you had to come out and bow three times."

His mother took a second look at Gracie. "That *was* you. My son doesn't miss much." She extended her hand. "I'm Rachel Adler. This is my husband, Reggie. And, yes, you gave an impressive performance."

She did a half curtsey. "Thank you. I wouldn't be much of an actor if I didn't want to make an impression."

"What a shame about the fire," Rachel said. "So much history in that charming, old playhouse."

"Yes, I'm still in shock." Gracie wanted to lighten the mood. "So, Miles, you like the theater?"

"Yup. I'm an actor like you. I was in *Pirates of the Maccabeans* in temple school."

"I bet you were terrific!" she said. "How about you, Miss Leighton, are you an actor too?"

Leighton was quick to answer. "No, I'm Daddy's W-Little Princess."

Miles lowered his head and mumbled, "That's what Daddy calls her."

"I see." *Could these two kids be any more delightful?*

The bow-tied restaurant manager waved his arms around at his staff as if he were the maestro of the Boston Pops. Gracie caught his signal, indicating there were patrons to be seated.

"Okey-dokey, pardners. I've got to mosey along. Ya'll come back now." She leaned in to whisper. "But not on Thursdays. That's my day off."

The Adler family returned twice that week—on Wednesday when Gracie came in as Anna from *Frozen*, and on Friday, when she wore a pink tee, purple leggings, and pigtails as Boo from *Monsters, Inc.* The glee on Miles and Leighton's faces told her she was the reason they were there.

As the foursome slid into a booth, she handed them menus. "Now that you've found the Cranberry Fare, I hope we'll see more of the Adler family after school vacation."

Miles shook his head. "We live too far away."

Leighton nodded. "We have to go on the highway and stop three times to go potty. Then we're home."

"Really?" Gracie said. "Where do you live?"

Miles squiggled in his seat. "Manhattan. Like in New York City."

"Then you live in the greatest city in the world!" She meant what she said. "My dream is to live there one day."

"Is that so?" Rachel shared a look with her husband before reaching into her purse. She handed Gracie a card. "Call me. My sister's moving to Los Angeles. We're interviewing for a nanny. Maybe we can work something out."

She read the card. "Juilliard: Rachel Adler, Drama Instructor."

The first free moment she had, she texted Ian and Tempie: "You'll never guess in a billion years ..."

Chapter Two

July, Postville, Iowa

After a busy, air-conditioned shift at the Postville Bowling Alley, Seymour Kaufman talked to the Lord as he strolled home alone on this sweltering summer night. *What a good day this has been.* He smiled. *What am I saying, Lord? Every day with you is a good day.*

Seymour had rented his garden apartment sight-unseen when he moved from Des Moines to the small town of Postville, Iowa. Unfamiliar with real estate euphemisms, he had not realized that *garden* meant basement. Instead of flowers, grass, and people, his view was of weeds, litter, and legs from the knees down.

In the three years he had lived there, Seymour planted flowers, removed trash, and spoke with as many passersby as would listen. He considered tending God's garden in front of his very first home a privilege.

He picked up a cigarette butt and a crumpled bagel bag in the stairwell outside his door. As he stepped over the threshold, his phone rang. "Shalom. Seymour Kaufman speaking."

"Shalom. Aaron Ehrlich here. Your second cousin on your mother's side."

"I do not know my mother's family well." He paused, waiting to hear what this "long lost relative" was peddling. *Will his sales pitch be for solar panels or a new mortgage?*

"No? Our mothers were raised one village over from each other in Moldova."

"Sorry, I came to the States to live with my uncle on my father's side when I was orphaned at fourteen."

"That's not so bad. Let me tell you why I'm calling. I've heard about you all the way from New York City."

New York City. The home of Polina Zelenka. Seymour cleared that thought from his head. "Heard about *me*?"

"Want to know if the rumors are true. Are you a certified mohel *and* a follower of Yeshua?"

Seymour's interest piqued. "Yes … "

"Likewise. Mind if I ask you where you studied?"

"Not at all. I graduated from Ross Jewish Academy in Des Moines, then got my teaching degree at Drake University. After college, I got a position back at Ross."

"No, where did you study to become a mohel?"

Seymour thought back on the years of nights and weekends he had memorized the laws, sterilized instruments, and stocked supplies for Uncle Jacob.

"When God called me to the covenant, I apprenticed under my uncle, a well-respected mohel with an established practice. I attended him during all his *brises*. Once Uncle Jacob was satisfied I was sufficiently trained, I was certified by the Iowa Board of Rabbis."

"You continued to teach school as well?"

"Yes, for twenty-five years."

Aaron grunted. "And your mohel practice?"

Seymour cringed, remembering the years that had passed after his certification without him being asked to perform one single circumcision. "Des Moines had more than its fair share of mohels. Three years ago, I moved my practice—not that I had much of one—to Postville, about as far away from Des Moines as I could go without crossing into Wisconsin."

"You gotta gripe with Wisconsin?"

"None whatsoever. I just felt a certain allegiance to the Iowa Board for their certification. I do confess becoming a follower of Yeshua while residing under my orthodox uncle's roof may have expedited my relocation."

Aaron laughed. "I can see how that could happen. Tell me, are you committed to staying in Postville?"

"I am committed to obeying the Lord."

"Well, here in the tri-state area, we have a great shortage of mohels to serve our Messianic congregations. You won't have to be recertified either. I've got an extra room in my apartment, and I'm hardly ever there."

Seymour stroked his beard. "When did you have in mind?"

"I have nine brises on the books for tomorrow, and there are only three of us. The sooner you can get here the better. *Fershtay?* Understand?"

"I will need some time to pray." Even as he said the words, he sensed the Lord had already given him the answer.

With some trepidation, Seymour left Iowa, his sporadic mohel practice, and his bowling alley position for New York City. He trusted God to guide his every step. His sole obligation was to obey, even if obedience meant those steps might circle right back to Postville.

Which, he surmised, was a very real possibility whenever he thought of himself in the same city with someone as grand as Polina.

Chapter Three

August, Palm Beach, Florida

Hubris and greed were the downfalls of most professional thieves, but that would never be him. The Chief stuck to three hard-and-fast rules: One, he worked alone. Two, he stayed away from jobs that would make headlines. Three, he stole only what he needed to live well for six months, which enabled him to enjoy the finer things in life without the burden of ownership.

His business model made his spoils easier to fence and harder to trace too.

The Chief had taken advanced courses in sleight of hand and running a con from one of his non-royal classmates at an all boys boarding school in West Sussex, England. He'd honed these skills and added safecracking to his résumé during his four years at the University of London where he majored in jewels.

His natural affinity for languages was a boon in his trade. He was fluent in four and had mastered every accent he'd ever attempted. As a bonus, sign language and lipreading had come easily. If needed, he could stutter, stammer, and lisp with the best.

Because he worked alone, he stuck to smaller venues like art exhibits, charitable dinners, intimate political fundraisers, celebrity gatherings, private estate parties, and society weddings. His smile, charm, and style got him in the door. His mental acuity and physical agility got him out.

After only two weeks in Palm Beach, he'd vetted his latest mark—a nouveau riche, middle-aged divorcee with an insatiable need to be accepted by old money high society and enough pride to brag about everything she owned. The kind who'd rather collect the insurance settlement than admit she'd been duped.

To blend in at this black-tie-optional end-of-summer event, he wore his navy blue tuxedo with the peaked lapels and his patent leather slips-on. He slicked his hair back and added conservative glasses—the style eccentrics like Johnny Depp would never wear.

The limousine was waiting when the Chief exited the five-star hotel. Javier, his Cuban-born driver, stood by the door. He used Javier whenever he was in the area because he was prompt, discreet, and never asked questions.

The Chief tossed his leather carry-on in ahead of him while Javier put the rest of his luggage in the trunk. Although the party began at seven, he planned to arrive at 6:15, giving the illusion of a more intimate friendship. Being fashionably late was for amateurs. He'd be out of there by nine o'clock.

The car entered the estate through a set of white iron gates. The driveway swept around to the front of the massive two-story Georgian. Before he got out, he instructed Javier, "Call me precisely at 8:45. Lo entiendes? Understand?"

"Sí, yes, Chief."

Chief. He never tired of the moniker he'd earned in boarding school.

The over-tanned, over-bleached, over-Botoxed hostess greeted him at the door. "Bill Mason! I was so hoping you'd be the first to arrive."

"I as well." He smiled, not so much at her, but at himself for adopting the name of an infamous jewel thief from the 1970s. "Tiffani, you're a vision. That necklace—are those emeralds?—brings out the green in your eyes."

She offered him a drink, then gave him a full tour of the house and grounds, including the master suite and her custom dressing room. While he raved about the craftsmanship and character of the old home, the silly woman boasted about her impregnable safe.

As they'd agreed beforehand, Tiffani introduced him to her guests as an import-export executive. When she did so to select female friends, she held his arm and purred as if there were more to her relationship with him.

As the evening wore on, the guests wore on him. The noise level increased exponentially with their alcohol intake. About 8:20, he slipped upstairs and got what he came for. Tiffani had left her hard-to-crack safe door ajar—pathetic woman—so his main event was rather anticlimactic.

A few minutes later, he was standing by his hostess when his phone rang. "Yes? ... What happened? ... How bad is he? ... Of course, I'll get a flight out to Chicago tonight."

Dripping with sympathy—for what, she didn't know—Tiffani said, "Bill, dear, is there anything I can do to help?"

He hung his head. "No. My father had an accident. I must go." He kissed her on the cheek and promised to call her in the morning.

Walking through the crowded room toward the front door, he challenged himself with some sleight of hand. He pocketed four jewel-encrusted gold bracelets and two watches—a Breitling and a Rolex. He left the lesser of the bracelets hanging out of the tuxedo pocket of one of the more priggish guests.

Javier was waiting. "Any stops before the airport, Chief?"

"No, my flight leaves in an hour."

On the short trip to the airport, he rearranged things in his carry-on. The car stopped a few feet from an express mail drop box.

How perfect.

After tipping Javier well, he climbed out. The Chief waited until the limo had eased back into traffic before he dropped a package into the gaping, orange mouth of the big, white box.

Stretching out in first class on his flight to New York, he amused himself, imagining how the police investigation might go …

> "Ma'am, what can you tell us about this Bill Mason, the man who left early?"
>
> "It's *Miss*, Officer."
>
> "Miss, yes. He was in the import-export business?"
>
> "Well, no. That's what he told me to tell everyone so he wouldn't be bothered."
>
> "What was he really?"
>
> "He was an investment banker from Switzerland."
>
> "Was he Swiss?"
>
> "Well, he had an accent. But I'm certain of one thing, he's not a thief. I would have known."
>
> "Of course, ma'am."
>
> "Again, Officer, it's *Miss*, but you can call me Tiffani."

> The officer turned his attention back to the cocky man with the movie star sunglasses. "Now, Mr. Pomfrit, tell me again how you came by this bracelet?"

The Chief put his seat back, closed his eyes, and smirked. I should write a book someday.

Chapter Four

September, Manhattan, New York

During the past six months as Reggie and Rachel Adler's live-in nanny, Gracie had fallen in love with their children. Seven-year-old Miles was a prodigy of sorts—and a challenge with a bent toward drama. Four-year-old Leighton with her Minnie Mouse voice and sweet spirit was a champion at melting hearts.

As on many of their mornings together, Gracie stood on a milk-crate stage in the middle of her airy, third-floor suite, playacting with her charges. Dressed in a green and gold brocade vest atop her pink flannel pajamas, she donned a silk, Elizabethan plumed cap, then smiled at the memory of Tempie's repeated admonition: "Remember, one always *dons*, never puts on, an Elizabethan cap."

Gracie began her monologue: "If 'All the world's a stage, and all the men and women merely players …'" She paused for dramatic effect. "… then New York City is Central Casting."

Leighton clapped and cheered, but Miles popped up from his front-row-center seat on the floor and waved his hands like a mad director. "That's not how it goes!"

Stepping off the stage, Gracie bowed low and made a sweeping arc with her feathered cap. "Then might you help me, kind sir?"

He exhaled and reached for the cap. "I'll show you one more time." Climbing onto the crate, Miles positioned himself on an imaginary mark. He folded one arm behind his back and held the cap over his heart with the other. Echoing a juvenile Sir Lawrence Olivier, he projected, "'All the world's a stage, and all the men and women merely players. They have their exits and their entrances. And one man in his time plays many parts.'"

Gracie yelled, "Bravo! Well done."

Leighton scrambled to her feet and clapped. "See, Milesy, I'm giving you a standing novation."

He beamed at his sister without bothering to correct her—just this once.

Though clearly, Miles inherited his talent from his mother, Gracie was still amazed a second grader could recite lines from Shakespeare … or would want to.

Her mantle clock chimed on the half hour. "Take one last bow before Daddy comes looking for you. You can't be late for your first week of school."

Leighton snuggled up to her. "How come you're not taking us?"

"Because I have a casting call today, remember?" She loved saying that, even if the call was only for an NYU student film, not paid, with no guarantee of an audition.

Miles laughed. "Hope you remember your lines better than you did this morning."

She tickle-chased them into the hallway, where they promptly collided with their dad.

Reggie Adler recovered his balance and grinned like he always did when his kids were around. "Easy you two. If you break Daddy, I'll miss my important meeting."

He straightened his tie, a perfect complement to his navy blue suit and plaid shirt. His hair was still damp from a shower after his usual morning workout at the nearby gym.

Gracie never did have a full grasp on what Reggie did for a living. He had one of those ambiguous VP-of-Something titles, which seemed logical for someone in his late thirties, in some sort of boring investment—or insurance?—company. After a while, she was too embarrassed to ask him again.

She had no problem remembering what Rachel did—especially since part of her benefits package as their nanny included coaching from Rachel, a drama instructor at Juilliard. Gracie was convinced getting this job was one of those "God things" Tempie always went on about.

Stop musing, Camden, and get dressed.

She treasured her collection of knock-off designer clothes and costumes. But being in this city surrounded by professionals, there'd be no more playing dress-up to recreate parts made famous by others. Now her mission was to own every part she played. Still, despite her declaration, whenever Gracie slipped into a famous costume or dress, she slipped into a character she loved.

What to wear today? Since the student film was set in the early 1950s, the iconic look of Audrey Hepburn in *Roman Holiday* while riding behind Gregory Peck on his Italian scooter would be perfect. She picked out a flared skirt, wide belt, white short-sleeved blouse, and a small striped scarf. The outfit was reminiscent of Audrey's less formal, pre-Givenchy, pre-*Breakfast at Tiffany's* days.

Surveying her reflection in her full-length, three-paneled mirror—her biggest and most useful bargain find since her move to New York—she twirled to see herself from all angles.

"Magnifique! If Edith Head's costume design style could do it for Audrey Hepburn, then the same can do it for you."

She curled her hand around her French twist, checking for stray brunette wisps, and fiddled with her bangs. Gracie could have penciled in thicker brows, added red lipstick, and shaded her cheekbones to make them appear higher, but she would have looked too much like Audrey. She wanted to exude the *feel*, that *je ne sais quoi*, which had catapulted the young gamine into fame.

She studied her outfit again. A touch of modernity was needed. No way did she want Harper Bellamy, her friend with the too-perfect stage name—and face and figure to match—to accuse her of cloning Audrey. She switched her striped scarf for one with a bold, botanical print, added a royal blue cardigan, and exchanged her black flats for her apple-green platform sandals with the floral detail.

Now she was ready. Click! And post.

When the subway train began to move, Gracie closed her eyes to calm herself. She conceded she had substantially more competition in New York City than on Cape Cod. A casting director could fill any part in any movie in any language with one walk through Lincoln Center, Times Square, or Greenwich Village, if the film were quirky. As culturally rich as New York was, the Cape was not. Well, except for a smattering of Wampanoag Indians, Cape Verdeans, Brazilians, and the ever-growing population of AA members.

When the car jerked to its first stop, her eyes flew open, her apple-green platforms in full view. She smiled, wiggled her feet, and mouthed, *Love these shoes.* She drew her feet under the seat as new commuters climbed aboard and shuffled by.

A plumpish, bearded man, maybe a few years older than her father, sat across the aisle. He was dressed all in black—suit, overcoat, shoes, and gloves. He could have been Amish, but for the fact he was on the subway. She decided on Jewish, maybe orthodox.

The one unorthodox thing about his appearance—if anything could be classified as unorthodox in New York—was his multi-colored, crocheted eye patch. She wondered about his eye. Was he hiding a sty? Was the eye black and blue? Or was it missing? And how tricky was it to get his temple leaders to agree to this colorful patch?

She knew staring wasn't polite, so she only did so when he wasn't looking.

On his lap, he held a medium-sized, black nylon bag with pockets on both sides. He had the wide shoulder strap wrapped around his gloved hand. *Lunch sack? Camera case?* No, his tight grip suggested the contents were more valuable.

When their eyes met—all three of them—she and the man nodded politely at one another.

Gracie deduced he must be one of the many Jewish men who work in the diamond district. If so, his case would contain tools, maybe even uncut stones. And spending monotonous hours peering through a monocular loupe, evaluating diamonds for color, clarity, cut, and carat, could be exhausting to an eyeball, which could explain the patch.

By the time the train squealed to her stop, and the doors whooshed open, Gracie and the man had made a connection, of sorts. She smiled at him before stepping out onto the platform. If she'd had a few more minutes, she might have given him a tip—"Hold onto that bag. If I figured out its contents were valuable, then others more streetwise than I will too."

At the casting location, Gracie scanned the mooing herd for Harper, the first friend she'd made in New York. They'd appeared together in a garage-band-type play, *Powerless to Pump*, a story of urbanite breastfeeding angst.

They hadn't exactly *won* their roles in that production. The producer-playwright was one of Rachel's former Juilliard students. Since the young woman couldn't afford to pay cast members *and* the rent for audition space and a theater, Rachel helped her glean a cast of seven from her drama classes, throwing Gracie in with the deal. As for Harper, her father owned considerable interest in the building where the sixty-seat theater was located.

Although *Powerless to Pump* had been advertised as a satire, half the breastfeeding audience hoped the play would lessen their anxiety. The other half came to laugh. The acrimonious mix resulted in some loud heckling and at least one hair-pulling match. Sadly, the opposing online reviews contributed to the play's short run.

She waved when she spotted Harper. "There you are! What time did you say the doors open?"

"Ten." Harper reapplied her lipstick.

"Did you find out the director's name?"

"No, but he's some hunky up-and-comer." Harper paused a second. "I've got first dibs."

"On what?" she laughed. "A part or the director?"

Harper tossed her blonde hair and batted her magnetic false eyelashes. "Why not both?"

Gracie perused the line, recognizing many from previous auditions. But there were always new faces. The girl in front of them had flown in from South Dakota. The sisters behind them were from Philly. Another actor was from Australia.

Sheesh. As if New York didn't have an overabundance of wannabes already.

Like you, Gracie?

She ignored her conscience, which could be so sarcastic.

The closer she moved to the head of the line, the more psyched she got. She'd read the script and character sketches. She matched the physical description of at least one of the major roles. All she needed was a chance to act.

"What's with the grin?" Harper nudged her. "Know something I don't?"

"I have a feeling, that's all. This audition might be a breakthrough."

"A breakthrough for you or for both of us?"

Harper would never understand about God and the gifts and talents he'd given Gracie and how he planned to use them, so all she said was, "We'll see."

She reached the front of the line a moment before the crew broke for lunch. Every bit of her wanted to cry. Why would God make her wait now? She answered her own question. *Because the reward with be worth the wait.*

When the crew returned forty-five minutes later, Gracie was poised for her cue.

Instead, some guy dressed in skinny jeans and an NYU tee shirt shouted, "Thanks, everyone. We've got what we need. The rest of you can go."

She stiffened. "I can't believe he just did that!"

Harper puffed. "No? After six months, you're still not used to rejection?"

Gracie surveyed her carefully planned outfit. "And whoever said 'clothes make the difference' was wrong."

All the way home she mentally laid on the floor, kicking and screaming. *What was that all about, God? Not even a reading? Why give me the gifts if you're not going to use them?*

Chapter Five

The girl on the subway reminded Seymour Kaufman of the young women in the art deco posters he had seen years back at the Des Moines Art Center—fresh-faced, good-natured, and colorful. When she stretched out her legs and moved her feet back and forth, smiling like a preteen at her bright green shoes, Seymour smiled too ... on the inside.

My! Such a simple thing as shoes can make a woman happy. I have so much to learn. And so kind she was to bless me with her smile. Yes, I smiled back, he argued with the Pharisee lingering in him. *What? A person should not be polite to someone dressed in colors? God created color! He would never be so rude.*

Like this young woman, Seymour was not ashamed to show his joy. He knew he was blessed. Not because of his shoes, which were plain, black, and utilitarian, but because God had a perfect plan for him.

Seymour had refused to be dissuaded from his calling as a mohel, even when those of lesser faith pointed out conditions that might not bode well for his business: First, he had only one eye.

Second, he had two fingers missing from his right hand. Despite these anatomical shortcomings, God had *called* him, which to him meant his abilities were more than sufficient.

His answer to naysayers had always been the same: "Hallelujah! Having one eye has sharpened my peripheral vision, and my two missing fingers merely give me more room to work. Such a blessing every mohel should have."

He had lived long enough to know wherever he settled, most families would likely prefer a mohel who had both eyes and all his digits. However, since there had been a dearth of mohels in the poor town of Postville, Seymour had found clients. His practice had grown there as well as his faith in Yeshua.

That was then. Now, he was on his way to perform his first bris in Brooklyn for a Messianic Jewish family. Seymour repositioned himself in his seat, raised his eye to heaven, and whispered, "Praise, God! Your plan is even greater than I ever imagined."

As miles go, Brownstone Brooklyn seemed much closer to Manhattan on the map than in the subway with all the stops and train changes. He was relieved he had listened to his cousin Aaron and left early.

Although Seymour had lived in the United States for thirty-seven years and had had formal lessons in English, he often fell into the cadence of his Eastern European accent. The closer he got to the house, the more his concern grew. His fears were allayed when he entered the three-story brownstone and met the family and friends whose accent far outweighed his.

"*Shalom aleikhem*, peace be upon you." The host greeted him with more honor than he had been accustomed to in Postville. Seymour could not ignore the irony, for he was the one who felt honored to perform the *mitzvah*, commandment, on their eight-day-old boy.

He returned the greeting. "*Aleikhem shalom*, upon you be peace."

The parents directed him to the living room where the ceremony would take place. He washed his hands before and after he laid out his sterilized instruments on a clean white cloth. After the grandmother carried the baby into the room on a large pillow, she handed him to the grandfather, whose role as *sandek* was to hold the baby during the circumcision.

"*Baruch Ha-Ba*. Blessed be the one who has arrived." Seymour recited a blessing to acknowledge the commandment about to be fulfilled.

Once he completed the circumcision, with only a few cries from the infant and one whimper from the father, he took a cup of wine and recited a special prayer announcing the baby's Hebrew name before placing a drop of wine in the infant's mouth. The parents drank the rest of the cup.

The whole bris took less than fifteen minutes.

No celebration was complete without food. *Mazel Tov!* Jewish people knew how to feed their guests. The dining room table was loaded with lox and bagels, tuna salad sandwiches, latkes with *smântână* or sour cream, stuffed peppers, and a variety of baked goods.

Once he had enjoyed a small feast and spent an hour kibitzing with the family and their guests, he rose to leave. As he said his goodbyes, the baby's proud father thanked him again and handed him an envelope.

Considering the service a privilege and a commandment, mohels do not often price their services. If asked what amount was acceptable, most would reply, "Whatever you can afford." In Postville, that usually meant between five and twenty dollars.

The grandmother followed him out the door and handed him three freezer bags of food. She grinned. "I put extra sour pickles in there, the ones you like."

"*A sheynem dank!* Thank you very much! There must be a full week of lunches here."

Seymour guarded the food on the subway almost as well as he did his mohel kit. When he arrived home, he stowed the bags in the refrigerator.

Aaron scuffed into the kitchen, still wearing his slippers and plaid robe. The sparse hair on his head flew in all directions. "Tell me, how did your first bris go?"

"Very well, thank you. And your day off?"

"Quiet. Slept in, read the *Post*, did the crossword puzzle." Aaron opened the refrigerator door and grabbed one of Seymour's bags. "You mind?"

"Not at all." Well, he did mind a little, but there was plenty to share.

When Seymour draped his suit jacket over a kitchen chair, the envelope he'd been given slipped out of his pocket. He lifted the flap. "What is this? Benjamin Franklin?" He looked again. "Oy vey! Someone made a mistake. There is five hundred dollars in here."

Aaron took a bite of a pickle. "You expected more?"

"More?" Seymour was confused. "Is this *usual* in New York?"

His cousin laughed. "There is no usual in New York. Sometimes you get less, other times triple that amount. You're not in Postville anymore."

Seymour contemplated the economies of scale in both locations. Then, remembering his freezer bags, he was grateful both Postville and Brooklyn had this one custom in common.

Chapter Six

"Miles, Leighton, guess what we're doing after school today?" Gracie knew they'd be excited.

Miles eyeballed her. "You're not taking us to the dentist, are you?"

She chuckled. "No. We're meeting Zeke and Eli at the park." Zeke was in Miles's class at school, and his brother Eli was a year behind.

Leighton squealed, and Miles pumped his skinny boy arms. "Yes!"

With no pre-K that day, Leighton was home. The afternoon passed slower than a four-year-old could handle. Her refrain every few minutes was "Can we go now?"

Around two thirty, Gracie packed her nanny ICE backpack with the mini first aid kit, yellow ducky owie freezer pack, crackers, and juice boxes. And, because she never knew when a need would present itself, she added her makeup repair case.

Leighton skipped and sang by her side the whole way to the school. Gracie collected the three boys, then sidetracked a few blocks to the park. As soon as they reached the playground, the children ran straight for the jungle gym.

"Kids, I'll be on the bench if you need me."

Halfway to the top already, Miles yelled, "What bench?"

"That one." Gracie swung her arm around to point to the bench behind her ... and smacked a man right in the face.

He jerked back. "Ahh!"

"Yikes! I am so sorry. Are you okay?"

The man from the subway. The diamond cutter. The one with the multicolored eye patch.

His hand flew to his injured eye. She wasn't sure if he was signaling "rock on" or signing "I love you," until she realized he was missing his two middle fingers.

Was diamond cutting that dangerous?

"I will be fine." He chuckled. "I stooped to avoid a tree limb and hit your limb instead."

She took hold of his arm to guide him to the bench. "Let me give you a hand ... uh, help you. I didn't mean to blind you, um, blindside you." *Really, Gracie?*

She dug through her backpack and handed him the cold pack tucked inside its yellow ducky terrycloth cover. "Hold this on your eye to prevent swelling."

"Thank you, miss." He scrunched the pack against his eye.

The cockeyed duck scowled at the man's psychedelic patch.

To distract him, as if she hadn't already, she raised her voice. "You know, I believe I was seated across from you on the subway yesterday."

Why was she loud-talking to a blind man?

He dabbed at his watery eye with the duck. "The subways are

so crowded. You must have an excellent memory."

"How could I not remember a man dressed in black with a …" She was about to point to his crocheted patch but ran her hand over her hair instead. "Uh … you were holding a black bag." Confessing that sounded kind of creepy, like she'd been watching him. Which, of course, she had. "How's your eye? The one I hit?" *D'oh.*

"Much better." He removed the pack and peeked out. "Ah, the girl with the pretty green shoes."

She teased him. "Now who's the one with the excellent memory?"

Miles yelled over to her. "Look! I'm almost at the top."

Zeke chimed in. "Me too."

"I'm watching," she called back. "Be careful."

Eli and Leighton played nearby in the sandbox.

Holding the ice pack in his hand, her new acquaintance said, "Your children are quite charming."

"I can't take the credit. I'm the nanny for two of them, and the other two are their friends." She extended her hand. "Grace Camden."

He shook it. "Seymour Kaufman."

"I don't think I've seen you at the park before, Mr. Kaufman."

"Seymour, please. I have been in New York less than a month. Staying with my cousin, two blocks south. Formerly of Des Moines, here by way of Postville, Iowa."

"Mind my asking what brought you to New York?"

He gazed beyond Gracie like he was unsure he wanted to answer her question. Repositioning himself on the bench, he faced her. "I could say work. However, that would not be the entire truth. If I am to be honest, I am pursuing a woman, quite possibly love."

Now that she had not expected. "How romantic."

"My pursuit is not an easy one. Of course, you may know about these matters already."

"The only thing I know for sure is romance can get in the way of my career."

"As a nanny?"

"No, as an actor."

His head bobbed slowly. "An exciting profession to be sure."

"Not too exciting yet. But Tempie, that's my grandmother, says she recognized natural talent in me when I was five. She says the Lord will make good use of what he's given us." Since Gracie was convinced he was Jewish, she felt comfortable in bringing up God.

"Your grandmother sounds like a great encourager."

"Yes, she is. And I've been very clear with the Lord, so he knows how to answer my prayers."

He stroked his beard. "I see. You have been instructing God?"

Gracie hesitated for a moment. "Well, not instructing so much as praying specifically."

"There is a difference?"

She snorted. "Now you sound like Tempie."

Before their conversation could continue, she had to break up a fight between Miles and Zeke. Once the matter was settled amicably, Leighton complained Eli had fallen asleep.

Gracie sighed. "I'd better check on him."

"I will let you get back to your duties." Seymour stood.

"I enjoyed our chat," she said. "I hope we bump into each other here again."

He tipped his hat and handed her the half-melted ducky. "That would be lovely, Grace. We can report on how God chooses to intervene in our quests."

"I like that idea. Maybe we should exchange phone numbers?"

Seymour hesitated a moment. "Why not?"

They pocketed each other's business cards.

"To good news then," Gracie said.

"Indeed." He waved as he walked away.

Gracie gently nudged Eli awake. "Are you okay, sweetie?"

He yawned, then closed his eyes again.

She called over to the other boys. "Come along, kids, I think we need to get Eli home."

A minor protest by the two older boys was handled with one no-nonsense nanny scowl.

Leighton fashioned a telescope by curling her hands, then peeped at Seymour. "Mommy says not to talk to strangers."

"Mommy's right. But I know that man from the subway."

Leighton spoke with matter-of-fact innocence. "Then why did you hit him?"

Miles stopped midstride. "What?" A look of vague alarm crossed his face. "You hit a man?" He sounded like he was going to report her to the police.

Wide-eyed, Zeke asked, "Why? Is he a mugger?"

"It was an accident," Gracie said. "And, no, he's not a mugger."

Miles asked, "What is he?"

"He's ... he's a diamond cutter."

"Why does he cut diamonds?" Miles ran past her.

Gracie sighed. "Miles, has anyone ever told you that you ask too many questions?"

"Yup." He laughed and scuffed on ahead. "You!"

To get their mind off strangers and muggers, she had them all race to the sidewalk. Miles and Zeke took off. Leighton did her best to keep up, but Eli lagged behind.

Gracie took his hand in hers. "Eli, do you feel okay?"

He rubbed his eyes. "I'm sleepy."

When they reached the boys' home, Gracie spoke with their nanny, Marisol, who'd been with the family since before the boys were born.

Marisol hugged Eli. "He hasn't been himself lately. No fever, but his energy seems low."

"I noticed. You might want to tell his parents he fell asleep in the sandbox with a bucket on his head."

Chapter Seven

Seymour chided himself as he walked back to his cousin's place. "You old fool. What prompted you to reveal such personal information to a complete stranger, when you have not even told the one you hope to see here?" At the tail end of a deep sigh, he whispered, "Polina, what will you think when you learn I have moved to New York?"

He had been introduced to the famed opera soprano Polina Zelenka six months back when she had come to Postville for her nephew's bris where he was the attending mohel. Seymour had never met a woman like her before, such grace and presence. He could still see her creamy, flawless complexion and her golden hair swept up on one side, held by a mother-of-pearl comb. Even her smile was not put-on like other famous people on magazine covers.

Having lived like an old bachelor *with* an old bachelor for most of his life, Seymour had no experience with single women. Unless you count the time he had his hair cut by Batya, the lady barber, who filled in for Irving when he had gout in both elbows.

Or the time he trimmed the fat off a brisket for Uncle Jacob's seventy-five-year-old housekeeper with arthritis. Or more recently at the park when he got tangled up with that angry woman walking all those dogs.

Seymour did not immediately attribute the discomfort he had felt in Ms. Zelenka's company to any sort of physical attraction. Instead, he blamed the MSG in the gefilte fish he had had the day before. No matter the reason, the world spun faster the moment he met her, which was disconcerting since he had yet to perform the bris.

Yet, God was faithful to answer his prayer. Seymour completed the ceremony with steady hands. No one was the wiser, except perhaps the eight-day-old child who had been crying the whole time anyway, so it was hard to tell.

When the *seudate mitzvah* meal was laid out after the ceremony, Polina was the one who filled a plate, served him, and sat beside him. Instead of recounting stories from her glamorous life on the opera stage, she expressed interest in him, marveling at his simple service to God as a mohel.

She was as enchanting as her public claimed. Considered royalty by many, yet she made Seymour feel like a king. Learning they shared a common faith in Yeshua confirmed Seymour's infatuation.

The following morning, he purchased one of her CDs, "Arias by Polina." Her voice was as strong as steel and as smooth as silk, taking his breath and making him shiver.

For weeks after their meeting, Seymour sought God for relief from these unfamiliar feelings and for wisdom on what to do about them. "God, what do you want me to see about this woman? Are we to become friends … or more? Please, Lord, direct my path and confirm your will to me."

A few months later, Polina reappeared at a *bar mitzvah* celebration for her third cousin who happened to be his butcher's son. Seymour's heart danced the *hora* at the sight of her even before Uncle Moishy, an entertainer hired all the way from Des Moines, could start performing with his monkey. When Polina approached Seymour with another smile and another plate of food, he had to relearn how to chew.

He prayed daily, "Oh God, oh God, is this the confirmation I have been seeking?"

When Seymour woke the next morning, his fear of seeing Polina had been replaced by a determination to find her. *Why?* Was his new resolve connected to the conversation he had had with the young woman in the park? Perhaps speaking out loud of his search for answers, and possibly love, had made a difference.

Ershter das ershter, first things first. He needed to let Polina know he was here. Simple, but not so easy since they did not exactly sing in the same circles. And, the two times they had been in each other's company, he had not thought to ask for her number. How does a man think of something when he cannot think at all?

Even if he knew where she lived, which he did not, he could not stop by unannounced, could he? No. That would be rude. He considered staking out the opera house on the remote chance of running into her. The idea that some might mistake his staking for stalking was not a risk he was willing to take.

Still lying in bed, he reached for his laptop and searched "Polina Zelenka." There she was. So lovely, so regal, so elegant. And so out of reach. He had been naïve enough to assume that since she lived in New York City, she would likely perform here solely. He was dismayed to discover she would be singing in San Antonio today, then move on to Sun Valley, Chicago, and Buffalo before she returned home. Even then, there were numerous venues in New York to consider.

The knowledge that the cities where she toured were far more sophisticated than Postville, or even Des Moines, was not lost on him. Indeed, he was the one who was lost.

"I know! I could attend one of her performances." An ideal solution until he checked the price of tickets. Based on his uncertain income and the cost of living in New York, he might need to tap his savings. Even so, his attendance did not guarantee he would win an audience with Polina.

Maybe he could write to her via her fan club or website? Did celebrities read their own mail? What exactly would he say? "Hello, I am the one-eyed mohel who looked like he had eaten some bad *kishke* at my butcher's son's bar mitzvah. Remember, we talked while Uncle Moishy danced the hora with his monkey?"

Seymour fell back against his pillow. "Impossible." But the second that word was out of his mouth, he sprang back up. "But my God is the God of the impossible! How could I, of all men, have forgotten?"

Chapter Eight

Whenever the Chief was in New York, he stayed at the Carlyle Hotel, which afforded him what he needed—classic style and a conservative clientele with potential. For this particular visit, the hotel's location near Lincoln Center was the greater asset.

In the few weeks since he'd been back in the city, he'd scouted the Center numerous times. Knowing the general layout of this large parcel of real estate and the floor plans of the Metropolitan Opera was imperative.

Once he got a feel for the place, he could more easily root out undercover security personnel and spot repeat visitors, often indicative of point men. The multi-million-dollar plunder would surely draw serious professionals. Nevertheless, since many were well known to both US and global authorities, he doubted they'd be here this early. And that was to his advantage.

The prize was worth the extra time and cost of his advanced surveillance.

When he observed an Air Tech HVAC team going in and out of the Met, he made small talk with one of the tradesmen. "Must be a big job. I've seen your vans around a lot."

"Yup. Have to bring all the units up to code in all fourteen stories. Serious time involved."

Raising an eyebrow, the Chief said, "And serious overtime pay."

The guy snickered. "Bingo! With all the nights and weekends I'm workin', the only thing I'll be shovelin' this winter is sand on a Cancun beach."

Hmm. Their presence might come in handy.

The Chief returned to his hotel room. After ten minutes of searching the internet for HVAC uniforms, he found the exact one the Air Tech team wore. A few phone calls later, and he had rush-ordered coveralls, a hard hat, dust masks, safety glasses, and work gloves. Then, he offered his Bronx connection for false documents a bonus to put Air Tech work order forms at the top of his list. Now, if another disguise was needed, he'd be prepared.

With that task accomplished, he dressed for the afternoon wedding. He'd been itching for an entertaining diversion when he'd read a half-page ad in the *New York Times* announcing the Third Annual Canine Nuptials Ceremony in the Conservatory Garden in Central Park. "Let's celebrate and affirm our dogs' loving relationships by helping them bond legally." Photos of previous ceremonies showed numerous pet parents flashing expensive ice and sparkle among the resplendent doggie brides and grooms.

At first, he couldn't believe what he read. Then he couldn't resist going.

The setting was like any other wedding, except for the barking and the poop patrol armed with teal green scoops and matching plastic baggies.

An usher of the human persuasion greeted him as he approached an aisle runner. "A friend of a bride or a groom?"

"Bride, please." He was seated on the left.

The vows were taken en masse, except for one basset hound couple who insisted on howling their own promises. The Chief made sure to congratulate only those who wore the most interesting and valuable pieces. More than once, that was a canine. Jewels were jewels.

Although the reception was decent, he couldn't take the barking and growling much longer than an hour. He was about to leave when a fiftyish woman sidled up to him. Her cocktail dress and jacket had the aroma of money.

"Such a lovely ceremony," she said. "Who were you here for?"

"Coco, one of the brides." Sounded feasible to him.

The woman searched his face. "I know you from somewhere, but I can't quite place where. Aspen? Maybe Napa? … I know, Palm Beach! You were at Tiffani's party the night she was robbed, weren't you?"

"Palm Beach? Robbery? I must have a double somewhere who's living a far more interesting life than I am. But I would love to hear more about Palm Beach." He tugged his jacket sleeve down to hide the Rolex he'd kept as a souvenir of that job.

"You must visit!" She rattled on about her *exclusive* gated community and her *exclusive* yacht club with its *exclusive* five-star epicurean menu.

When a third person joined their conversation, he excused himself "for a minute" and slipped out of the park and onto Fifth

Avenue. A half block up, he placed his glimmering take in a prepaid cardboard envelope, then dropped it in his friendly express mail drop box.

Fait accompli.

Chapter Nine

Gracie opened her laptop for her Sunday night video chat with her grandmother. "So, Tempie, what trouble have you been into this week?"

"None. Couldn't find any. Outside of my semi-regular lunch date with your Ian on Monday—he's a blessing, that one—I caught up on my correspondence and tried to fill a few journal pages, which wasn't easy since I had nothing to write about."

Gracie was charmed that her grandmother still handwrote all her notes and letters.

"To add to that bit of excitement," Tempie said with a hint of droll, "I put my years as a seamstress to good use and worked on some costumes for the playhouse."

"Construction hasn't even begun. How do ya know which shows they'll do and which costumes to make?"

"I don't. That's why I'm doing simple capes and hooded robes." She held two up to show Gracie. "Dark colors for the bad guys, light colors for the good guys. Between the Cape Cod

Confiscation Commission and the *Hysterical* Society, I have my doubts that playhouse will ever be rebuilt."

"But aren't they building on the same site?"

Furrows rippled across her grandmother's forehead. "Yes, and that's half the problem—historic King's Highway. The other half is the cost to comply with current regulations. Pffft. Maybe they'd approve the plans faster if we agreed to rebuild in the woods behind the old county jail."

Gracie chuckled. "Frustrated?"

"You think?" Tempie pressed her hands to her cheeks. "What's more, I'm bored. So much so your parents noticed and want me to join their bridge club."

"I didn't know you played bridge." Somehow, she managed to keep a straight face.

"I don't," Tempie grumped. "And, as long as I have a say, I never will."

Gracie couldn't hold back her laughter any longer.

"You think my dilemma is funny?"

"I can't help myself. The picture of you at a card table, bidding three no-trump and making polite small talk …" She started laughing again.

"Quit! What I need is an acceptable excuse so your parents will stop asking."

"For starters, don't tell them you're bored."

"What a brilliant idea." Tempie grabbed a pen and pad. "I must write it down, so I don't forget." She eyed Gracie over the top of her glasses.

"I'm the only one I know with a wise guy for a grandmother."

"You should feel special." Tempie winked. "Now tell me, how did the casting call go?"

"Not well. They made their choices before Harper and I got a chance to audition."

"Sorry, dear. That's show business, all hurry up and wait."

Elbows on her desk, Gracie braced both cheeks with the back of her hands. "At least we can commiserate with each other."

"Yes, we can. But you have Miles and Leighton to keep you occupied. Don't ever discount your gift with children."

"You'll love this." She snickered. "Miles quizzed me this morning on my homework from his mother. And Miss Leighton begged me to come to school for show-and-tell dressed as Belle from *Beauty and the Beast.* She told her classmates I was the real Belle."

Tempie laughed. "You'll never get old caring for children. That's what you did for me."

"You used to say I was 'exasperating and relentless.'"

"Oh, you were," Tempie acknowledged. "But keeping up with you is how I kept my mind sharp and my body active."

"Ha! I'm pretty sure I was the one trying to keep up."

"Maybe." Tempie fluffed her hair. "So, what do you have planned for your soon-coming twenty-sixth birthday?"

"Not much. Harper and I are taking a tour of Lincoln Center."

"*Again?* I should think you'd know that place well enough by now."

"I do, but rumors are there'll be famous Juilliard alumni teaching that week. Not sure who yet, but I'm hoping to get into a few of their workshops."

Tempie raised a brow. "Don't you mean *sneak* into?"

"*Sneak* is a strong word," she said. "I prefer to think of my attendance as auditing a class—a little birthday gift to myself, you might say."

"Seriously, Gracie, why not give yourself a priceless gift this year? Plant yourself in a good church and grow."

Gracie bit her tongue. "'You can't hurry faith.' Haven't you told me that before?"

"Still exasperating and relentless, I see."

"Guess I take after you. Tell you what, I promise to get Mom and Dad to stop bugging you about their bridge club."

"If you succeed, I'll put you back in my will."

She shook her head and smiled.

Tempie yawned. "Say goodnight, Gracie."

"Goodnight, Gracie."

They blew each other a kiss.

Chapter Ten

"*On* Broadway, not off Broadway?" Gracie switched the phone to her other ear. "Harper, what took you so long to tell me?"

"Well, you might be a bit too prudish for this one."

Gracie snapped. "What's that supposed to mean?"

"The play depicts the gritty side of life, not the fantasy world you live in. I'm not sure you can handle the playwright's interpretation."

"Me? You're saying *I* can't handle real life? I'm not the one with a rich father who spoils me rotten."

Harper laughed. "Okay, you got me there. If you want in, I might be able to help. The audition is still a few weeks away."

"I want in. What's the play?"

"*Little Black Lies* directed by Gerard Dupris. The part I'm auditioning for is the lead's mistress. This could get me noticed."

Gracie knew the sleazy play and its hands-on director. "Yeah, noticed for all the wrong reasons."

"And you wondered why I didn't tell you?" Harper sighed. "Remember, theater is art representing life. Sometimes life is pretty, other times not. Dupris always says, 'How can we educate our audience if we masquerade reality as piety and innocence?'"

She took a few seconds. "Maybe you're right. I need to be flexible if I ever expect to succeed in this business. You have any clout with the casting director?"

"I'll work on him. Hey, how about some stargazing later? I'm free in a few hours."

As they often did on weekend evenings, Gracie and Harper headed to Broadway. Even without tickets for a play, mingling with the theater crowd could be a show.

When they reached the Minskoff Theater on West Forty-fifth, Harper slowed to a stop. "Hey, isn't that Lux from *Hear It Here First?*"

Gracie followed her gaze to a scruffy, muscular guy pushing a mic in someone's face, while a cameraman leaned over his shoulder. "That's his MO."

Harper held up a finger. "I'll be back."

Lux was one of the many celebrity reporters her friend chased regularly. To Gracie, he and his bunch were nothing but ruthless bullies, gossip mongers, and privacy invaders. There was no line they wouldn't cross and no lie they wouldn't tell.

Unlike Harper, Gracie didn't chase celebrities. She went by the park ranger-lost camper rule. If she stayed in one place long enough, they would eventually find *her*. Not that they were looking, but still.

Not long after, Harper returned, fast-talking. "Need a favor. A friend of mine is on his way over. He might not be your type, but please, please be nice to him. I could get my dream role out of this."

"Uh ... what?"

"Here he comes." Harper gushed, "Chase, this is the girl I told you about. Gracie meet Chase Grayson."

His hand flew up like an auction paddle. "Ciao."

"Uh, nice to meet you." *Was it really?*

Chase Grayson did not look the part of a guy who could get others a part. His outfit alone disqualified him—a tight, tan cardigan worn over a paper-thin polyester shirt buttoned to the top and twill trousers, the waist too high and the cuffs dragging.

He smoothed his slicked-down hair until his bangs reached the top of his black thick-lensed glasses. "Harper tells me you can never say no to a good taco."

Sooo not the opening she had expected. "Uh, yes, I guess."

"I'm headed to the Mexicali truck around the corner. Wanna come?"

Standing at Chase's side, Harper's eyes pleaded with Gracie.

Gracie agreed for one reason only. She could never say no to a good taco.

Harper ogled the paparazzi. "You two go on." She patted her flat stomach. "Watching my weight, you know."

She branded Harper with a you-owe-me glare.

Chase used his greeting of choice—Ciao!—with the taco truck owner, the newsstand vendor, and the loquacious, old, skinny guy dressed in an ocean-blue Speedo, silver tights, and a green foam Lady Liberty crown.

They placed their order. Silence hung between them like a slack clothesline. A word or two dragged on the ground before they burst forth simultaneously, resulting in a snort-chuckle combo.

Chase motioned to her. "Ladies first."

"So, Chase, what brings you to the theater district tonight?"

"A meeting with one of my uncle's friends." He smooshed his taco filling into its shell, then licked his fingers. "He needs me to do some research."

"What kind of research?" She took a bite, glad the conversation was moving at any pace in any direction.

"Whatever they need. Lately, a lot of my clients have come from the entertainment industry."

He had her attention. "You mean like playwrights and directors?"

Chase shrugged. "Yeah, and set designers and movie producers."

"Your uncle's friend hired you to …?"

"Confirm the historical accuracy of a script."

She swallowed a bite without chewing. Faking nonchalance, she wiped the corners of her mouth. "Is the script one of *his*?"

"Don't know. Our meeting's in a half hour."

For a crazy second, Gracie considered inviting herself to tag along. "I envy you working with entertainment professionals. Must be fascinating." *How had Harper met this guy? And why had she let him loose?*

"Depends on the assignment." He shoved the rest of his taco in his mouth and talked through it. "Harper tellsh me you're an actressh like her."

"Yes, we met doing the same play. Mostly, I'm a nanny for two kids." She didn't want him to think she was so successful she didn't need his connections. "Their mother is a drama instructor at Juilliard."

"That's in Lincoln Center, right?"

"Yes." Gracie wondered how long before Chase noticed the guacamole on his shirt. "When did you say your meeting was?"

He checked his watch. "I suppose we better get back. Harper's going to think you deserted her."

"She's a big girl." Gracie scrambled for a way to suggest they stay in touch.

Chase beat her to it. "Maybe we can get together again."

"Sure. Call me." She gave him her card. "And thanks for the taco."

Harper found her after Chase left. "How'd things go?"

"He wants to see me again."

Harper grabbed her arm. "I hope you said yes."

"The things I do for a friend." Her conscience scolded her. *You're bad, Gracie.*

Chapter Eleven

Gracie's sleep had been fitful, dreaming about Chase Grayson introducing her to famous directors and playwrights. To clear the grogginess, she downed a cup of strong coffee before thumbing through her latest assignment from Rachel on the history of the American theater. A few minutes into the lesson, her mind time-traveled from the Lewis Hallam troupe in 1752 to Chase Grayson and Gerard Dupris in present-day, Tony-award-winning territory.

When she told Rachel about meeting Chase and the possibilities, Rachel cautioned her, sort of like a pin cautions a balloon. And she hadn't even mentioned her chance with Gerard Dupris.

Sheesh. The reason Gracie chose this career in the first place was because acting was all make-believe. She was fine with others infusing her hope with more hope, not deflating it with their boring statistics.

What was so difficult about this concept that people found so hard to understand?

She wanted to celebrate her impending breakthroughs, but with whom? Without saying as much, most of her fellow nannies thought her career pursuits were unrealistic and shallow. And Tempie and Harper weren't answering their phones.

Well, that's not exactly true. She hadn't called Harper yet. But she would. Maybe. When she knew more.

All this useless projecting landed her in a nail-biting state of anxiety. Some fresh air and exercise couldn't hurt, so she walked the tree-lined sidewalk to the park. How a cool breeze could find its way in and around the high rises and brownstones of Manhattan still amazed her. She found a bench in the sun, determined to enjoy the solitude.

Which she would have if peace and quiet hadn't itched so much.

Seymour Kaufman. Could he be the sounding board she needed? Was he sincere when he said they should report back on their journeys? Before she could talk herself out of calling, she dialed his number.

"Grace, how lovely to hear from you."

"I took you at your word. Are you free to talk?"

"At present, I am on the subway heading to the Lincoln Center for the Performing Arts."

"Really? I can be there in about twenty minutes. Meet me at Sixty-sixth Street and Broadway. That stop's only a block from the Center."

Did she give him a chance to respond? *Oh, well.*

He was easy to spot, all in black—suit, eye patch, and matching diamond-cutting tool bag. "Seymour!"

He waved back. "Grace!"

"Hope you don't mind my joining you."

"Not at all. I am pleased to share my adventure with you."

They chatted on their one-block walk, then entered Lincoln Center near Alice Tully Hall.

Seymour wobbled a bit as he gazed at the surrounding buildings in the massive space. "The goings-on here are dizzying!"

"There's a lot to take in. Why don't we sit for a minute?" She took his arm in hers and led him over to a long, concrete bench overlooking the glistening reflecting pool. "Is this your first time here?"

"You are correct, but I have thought about visiting many times since my arrival." His eye roamed the area. "Where is the Metropolitan Opera?"

"Right behind us. That's Juilliard in front of us. My boss, Rachel, is an instructor there."

Seymour did a double-take. "Do you know this place well?"

She grinned. "Some might say well enough to be a nuisance."

"I am sure that is not true." He fixed his gaze on her. "What has put that sparkle in your eyes?"

"That's sort of why I wanted to talk." She told him all about Chase Grayson and his show business connections. "Isn't it just like God to make this happen?"

"Well, he is a good God, I must say."

If only her wet-blanket friends could hear this man. Being optimistic isn't hard if you try.

"Yes, meeting the right people could turn my career around." Until she knew more about *Little Black Lies,* she thought it best not to mention it.

He sighed. "Waiting is not an easy task, is it?"

She laughed. "That's an understatement. How about you? Any progress?"

"In one respect, yes. I pushed my fear aside and made a concerted effort to contact the woman of whom I spoke."

"That's a start."

"Oy, but her fame may have rendered her unapproachable."

"Fame? Who is she?"

"Her name is Polina Zelenka."

Gracie wasn't sure she'd heard him right. "The opera star?"

"Yes. I met her back in Postville. We spent some pleasant afternoons together on two separate occasions. I never believed I would be in New York, so it did not occur to me to get her phone number or address. Now it feels near impossible, without divine intervention, to reach her."

Her back straightened. "I've got an idea."

A good-looking, well-dressed guy, wearing a newsboy cap and mirrored shades walked by them, derailing her train of thought. He sat a few rows up, a few feet to their left, and opened a copy of *Atlantic Monthly*.

Gracie brought her attention back to Seymour. "My boss and her husband attend the opera occasionally. Her last class gets out in about a half hour. She might be able to help."

Seymour's eye opened wide. "Do they know Polina?"

"Not personally, but at the very least, Rachel could get to one of her handlers."

Was it her imagination or had newsboy-man edged closer? She'd say it was odd, but this was New York.

"Perhaps God has sent you after all. I do not know anyone in the city who could have helped me."

Gracie was surprised. "Not even your cousin?"

"I do not know Aaron well enough to get him involved."

She chuckled. "Yet you know me well enough?"

He belly-laughed. "You make a fine point. Perhaps some things are easier to speak of with a stranger. Furthermore, Aaron's duties keep him so busy I hardly ever see him. That is why I am in New York, to relieve him of some of his workload."

"Really?" She motioned to his tool bag. "I always assumed New York had a whole district full of diamond cutters."

Newsboy-man stood, stretched, then moved down one row.

Would his next move be on her? To avoid that sort of encounter, Gracie got up. "If we leave now, I can show you around a bit before we catch up with Rachel."

"Sure." Seymour's brow wrinkled as they began walking. "Diamond cutters? Is that a term specific to New York?"

"Why? What do you call them?"

"Back in Iowa, most people call me a mohel."

"That's Jewish, right?"

"Hebrew, yes."

"Oh."

Gracie and Seymour's short walk to Rachel's classroom was delayed by a tour group. She was about to suggest he take a tour himself when the guide said, "This November, the Center will be honoring famed opera soprano Polina Zelenka on her twenty-fifth anniversary with the Met. The top international jeweler Harry Winston has pledged quite a sum for the privilege of having her wear a diamond and platinum necklace that evening worth an estimated $6.5 million."

Seymour suppressed a yelp. "Did you hear that?"

She chuckled. "Sure did."

"We are getting closer to finding her." He stared at Gracie like she'd been dropped from heaven. "I am certain the Lord had a hand in our meeting."

When they reached Rachel's classroom, it was empty. A sign on the door read: "Due to an unexpected faculty meeting, today's last class has been canceled. Don't pump your fists. There will be a makeup."

No slacking in Rachel's classes. And no calls allowed in faculty meetings. "Don't worry. I'll talk to Rachel tonight. We'll find Polina for you."

Seymour bowed slightly. "I have no doubt you will."

Chapter Twelve

The Chief caught his reflection in the storefront window. The indigo striped shirt, charcoal blazer, and straight-legged jeans were worth the thousand he'd spent on them.

The raw, vintage look of organic cotton does suit me.

He removed the newsboy cap, then ran a hand through his dark brown hair, admiring his versatile loose style. Adjusting his Dolce & Gabbana aviator sunglasses, he marveled how a good haircut and designer shades could influence people's perception of you—almost as much as a man's watch and shoes.

He'd learned long ago that hats could serve double duty. First, to partially hide his visage. Second, to be the main item of clothing a witness would remember. He seldom wore the same hat to the same place twice.

He'd seen the attractive brunette at Lincoln Center before, but never with the Jew. Her repeated presence and their mention of "diamond cutting" and "handlers" piqued his interest. A little competition among thieves could be fun. But these two were an amateur threat, nothing more.

The Chief returned to his hotel to change. He had one more errand to run before he could enjoy his favorite French restaurant.

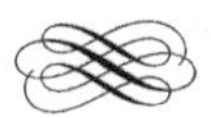

When he reached his destination on East Seventy-eighth, he tipped the cabbie well enough to be thanked but not well enough to be recognized in a lineup. Not that he ever intended to be in one. He entered Specialty Dry Cleaners, carrying a handful of shirts and a pair of slacks.

The clerk at the counter nodded to him once before turning back to an irate, old woman with perm-fried bluish hair.

She pushed the clear plastic cover up over a dress. "You pressed this? I bet you ran it through the dryer with a wet dishrag. I could do that at home. Why should I have to pay?"

The pallid, mild-mannered clerk spoke softly. "What would you like me to do for you, ma'am?"

What she suggested he do couldn't be repeated and didn't even sound possible.

She left the dress and stormed out.

The clerk made no attempt to stop her but addressed the Chief instead. "The usual, Chief?"

"Yes. And you might want to double check those slacks for dog hair."

He ticketed the Chief's clothing, then reached under the counter and handed him a key. "Pickup in two days acceptable?"

"Perfect."

The Chief walked past a clothes conveyor to the back of the building. Making sure he was alone, he unlocked a door marked No Admittance and entered an ordinary-looking storage room. He walked to the far wall, flipped a switch, and slipped behind a rotating shelf unit laden with dry cleaning supplies.

In the corner of this hidden room, an elderly man sat hunched over a workbench, a bright light shining on his thick gray hair. He held a jeweler's loupe to his eye as he worked on a replica of the Harry Winston necklace Polina Zelenka was to wear at the gala in her honor.

"How's it coming, Oren?"

"See for yourself." He hung the necklace on a black velvet display stand adjacent to an enlarged photo of the original designed by Winston himself. "My esteemed late employer assigned me to handcraft his design. What do you think?"

The Chief examined the fake with the loupe. "Excellent work as usual. I see some settings are still empty. Are we on schedule?"

The man rested his hands on his knees and swiveled his chair to face the Chief. "After all our years together, insulted I am you should ask."

He patted Oren on the back. "No insult meant and no hurry. Call me when you're finished." He walked to the front of the cleaners only to find that the acrimonious woman had returned—with a cop.

Her attention moved to the Chief. She pointed to her dress still hanging where she'd left it. "You work here? Are you responsible for this shoddy job?"

"No, ma'am, I'm not an employee. This kind gentleman allowed me to use his restroom." The Chief handed the key back to the clerk. "Thanks."

"Likely story. Are you a liar like this one?" She glared at the clerk, then harped at the pot-bellied officer. "Something fishy's going on. I wouldn't be surprised to find out they're dealing drugs out back."

The officer rested one hand on his holster and spoke in an even tone. "What would make you believe that, Miss Edna?"

Great. He knew her.

She ripped the plastic off her dress. "See! This has not been properly pressed, so what other activity might they be engaged in?"

The cop lowered his voice. "You may be right. I'll look into it."

The clerk stayed focused on the woman.

The cop placed a hand on her shoulder. "Until then, if the dry cleaner agrees to re-press your dress, will that solve your immediate problem?"

Miss Edna fumed and sputtered but finally agreed.

"My apologies, ma'am," the clerk said. "I will take care of this immediately. May I get you a cold drink while you wait?"

Once she was settled and quiet, the Chief and the cop left.

The officer said, "Sorry about that, sir. Miss Edna's dementia's gettin' worse. Her calls to me are increasing."

The Chief flagged a cab. "You're a credit to your uniform, officer. I was impressed by the way you handled the matter."

Thumbs hooked in his belt, the cop rocked back and forth on his heels. "After being a beat cop in this neighborhood for over thirty-five years, ya get pretty good at readin' people."

"I can see that." A cab screeched to a stop, and the Chief hopped in. He saluted the cop as they sped away.

Chapter Thirteen

Gracie packed the kids' lunches and organized their backpacks.

Miles cupped his hand over Leighton's ear and stage-whispered, "'Member, Gracie's birthday is today."

A secret played in Leighton's hazel eyes. She twisted a curl around one of her tiny fingers and peeked at Gracie. "Nobody's making you a birthday cake with yellow roses after school."

"*Leigh*-ton!" Miles bopped the top of his head with both hands, static electricity waking his cowlicks.

Pretending not to notice him, she stooped to hug Leighton. "That's okay. Everyone is so busy."

On their way out, Gracie found a sticky note from Reggie on the hall table. "G, a guy handed me this package for you as I was coming in from the gym. Have a great birthday."

She opened the gift-wrapped package—if you can call a cardboard paper towel tube wrapped in thin tissue *gift-wrapped*. She yanked a wad of paper from its core. Inside, she found a bracelet and a rolled note which read, "Mother told me most women like jewelry. I hope you like it too. Chase."

Super. Wait. How did Chase know it was my birthday?

Miles grunted. "Only a dumb bracelet."

Leighton bounced on her tiptoes. "Let me see!"

"Maybe later, sweetie." She shoved the bracelet into her bag and mumbled a warning to herself, "You might want to rethink Chase as a connection."

Once Miles and Leighton were safely delivered to their classrooms, she took a minute to pray, "Please, Lord, make this birthday one to remember. Amen."

Gracie had high hopes for this year. A starring role on Broadway would do nicely, thank you, God. Of course, being on location in Hollywood or Monaco wouldn't be bad either.

She speed-walked the two blocks to her regular coffee shop. With only one woman ahead of her in line, Gracie was golden.

Until the woman spoke. "I'd like a medium black coffee."

Gracie moaned as loud as she could without making a sound. One did not order a drink as simple as "medium black coffee" from a barista if one expected to make friends with the people behind you.

After an annoying back-and-forth about sizes, blends, and roasts, the woman and the barista worked out a reasonable compromise. The woman side-shuffled to the pick-up counter, and Gracie stepped forward.

"Tall, half-caff, soy latté." She queued up behind black-coffee woman. Within ninety seconds, Gracie was out the door on her way to the subway station.

After several failed swipes of her MetroCard, she got through the turnstile. She bounded down the steps to the dank underground with its melting pot of odors, sooty walls, peeling paint, and soiled concrete.

She focused on her word for the year: optimism … until the car doors closed, and the subway took off without her.

Fighting her instinct to whine on her birthday, she took a sip of her latté. After filling her mouth with the warm liquid, she choked. The scribbling on the cup read: "Med Bk Coff." The cup landed in the trash bin, but not before a backlash of liquid baptized her blouse.

She took the next subway.

A long-haired man in a stained muscle shirt wobbled to a stop a foot in front of her, self-talking about a recent romantic breakup. After staring at a photo—of the ex-girlfriend, Gracie presumed—he tore it in pieces and tossed them in the air. He swooped his hand over his greasy locks, then rummaged through his grungy backpack. Pulling out a stick of deodorant, he applied it liberally to his moist armpits.

Gracie held back a gag until he moved on.

Remembering Chase's gift, she pulled the tissue-wrapped bracelet out of her bag and fingered its nickel-sized, heart-shaped charm. Something sparkled. *Was that a diamond?* Squinting, she looked as close as she could without going cross-eyed. Holding it in the light, it sparkled again. *A piece of glitter?*

She examined the small white tag. *Genuine 10k gold.* A diamond paired with 10k gold? She didn't think so.

Now what to do? Thank someone for a diamond bracelet if what she saw shining was a microdrop of spittle? And if it was a diamond, how could she not mention it? The whole thing was unsettling.

Gracie doubted a reputable craftsman like Seymour Kaufman would have anything to do with creating a piece like this.

She amused herself by inventing a provenance for the bracelet—designed in the diamond *chip* district. Each piece came with its own magnifying glass and Certificate of Authenticity, which read: "The Diamond Chip Jewelers Association certifies that this is an authentic magnifying glass."

She chuckled at her silly story.

Not that she was a diamond or gold digger. She just wanted to know why Chase thought giving her jewelry appropriate, no matter how inexpensive, after one fix-up at a six-dollar Manhattan taco truck and two missed phone calls.

Had she misled him? Of course, she had. And now she had to make things right.

Even if Chase *was* a perfect match—and he most certainly was not—Gracie had no time to date. Between her nanny duties, auditions, and Rachel's mentoring sessions and assignments, her life was booked.

His industry connections aside, she needed to make sure Chase was clear about their relationship.

She leaned her head back and closed her eyes, running through lines from the *Romeo and Juliet* scene Rachel had assigned. Her head bobbed as the train lurched to a stop. She marked the spot: scene 2, Capulet's Orchard, as Juliet enters.

She hopped off and walked the block to Lincoln Center. Despite her delayed arrival, there was no sign of Harper in the plaza. Sitting on the fountain wall, she basked in the sun and crisp air of the early New York fall.

Using the solitary moments, she indulged in fantasy as she waited for her friend, contemplating characters she could portray—Oscar-winner hounded by the paparazzi? Understudy hoping the break-a-leg wish would come true this one time? Aspiring actor beleaguered by her family's advice to get a real job?

No, that one hit too close to home.

She jumped when her phone rang, interrupting her meanderings. *Ian*. She smiled. Even though they texted nonsense almost daily, they hadn't spoken for a couple of weeks. "Hey, stranger."

"How d'ya plan to celebrate this grand occasion, birthday girl?"

"I'm meeting a friend at—"

"Let me guess. Lincoln Center?"

"Wouldn't you like to know?"

He laughed. "I do know because you told me, remember?"

"Oh, right."

"I bet you're already there, sitting on the fountain wall, scouting the crowds for characters, dreaming about a leading role in your first big production."

He knew her so well it was eerie. "Wish you were here."

"Sure you do."

"No, really. My friend Harper is meeting me, but I could use another party guest."

"Then look behind you."

"Huh?" She twisted around and gaped at Ian striding across the concrete expanse.

"Good to see you, darlin'. Even better when you're speechless."

"What in all New York are you doing here?" She sprang to her feet and threw herself into his hug. "And don't tell me you came for my birthday. Must be business."

"I'm after meetin' with a potential customer."

"'After meetin'? You haven't been back from the old country long? You're still showing your Irish."

"Amn't." He flinched at his slip into Irish slang. "I mean, I am not."

"Are too, but let's not argue. How's your family?"

"Mum and Dad are doing fine. Their pub's busier than ever. Still can't believe my baby sister is old enough to be waitin' tables."

"I wish I had siblings so my parents could divvy up the guilt between us."

"Gracie, darlin', guilt is like love. With each child, it multiplies. I still get grief for not visiting more often."

"Speaking of visiting, how long will you be in New York?"

"As long as it takes to impress my potential client."

"Can you stick around to join my party? We're taking a tour of the Center."

"I don't know …"

"See the tall blonde with the red leather Gucci bag walking toward us? That's Harper." She waved her over.

Ian grinned. "Hmm. I may have found an opening in my schedule."

She gagged. "Behave. Don't make me lose one of the few friends I have here."

Gracie introduced them.

"A pleasure to meet you, Ian. I see Gracie's been keeping secrets." Harper flipped her long hair over one shoulder with the back of her hand.

Do guys really fall for that?

For his part, Ian kept the brogue going after Harper told him he sounded like Bono.

Pfft. As if she knew Bono.

"Before we get started on that tour," Ian said, "I have to check in with my office." He stepped off to the side.

Harper grabbed her arm, pulling her a few more feet away. "Are you and he ...?"

Gracie looked at an imaginary watch on her wrist. "Losing your edge? You took a whole thirty seconds to ask."

Harper crossed her arms. "And?"

She eased her friend's mind. "We're best buds. That's all."

"What's his story?"

"Are you asking if he has a girlfriend?"

"Maybe." Harper gazed in Ian's direction. "Put in a good word for me, okay?"

"For you? Ha! After you ambushed me with Ciao-boy?"

Harper tightened her hoop earring. "You don't like Chase? He seems nice, and he knows people."

"Seems nice?" Gracie's shoulders sagged. "You told me he was a friend of yours."

"Sort of. I met him that night near the theater. He asked me for directions, then we got to talking. Mainly about his connections."

Gracie's hands rolled into fists. "Then why didn't *you* go out with him yourself?"

Harper stuck her lower lip out. "Well, I could have, but after he told me one of his friends knew the director of the remake of *Tony n' Tina's Wedding*, I didn't want him to think I was using him to get the role of Tina."

"So you used me instead?" She didn't bother to comment on the preposterousness of a suburban, blue-eyed, blonde Scandinavian thinking she was perfect for the role of an Italian bride from Queens.

Sheesh. Even her roots are blonde.

Harper said "sorry" almost like she meant it. "They've cast the part already, so you don't have to see him anymore if you don't want to. After today."

Gracie shout-whispered. "What do you mean 'after today'?"

Chapter Fourteen

"Gra-cie! Har-per!" The voice called from a distance behind them. Chase galloped toward them, his arms flying about, his glasses bouncing diagonally across his nose.

Gracie hissed at Harper. "What's he doing here?"

"He called me last night to get your number. When I mentioned today was your birthday, he asked if we were doing anything. I couldn't lie, could I?"

"I thought you were my friend."

Harper took Gracie's hands in hers. "Be nice. He's not such a bad person, is he?"

Despite Harper's misguided attempt at matchmaking with an ulterior motive, Gracie knew she wasn't all bad. And she'd tell her that—right after she killed her.

Chase reached them sweaty and out of breath from his twenty-yard run, grinning like a sixth-grader who'd won first place at a science fair. He flattened his 1960s Beatles hairdo until it covered his eyebrows. "Phew! I ... almost ... didn't ... make it."

She wanted to tell him he could run faster if he'd shorten his pants by three inches, and he could breathe easier if he'd unbutton the top button of his shirt. Instead, feeling guilty because he seemed so happy, she kept it short. "But you did and right on time."

Ian ended his call and joined them.

Gracie introduced the men to each other. "Old friend, Ian. New friend, Chase."

Still panting like a dog after fetching a stick, Chase gasped, "Ciao!"

Ian reached for his hand. "Nice to meet you."

Harper simpered. "Glad you could join the birthday celebration, Chase."

"Thanks." His whole face glistened. "Hey! A double-dater!"

"Double-dater?" Did Gracie hear Chase right?

"You know, Harper and Ian and you and me."

What is wrong with this guy? She had to fix this soon.

"Did you find my present, Miss Birthday Girl? Your boss said he'd make sure you got it."

A bit of saliva gathered at the corner of his partially-opened mouth. She wanted to hand him a tissue but pretended she didn't see it. "You shouldn't have, really."

He frowned. "Isn't that what couples do? Exchange gifts?"

This whole thing was getting away from her. No sense prolonging the inevitable, so she pulled Chase off to the side. "Yes, that is what couples do, but you know we're only friends, don't you?"

He registered shock for a split-second just before he snorted. "You're such a kidder, Gracie."

This wasn't going to be easy.

The foursome proceeded toward the Rubenstein Atrium to register for the tour.

When they entered the Atrium, Ian scanned the media wall and the impressive vertical gardens. "What? No streamers and balloons?"

Gracie followed his sightline. "I was going for a classier setting."

He said, "Spoiled American. Balloons were a luxury growing up in Kilkenny."

She snarked, "Ian Quinn, are you going to make us listen to that poor-me-I'm-Irish-and-all-I-got-on-my-birthday-was-a-potato ballad?"

"Nothing pedestrian for my mother," Harper said. "When it came to my birthday parties, she was the queen of lavish. Always outdoing her country club friends. I hated her for it. As did my father. That's why we divorced her."

Chase tripped into the conversation. "Every year on my birthday, Mother takes me to the Museum of Natural History, then to the pet store to get a new turtle. I got my first one when I was ten."

Gracie's mind stumbled over his use of the present tense. "Every year? Even now?"

"Yup. This year will be my eighteenth." Chase's chest puffed out.

Harper adjusted the strap on her bag and asked the question which was on Gracie's mind. "What happens to them?"

Chase cocked his head. "I'm not sure what you mean."

"You know, uh," Harper struggled, "why do you have to keep, uh, replacing them?"

He pushed his glasses back up. "No, no. Turtles live long lives. I still have all seventeen. Five red-eared sliders, three African side necks, four painted, two Greek tortoises, and three ornate woods."

Ian took his time, nodding like he was trying to think of an appropriate comment. "So-oo, you like turtles?"

Chase shrugged, palms up. "Who doesn't?"

Harper's smile flattened, her eyes misted. "My first and only pet as a child was a timid, miniature lop-eared bunny named Lancelot. While I was at school one day, my mother's psycho Chihuahua yapped him to death."

Chase touched her arm. "That's so sad."

Gracie had to ask. "So, Chase, where do you keep seventeen turtles?"

"We share a room. You'll see when you come over to meet Mother."

Oh, Chase, there will be no meeting Mother ... or the turtles.

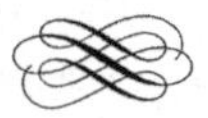

Gracie was well-acquainted with their tour guide, Tall Ralph, a transplant from DC. He had no trace of an accent whatsoever, which was refreshing if not as interesting as Short Ralph from the Bronx. Though she'd memorized much of his presentation (and those of others) from her numerous visits, the impromptu backstage detours and unscripted bits of insider information kept her coming back.

They began at the Metropolitan Opera. Gracie loved the interior design of the Met. Not that she knew much about opera or architecture, but to her, it looked like an opera house should look. Dozens of starburst-shaped Lobmeyr crystal chandeliers illuminated the lobby. Colors of gold and white throughout served as the perfect backdrop for rich oil paintings, woven damasks, and sculptures. The two huge Chagall murals were rumored to be worth over $20 million. The scuttlebutt was that they'd been used as collateral for a long-term loan.

As the tour proceeded to the massive cantilevered stairway, an older woman trailed behind them. To Gracie, she looked like she stepped right out of a British World War II movie filmed in sepia.

Seasoned visitor that she was, Gracie felt obliged to help. "Hold up while I collect a lost lamb." She took a few steps toward the woman. "Ma'am, you can follow me. I know my way around this place better than most."

The woman protested. "But I need to go down *coridor*."

Poor thing, she had an accent, probably couldn't read the signs. Gracie reached out and touched her arm. "That corridor leads to the stars' private dressing rooms. Even regulars like me aren't allowed back there."

Hearing the buzz, Tall Ralph peeked back at the group. "Is there a problem?"

She answered, "No, I was helping this lady find her way."

He backtracked a few steps. "The lady is Mrs. Lonnit, Ms. Zelenka's personal assistant. I am sure she knows where to go." Then to the woman, "I apologize, Mrs. Lonnit."

Ian hid his laugh with a cough while Harper mimicked Gracie in a sing-songy whisper, "'Even regulars like me aren't allowed back there.'"

Ms. Zelenka's assistant? How was I to know? "Wait! Mrs. Lonnit, could I have a word?"

Tall Ralph tried to herd Gracie back to the pack.

Mrs. Lonnit raised her hand to stop him. "Is okay. What I can do for you?"

"My friend—he's a friend of Ms. Zelenka's—Seymour Kaufman, well, he's been trying to find her. I told him I'd help. Here you are … but he's not …and, well, here I am."

The woman laughed. "I should tell Ms. Zelenka that Mr. Kaufman wants to speak with her?"

"That's what I'm trying to say. He's been in New York a month but didn't know how to reach her." Gracie remembered Seymour's card. "Wait." She fished around in her purse until she found it. "Here."

"*Mulțumiri*. Thanks. I give to Polina when she come home."

As soon as Mrs. Lonnit was out of sight, Gracie stuck her tongue out at Harper and Ian, and thanked Chase for not stooping to their level."

Tall Ralph called out, "With your permission, Grace, may we continue our tour?"

I should have never told him my name.

Chapter Fifteen

Tall Ralph led them to Alice Tully Hall, where he recited boring quotes from an architectural magazine about the design of the many Juilliard buildings.

"Here's a tidbit for our group," he said. "Extra security has been added to keep the paparazzi in line because three of our most famous alumni will be leading drama workshops next week."

What did he mean *next week?* Gracie raised her hand. "Are you saying there are no workshops today?"

"Yes." He continued, but she didn't hear a word after that.

Rumors! When did they become so unreliable?

When the tour ended, Gracie held her threesome back while the remainder of the group rounded the corner to the exit.

Ian crossed his arms. "What are you up to now, Gracie?"

"Shh. Follow me." They backtracked to Alice Tully Hall. "No time like the present to make my stage debut."

Harper's breath quickened. "You can do that?"

"Why not?" Gracie whispered.

"Then why are you whispering?" she said.

Ian raked a hand through his hair. "I'm not so sure about this."

Gracie was frustrated. "Where's your sense of adventure? No one's going to arrest us for returning to a place included on the tour."

Chase jogged in place and raised both arms like he was crossing a finish line. "I'm with you, Gracie!"

She scowled at her wannabe boyfriend. *Oh, please don't do that.*

The foursome entered the soaring, three-story, all-glass lobby. Gracie opened the heavy doors and peeked inside the concert hall to make sure it was empty. The seating area was dark, but the soft light from the wall sconces made it possible to navigate. After waving them in, she headed toward the stage.

"I'm doing a scene from *Romeo and Juliet*. You three can be my audience."

Chase rubbed his hands together. "This is going to be good."

Ian said, "Not much of an audience, Camden."

She sighed. "Well, you're all I have at the moment."

"Your cast is kinda thin too." Ian pointed to Harper. "Maybe Harper could join you."

What was he saying? Harper didn't know the scene. She slowed, trying to think of a response that didn't sound selfish. But when Harper's whole countenance lifted, the only thing she could say was, "How about it?"

"Sure, but I don't do Shakespeare." Harper tossed her purse to Ian. "Let's do the opening scene we had in *Pump*. I think I can remember my lines."

"I doubt our audience will know if we flub them." Gracie handed Ian her phone. "Video our performance, will you? I want to post it online."

Harper's eyes shined like spotlights. "Chase, think we could get a copy of the video to your uncle's friend?"

Gracie growled inwardly. *This isn't all about you, Harper.*

"Sure!" Chase shouted. "I can do that."

Gracie and Harper found their way onto the stage. Even if the audience was conscripted and her production changed without notice, Gracie was standing where so many of her heroes had been before her. For a moment, her legs trembled.

They stepped to their imaginary marks. Gracie cleared her throat, then spouted lines from the satire. Harper responded. They stuck to the script as much as they could and improvised when necessary.

As they finished their scene and bowed, a voice bellowed from the back of the darkened hall, blocking out the applause. "What are you doing in here?"

Harper deferred to Gracie.

"Um, a scene from the first act of *Powerless to Pump*," she said, perhaps taking the man's question too literally.

"Are you Juilliard students?"

Gracie hedged. "Well, not exactly." From what little she could see of this shadowy figure, he had put his hands on his hips.

"What exactly does 'not exactly' mean?"

"Means no, I guess. We were on the tour. But one of the drama instructors is my mentor. She can vouch for us." She hoped her connection to Rachel would suffice.

"Your name, please."

"Grace Camden and, uh, this is Harper Bellamy."

Harper mumbled, "Why'd you have to give him *my* name?"

She ignored her. "Are we in trouble, sir?"

"Nah, you're not the first people to sneak up on this stage. That's how producers discovered their last four leading ladies."

Harper rushed past her to the edge of the stage, cooing, "Really?"

"No. Now, which instructor do you know?"

With confidence, Gracie spoke. "Rachel Adler."

"Adler. And Grace is your name, right?"

"Yes. And you are?"

"The guy who gets paid to kick you out of here."

Ian and Chase stood as Gracie and Harper made their way down the stairs. Neither of the guys said a word.

"One more thing," the man said. "My sister told me that play was pretty awful. But your performance just now was not."

Gracie shaded her eyes and looked to the back of the theater, but all she could see was the outline of a tall figure wearing a ball cap.

Before she could speak, Harper gushed, "Thanks, but it was far from my best work."

The guy took off before she could see his face. Not wanting to chance getting banned from the Center altogether, Gracie rushed out into the lobby, hoping to have a word with him. The only people around were a teenage girl off in a corner texting and a man on a scaffold washing windows.

Ian reached into his pocket. "Here's your phone. Is getting kicked off the stage what you had in mind for your debut video?"

She mugged. "That's why God created film editors."

Chase crowed, "Good answer, Gracie!"

Ian gave him a sour look.

She led the group back to Juilliard. "If we bump into Rachel, don't mention the whole stage thing. I'll tell her later."

Rachel stepped out of her open classroom door. "Tell me *what* later?"

Gracie shot a warning glance at her friends. "That we had a good time on your free passes. Thanks again."

The others nodded and mumbled a jumble of one-word answers.

Rachel tapped her cheek. "So, any potential Juilliard students here?"

"Harper's a viable candidate," Gracie said. "The guys, not so much."

Harper vented, "'Viable' is not a word Father would use. He's still not convinced my commitment to the profession equals the tuition."

Rachel said, "Well, you don't have to attend Juilliard to have talent and an artistic soul. Gracie's a prime example."

"I'm no dummy," she said. "In some ways, I have it better than the students—the personal attention of a mentor *without* the student loans."

Rachel chuckled. "Well, there's that too."

At the end of the hall, Gracie noticed a man in a navy suit conversing with a uniformed guard. "Rache, is that Reggie?"

"My husband? I doubt it. He's at work …" She followed Gracie's glance. "Huh?"

The guard exited a side door while Reggie walked toward them.

He kissed Rachel's cheek, then said to Gracie, "Who does the birthday girl have with her today?"

She introduced her mini entourage.

Rachel interrupted. "Are the children all right, Reggie?"

"They're fine, dear. Do I need a reason to visit my wife?"

Her brow smoothed. "No, I suppose not."

But Gracie could tell by Rachel's expression this was not the end of the story.

Once she and her guests were outside, Chase said, "I need to use the boys' room. Ian, you want to come with?"

Ian's cobalt blues sliced back and forth between Chase and the girls. "Uh, that's okay. You go on without me."

Chase nodded. "Okey dokey, be back in a few."

Ian tugged at his shirt collar. "That was weird."

Gracie stifled a laugh.

Harper sidled up to him. "I think Chase wants to make friends."

"Well, he's not going to make them that way." Ian looked over at Gracie. "What are you laughing at?"

Chapter Sixteen

At Harper's suggestion, they continued Gracie's birthday celebration over lunch. But as soon as they were seated, her girlfriend's attention was all on Ian. The basic body language Gracie had learned in acting workshops told her Harper was flirting, and he was falling for it. Classic signs—smoothing his hair, raising his eyebrows, straightening his back. *Silly man.*

Gracie was stuck with Chase who talked turtle, using his hands as much as his words. She tried to be polite, but she'd never been into reptiles. Her mind wandered, searching for a woman she could fix him up with. When she cut Chase loose, she'd rather their "good connection" remain intact. She imagined a match, leading to a happily ever after ending. Chase and his wife with turtles and children ... four boys ... named Leonardo, Raphael, Michelangelo, and Donatello.

Chase waved a hand in front of her face. "Did you hear me, Gracie?"

"Huh?" She hit delete before he could read her thoughts. "I'm sorry, what did you say?"

"The name for my next turtle. Pecan. What do you think?"

Harper and Ian were lost in each other, and Gracie wanted to gag. "Pecan is a fine name, Chase." *How long can I feign interest? Act, Gracie. Not the first time you've had a lousy part in a horrible play.*

Chase tilted his head back and forth like he was trying to keep pinballs from falling into holes. Wagging a finger at her, he said. "You know, I spent most of last week at Lincoln Center studying the architecture for my client. I saw a Jewish man, maybe a rabbi, speaking with someone who looked a lot like you."

"If it was Tuesday, it *was* me."

"Mind my asking what you were doing with a rabbi?"

Gracie chuckled. "Our own bit of research, but nothing like yours. Technically, he's not a rabbi."

Chase slurped the last bit of soda from his cup. "A religious thing, huh?"

"No. We're working together on a special project." Gracie didn't feel the need to elaborate on her personal relationship with Seymour.

"Oh. By the way, I forgot to ask you. Would you like to meet my uncle?"

First his mother, then his turtles, now his uncle? She hesitated. Was this the uncle who was friends with the director Harper had mentioned? She played it coy. "Your uncle?"

"Yes, he's some big deal Broadway director. His name is Bennett Noble."

Gracie practically swallowed her fork. She lowered her voice. "Bennett Noble is your uncle?" She peeked to see if Harper had been listening. *Nope.*

"You've heard of him?"

"Even people in Peoria have heard of him. He's either won or been nominated for at least a dozen Tony awards: *Slick, Panacea,* and my favorite, *Children of Duluth*."

"Hmm. Guess that's why he's got a whole library full of statues and plaques. I'm meeting him at seven-thirty Sunday night at the Grove Street Starbucks in the West Village. You're welcome to join us."

"Seriously? Thanks." She was too charged to feel guilty about using Chase or leaving Harper out. Served her right for being so obnoxious.

A meeting with Bennett Noble. She couldn't wait to tell Tempie.

Now *this* was God.

Chapter Seventeen

Miles and Leighton told Gracie she could open her eyes. She oohed and aahed over the homemade birthday cake decorated with yellow store-bought sugary roses.

"Do you wuv it?" Leighton asked.

"I do! Yellow is my favorite color."

Leighton pressed her little hands together. "I knowed that!"

With eyes as bright as this child's, Gracie didn't need candles.

Miles couldn't stay still. "Leighton almost blew it this morning, but not me!"

"No, you didn't. You positively know how to keep a secret."

He looked like he'd flown to the moon and back. "Now, Mom?"

Rachel nodded. "Yes, Miles, now."

He and Leighton each pulled a gift out of the hutch. They'd used almost as much tape as paper to wrap them.

"For me? I wonder what they could be."

Leighton started to speak, but Miles covered her mouth with his hand.

The first was a framed photo of Miles dressed as Julius Caesar, complete with toga and laurel wreath. The second was of Leighton in a Little Orphan Annie costume, holding her stuffed dog, Sandy. "Love them! And I have the perfect shelf to display them."

Miles moved in closer to Gracie. "Is my present better than that guy's?"

"Miles." Reggie tapped the table with his finger. "That is not a polite question."

Rachel said, "I think someone may be a tad j-e-a-l-o-u-s."

Miles shook his head. "No, I'm not."

Gracie stooped until she was face-to-face with him, then rested her hand over his heart. "Your gift came right from here. That's always the best kind."

He almost knocked her over with a hug.

"Okay, kids, bedtime. Leighton, Daddy's going to run a bath for you. Miles, you can take a shower in Mommy's bathroom again."

Miles's ribcage seemed to expand as he explained in his deep, man-boy voice, "I take showers now, Gracie."

She gave him a thumbs-up. "Wow. I did not know that."

Reggie corralled the kids and led them upstairs while Rachel began cleaning up. "You're so good with them. I hope you know how grateful we are."

Gracie stacked some plates in the sink. "You might have mentioned it once or twice."

Rachel made a face at her.

She made one back.

"How're you doing with Jacques' monologue from *As You Like It?*"

Gracie wiped the cake crumbs and frosting smears off the table. "As a matter a fact, I held my own dress rehearsal with the kids last week."

Rachel rinsed a plate and put it in the dishwasher. "That's right, you did. Miles told me he had to bail you out."

"Snitch. Of course, his execution was flawless. How does it feel raising a genius?"

"Most of the time it feels like he's raising me. He might have inherited my creative bent, but he gets his bossiness from his father."

"That reminds me, do you know the guy Reggie was talking to this morning outside your classroom?"

"Might have been Dan Favor, the new chief of security. Why?"

"Well, after I made my debut today at Alice Tully Hall, he kicked me off the stage."

Hands on her hips, Rachel said, "Gracie—"

"I gave him your name as a reference."

"If I get fired, you'll be out a job, you know." She tried to look stern but blinked.

"No chance." Gracie gave her a hug, then gathered her gift bags. "Thanks for everything. I've gotta get back to my place. Ian's stopping by."

"Why didn't you say something? He could have joined us."

"I invited him, but he acted all mysterious. Said he had something to take care of."

"Ooh. Maybe a birthday surprise?"

"Ian? Not likely. He's all about business."

Or all about Harper? He'll never tell—the brat.

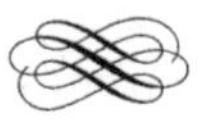

Gracie handed Ian a can of soda.

He popped the top and took a swig, then perused her nanny suite. "Nice flat."

"Right, huh? Decades ago, the third floor used to be the servants' quarters. There's even an elevator." She took a sip of her bottled water. "So, you seemed to impress the hard-to-impress Harper Bellamy today."

"Think so? She's pretty cool."

"Yes, she is, if you're into looks alone and like shallow people."

Ian choked as a laugh bubbled up.

"What's so funny?"

He caught his breath. "You mean like you?"

"I'm not shallow."

He got comfortable on the love seat. "Perhaps a bit self-absorbed, that's all."

"I am not." She dropped next to him on the couch and put her feet on the ottoman.

"No?" He stretched his arms and cracked his knuckles. "Then answer me these. Specifically, what does my company manufacture? When was the last time you went an hour without looking in a mirror? What exactly does your boss Reggie do for a living?" He smirked. "Need I go on?"

"What makes you so sure I don't know what Reggie does for a living?"

He folded his arms. "Well, do ya?"

She glowered. "I don't like you."

Ian gave her hand a tap. "I know. Would it help if I told you I liked your three o'clock selfie? Best one today."

"Think so?" She liked him again. "As for the mirror thing, Tempie always preached that one smudge of mascara, smear of lipstick, or hair out of place could cost me an introduction or even a part."

"That's what you've said. Speaking of hair, I like the color you picked this time. What's this one called?"

"Born with it brunette."

"Clever."

"Not really. This is my natural color. I grew it out—except for the highlights. Don't change the subject. My appearance is a huge part of my career. I have to do all I can to get noticed before I'm too old."

"Twenty-six is not old. You knew it could take longer to become a fulltime actor, considering your agreement with God. You are keeping that agreement, aren't you?"

"Yes, no vulgar dialog, no gratuitous violence, no nudity, and no sex. And no problem, since I haven't been offered a single role since *Pump*." *Little Black Lies* crept into her conscience, but she booted the thought out.

"As Mr. Anderson always says, 'Your original plan is usually best.'"

"How are Will and Elizabeth doing anyway?" The Andersons had been two of her favorite customers at the Cranberry Fare. They'd met there at Party of One, a Friday supper club for singles.

Ian leaned back. "Finding love in their later years suits them."

Gracie recalled the Andersons' travelogue video and drama company. "How's their business, We'll Always Have Paris?"

"They're booked solid almost every week at nursing homes, senior centers, and assisted living facilities."

Ian quieted and stared off into space.

His tilted grin made her ask, "What's going on in that scheming mind of yours?"

He opened his arms wide. "Tempie! She's been at loose ends since the playhouse burned down. I'm sure the Andersons could use her help. Why don't you give her their number?"

"That's a great idea!" Then why hadn't Gracie thought of it first?

Because you were too busy thinking of yourself.

She changed the subject. "Does Mr. Anderson still serve as your advisor?"

"There aren't many important decisions I make without his input. He helped me negotiate the lease for my rental space and sat in on my interviews for a shop manager. I couldn't believe how much he knew about electronics. Even this meeting in New York is because he knew someone who knew someone." He hesitated a few seconds. "I think it was a God thing."

Gracie grinned. "Your lunches with Tempie are rubbing off."

"You may be right. She's a grand cheerleader, your grandmother."

"That's what you and Tempie were to me. I never would've had the courage to move here on my own."

"Nah, you had the courage. Who else could have played all those roles and worn all those crazy costumes while seating restaurant guests?" He nudged her foot with his. "Your star's going to rise so high your hometown chums will fade from view."

She struck a pose, putting her hand aside her face. "A star never forgets her first real fans."

"Speaking of fans, what's up with this fella of yours, Chase the turtle-lover?"

"Ha, ha. Besides, you, of all people, should know serious career plans don't leave room for a relationship." To prevent herself from sliding back into self-absorption, she said, "I want to hear more about this client you're here to impress."

"*Potential* client. If I land the job, it would be a huge boost to my business. But before the customer decides, I have to pass a test."

"What kind of test?"

"I have to prove the effectiveness of the components I manufacture by putting them to work in a practical situation."

"Like an audition?"

A slight grin appeared. "Yes, like an audition." He shifted on the love seat. "Hey, you never told me whether your birthday prayer was answered today."

She was fuddled. "Prayer?"

He laughed. "You prayed for a birthday to remember … remember?"

"Oh, right. Let's see. I started my day with the wrong coffee order, missed my train, and had a smelly encounter with a lovesick vagrant on the next one. Then I made a fool of myself in front of Polina Zelenka's assistant. My solo debut was hacked by Harper, thanks to you, then I got kicked off stage. I followed that with a lunch watching you and Harper drool over each other while Chase drooled over his turtles. What do you think?"

"Prayer answered." Ian brushed his palms together. "A day to remember, I'd say."

"You would." With one swift move, she pushed his feet off the ottoman.

So, Gracie, any reason why you left out Chase's invitation to meet Bennett Noble?

Stupid conscience.

Chapter Eighteen

Gracie was waiting by her laptop for her grandmother's video chat signal. The second it beeped, she clicked on the icon and blurted, "Tempie, guess who I get to meet next week."

"And hello to you too, dear."

"Sorry. Hi. But guess!"

"Why that shouldn't be hard at all …" Tempie adjusted her webcam. "… since New York only has a population of 8.5 million."

"I'll give you a hint. He wrote and directed *Love and Waffles*."

"Hmm, a trick question. Could he be Bennett Noble?"

"Can you believe it?"

"My, my, Cape Cod's very own Kat Hamilton will finally get to meet her hero. How did this come about?"

"Harper introduced me to this guy who happens to be Noble's nephew. We're meeting for coffee."

"A small world after all. Here's a tidbit for you. Noble is one of the few directors who still uses storyboards for his plays."

"Really? How do you know that?"

"I read. Now here's an idea. Create a Grace Camden storyboard. Sort of like scrapbooking. Include all the plays you've been in since you were a child. I'll email you some pictures. You can find storyboard templates online."

Tempie knows about templates?

"Have the storyboard with you. But, now this is key, wait for God's prompting before you give it to him. Don't run ahead of him as you're prone to do."

Gracie twirled her hair around a finger. "I have no idea what you mean."

"I could give you a few examples if you'd like?"

"No, I would not like, thank you very much."

Tempie laughed. "Let me know how it goes for you girls."

"No *girls*. Just me and his nephew, Chase."

"Didn't you tell me Harper introduced you to this young man?"

"She did, but—"

"But she doesn't know about the meeting with Noble?"

Gracie averted her eyes. "Well, I, uh … Harper can be so competitive and jealous sometimes. Our friendship works best when we both have a reason to celebrate."

"Perhaps a joint meeting with Bennett Noble would do?"

"Yes, ma'am." Gracie tried to redeem herself. "Before we go, I've got something that might interest *you*. Do you recall me telling you about Will and Elizabeth Anderson, two of my favorite customers at the Cranberry Fare?"

"Of course, I do. Why?"

"Well, after they married, they started a company called We'll Always Have Paris. They put on shows for residents in fifty-five and older communities and nursing homes. Elizabeth has a ton of props from her years as an international travel guide. They need help. You'd be a great asset to them."

"Sure beats bridge. Thanks for thinking of me, dear."

"The idea was Ian's. You can thank him. Will is his business mentor." Gracie gave her the Andersons' phone number.

"Next time you see that young man, give him a big hug for me. Tell him I miss our lunches."

Soon after they signed off, Gracie found a storyboard template online, which she titled "Grace Camden: Actor." She listed all seventeen plays she'd ever been in from *Bears Don't Cry* in first grade, to her starring role in *Love and Waffles* on the Cape, and to her recent role in *Powerless to Pump*. Since she doubted she'd get to say all she wanted to say when she met Noble over coffee, the storyboard would have to speak for her. At the very least, it would show her range and commitment.

While researching Noble, she learned he'd once served as head of the drama department at Juilliard years before Rachel began there. This guy wouldn't be easy to impress. A deep search of insider entertainment blogs confirmed this particular Starbucks was a hangout for him and others in the theater. How had she missed that?

As for inviting Harper, I'll see.

Chapter Ninteen

Indian summer greeted Gracie the next day, convincing her that the air in the city smelled fresh, and fall was the best season of all. She'd invited Seymour to join the children and her at the park. She could've given him her news over the phone, but she wanted to see his reaction when she told him his phone number was in the hands of Polina Zelenka's personal assistant.

Seymour was waiting. "Shalom! Who do we have here? The incredible children I saw when we first met?"

Gracie placed her free hand on Miles's shoulder while Leighton held tight to her other. "This is Miles, an aspiring actor like me, and his sister, Leighton, an aspiring angel—unlike me. Children, say hello to Mr. Kaufman."

Leighton stepped closer to Gracie and snuck a peek at Seymour. "Hi."

Seymour bowed. "Hello, Miss Leighton. You are the first angel I have ever met."

She released her grip on Gracie's hand, pressed her thumb against her palm, then held her fingers up. "I'm four."

"That is astonishing! I was four once too."

Leighton pointed to his patch. "Do you have a boo-boo?"

"I did a long time ago, but it is all better now."

Miles assessed Seymour with the intensity of a cold war border guard. After ten seconds of silence, a suitable period for any seven-year-old, he said, "Do you know any songs from *Fiddler on the Roof*?"

Gracie folded her arms. *Unbelievable.*

Seymour clasped his hands together. "I do! A most powerful story."

Miles climbed on the bench and spoke the opening words to the song "If I Were a Rich Man." He beamed when Seymour joined him, starting right where Miles left off. The unlikely duo belted out a rousing rendition of Tevye's lament, then gave each other an enthusiastic ovation.

When Seymour sat to catch his breath, Miles and Leighton raced to the swings.

"You passed Miles's litmus test with extra credit. There's not a week that goes by that we don't have to download *Fiddler* music videos. 'Rich Man' is his favorite. Thanks for being so patient."

"No patience needed. Singing with that child—what a joy!"

"Yes, it can be." She joined him on the bench. "I have some news."

His eyebrow lifted. "About your future?"

Gracie said, "About *both* our futures."

"Is that so?"

"Yours first. By some miracle, I was able to give your phone number to Polina Zelenka's personal assistant. Her name is, uh,"—She pulled a slip of paper from her pocket.—"Simka Lonnit. Sounds foreign to me."

His brows snapped together. "Polina has my phone number?"

"Well, Simka Lonnit does. I have no way of knowing when or if she'll give it to Polina."

"Perhaps upon her return from Buffalo on Sunday." Seymour flushed then shrugged. "I found her schedule on her website."

"You know, Polina doesn't need to be home to call you."

Patting his coat pocket, he pulled out a flip phone. "It is on." He exhaled then smiled. "And your news?"

"I met this guy, Chase Grayson, who's going to introduce me to his uncle who happens to be the playwright and director Bennett Noble."

"That is wonderful news, Grace."

"I know. God gave me this talent and the desire to use it, so I need this meeting to go well."

"The Lord is sovereign," Seymour said. "If meeting Bennett Noble is best for you, and if meeting Polina is best for me, then both will go well."

"No, really, this is my big chance."

"Grace, you will have many big chances. However, some of them may not be from God."

"But, Seymour—"

"Let me tell you about my 'big chances.'" He got as comfortable as he could on a steel park bench. "I was the new mohel in Postville. Like many in my profession starting out, I needed a second job to supplement my income, which to that point had been zero."

Gracie interrupted, "With your years of experience, couldn't you have gotten a teaching position?"

"Postville's population could only support a combined elementary and middle school and one high school. And homeschooling was quite common in that rural area, so children could help on the farms."

"What did you do?"

"I prayed, pondered, and waited. Since I had come from a long line of Moldovan furriers—six generations to be precise—I sought a job in that industry."

"Diamond cutting *and* furring? Both high-end businesses—I'm impressed."

"I do not know about that, but I believe as you do that God does not waste a thing. Yet no amount of knowledge could help when I discovered a dearth of furriers in Postville or in the surrounding towns. None to be exact."

She took her jacket off and tied it around her waist. "Were you bummed?"

"I was not *bummed* but curious and thrilled because I knew it meant God had a better plan for me. I praised God the way my parents had taught me, then I prayed, pondered, and waited some more."

"What happened then?"

"I soon learned that Postville was home to a large, kosher, meat-processing plant. Even though I had never processed meat, I reasoned my familiarity with animal anatomy might give me an edge over the competition." He removed his wide-brimmed black felt fedora and fanned himself with it. "The hours were steady, and the pay was good."

"I bet you're glad you waited." Gracie craned her neck to check on the children.

"Yes, though not for the reason you think. As a boy, I had seen the way furriers and butchers glared at each other, each thinking their part of the carcass more important. Before I applied for the position, I had to examine my conscience for such pettiness."

She dropped her head. "Of course, you did. How long did you work there?"

He leveled his gaze at her. "No time at all. In the brief period it took me to determine my heart held no bitterness, the slaughterhouse filed for bankruptcy under allegations of mistreatment by an animal rights activist group. Kosher rules or not, technically they were killing cows, so I guess some might mistake that for mistreatment."

"Are you kidding me? Weren't you discouraged?"

"Discouraged? Why would I be when I knew the Lord had an even better plan for me?"

"Okaaay. And what exactly was that plan?"

"Well, the only other industry professionals the furriers and butchers trusted less than each other were taxidermists, whom they believed were hypocrites for letting others do the killing. I was willing to overlook this tiny hypocrisy to secure employment."

Gracie shivered at the idea of performing any of those jobs. "I suppose transitioning to taxidermy wasn't that much of a stretch."

"I never found out. The only call for taxidermy in the county came from two old maid sisters who refused to part with their pets for any portion of forever. A cat here, a bird there, was hardly a reliable source of income."

"Don't tell me. You praised God because he had an even better plan for you."

"I did and he did." Seymour checked his watch then stood. "But I must leave that story for another day."

"What? You're not going to tell me how it ended?"

"I cannot be late for my appointment." He adjusted his hat. "My counsel is to wait on the Lord. You will recognize his plan when you see it."

"In case you haven't noticed, patience isn't one of my stronger traits." She called over to the kids. "Come say good-bye to Mr. Kaufman."

Leighton ran over and hugged Seymour.

Miles shook his hand. "D'ya have to go cut diamonds now?"

"You know, Mr. Kaufman," Gracie said, "the Adlers are Jewish. Miles may be more familiar with the Hebrew word mohel than I am."

Miles scrunched his face into one big question mark. "Isn't a mohel the man who circumcises baby boys?"

Gracie looked from boy to man, then back and forth again. Truth broke over her head like a raw egg. She gawked at Seymour. "You don't cut *diamonds*, do you?"

"I do not." Seymour tried not to laugh but failed completely.

Gracie muttered something she didn't want the kids to overhear.

Seymour patted Leighton's head and gave Miles a high five. "Until we meet again, 'yubby dibby dum.'"

Miles sang back, "Deedle deedle dum."

"Shalom, Grace. Thank you again for your help." He walked briskly down the pathway.

She called after him. "Let me know if you hear from Polina!"

"I shall indeed!"

Chapter Twenty

Rachel hugged her children when they entered the house with Gracie. "Did you have fun today?"

Leighton snuggled closer to her mother.

Miles squirmed away. "Know what, Mom? I beat a kid climbing to the top of the jungle gym and sang 'Rich Man' with a mohel. And I saw a guy spying on us."

Gracie rolled her eyes. "Don't scare your mother, Miles. No one was spying on us."

"Yuh-huh! He was behind the trees when I was at the top of the jungle gym."

"Perhaps you imagined it." Rachel patted down one of his cowlicks. "Okay, you two, you have time for one show before dinner, so go!"

He and Leighton bolted down the hall to the family room.

"I need to curb that boy's imagination," Rachel said.

"I can relate. He makes things up to have fun."

"Did he imagine singing with a mohel too?"

"No, that was real. He did a *Fiddler on the Roof* duet with Seymour, who, by the way, thinks your children are a joy."

"They are, mostly when I'm not around."

Miles sprinted back down the hall. "Mommy, I forgot to tell you! Gracie thought a mohel cut diamonds." Then he rushed back to his show.

Rachel eyed Gracie, then put up a hand to stop her. "I don't even want to know." She opened the refrigerator door. "Stay for dinner? We're having leftovers."

Gracie's mushy avocado, film-covered canned soup, and soggy half sandwich from three days ago didn't seem appealing. "I accept. Your leftovers are four-star compared to mine."

"Good. Reggie's been working overtime a lot lately, but he said he'd be home on time today."

Rachel got dinner in the oven while Gracie set the table.

The door flew open, and Reggie walked in. "Where's my dinner, woman!" He raised his arms to protect himself from a possible swat.

"Such a funny man." Rachel kissed him. "Go say hello to your children. They're watching one of their shows. Dinner will be a few minutes yet."

He set his briefcase on the floor, put his phone on the hutch, and hung his coat. "Let me know. I'm starving." He headed for the family room. "Daddy's home!"

Rachel put on her oven mitts. "Gracie, can you get me a platter from the hutch?"

Reggie's phone buzzed as Gracie opened the glass door. "Your husband's phone is vibrating."

"Normally, I'd say ignore it, but he's been so hyped about his latest project, I don't dare. Would you mind running it to him?"

Gracie grabbed the phone and quickstepped down the hall. The screen lit up, the caller ID read "Ian Quinn."

Huh? Maybe Ian was looking for her. But how would he know Reggie's number? To be sure, she stole another glimpse before she handed the phone to Reggie.

He glanced at the phone then at her. "Thanks. I'll take the call in my office."

Why would Ian be calling Reggie? As far as she knew, they'd only met briefly that one time at Juilliard on her birthday. What had she missed?

All through dinner, Gracie waited for Reggie to comment on the call. He didn't. And she couldn't ask him about it because then he'd know she'd been nosey.

Is Ian checking up on me? Why would he do that? Nah, this has to be something else.

Back in her apartment, she texted Ian. "Hey, Quinn, what's going on between you and my boss?" She deleted her question and typed, "Doing anything tonight?"

No response.

The day before Gracie was scheduled to meet with Chase and Bennett Noble, she caved and called Harper. "Want to tag along on my meeting with Chase and his uncle tomorrow?"

"His uncle?"

"Yes, Bennett Noble." She giggled, picturing Harper's face.

"Are you joking?"

"Nope. But you owe me, remember, for inviting Chase to my birthday party. Your job will be to distract Chase while I talk to Noble."

The next evening, she hurried Harper along in case they had difficulty finding the right Starbucks. They were early. Gracie prided herself on always arriving five minutes before a meeting, certainly not fifteen. She and Harper dawdled, window shopping until it was time.

When they walked in, Chase was there. Alone.

"Ciao!" When he tried to stand, his chair fell backward hitting the customer behind him. "Sorry, sorry."

The man glowered and grumbled.

The clock on the wall matched the time on Gracie's phone. "I hope we're not too early?"

"Not at all." Chase adjusted his clunky eyeglasses and patted his hair.

Gracie's attention was drawn to an errant shock of pure white hair in one of his brown-black eyebrows. A birthmark? Early onset old age? Toothpaste? She hadn't noticed before.

"What would you ladies like to drink? Uncle Bennett should be here soon. That's if nothing more important comes along."

Not like Gracie could ask him what that might be since she could list a hundred more important things in one breath. This wasn't her insecurity; this was a fact. Why hadn't she considered the possibility?

They gave their order to Chase. As he went to fill it, Gracie glanced around to see if she recognized any celebrities. Nope.

Putting heel to toe like he was walking a tightrope, Chase managed to deliver their coffee without spilling. After a brief, weird period of dead air, he said, "Anyhow, Gracie, what have you been up to?"

"Not much. Usual nanny duties and getting ready for this meeting." She pointed to her portfolio propped against her chair.

Chase leaned over and looked. "Are those glamour shots?"

"No, more like a visual history of my acting experience."

"Oh." He stirred another packet of sugar into his coffee. "How about you, Harper?"

"I'm auditioning for a role in a Gerard Dupris play. Gracie might try out too."

"That's good." He held his coffee with both hands and slurped. "I haven't seen you at Lincoln Center lately. No more secret meetings with your rabbi, huh?"

"No. And like I said, he's not a rabbi, exactly."

Harper said, "Rabbi? What rabbi?"

Gracie wished the conversation would move on to turtles. The time was ten past eight. She felt like she was auditioning for a part in *Waiting for Godot.* But unlike Samuel Beckett's characters, she wasn't willing to wait endlessly.

Chase's phone rang.

She prayed his uncle wasn't at the end of the smooth jazz ringtone calling to cancel.

"I have to take this. It's Mother." He sat sideways in his chair. "Hello, Mother ... Oh yes, I am here with my friends waiting for Uncle ... I did ... Nothing to worry about ... Yes, Mother ... Love you too. Ciao."

He lowered his head. "Mother is worried about one of my turtles. He wasn't eating this morning."

"Oh no, which one?" Harper asked.

Like Harper cares. Gracie changed the topic. "Chase, maybe you should call your uncle."

"Good idea." He stood without knocking his chair over. "Right after I get back from the little boys' room."

After he excused himself, Gracie panicked. What if Bennett Nobel came in while Chase was gone? Would she dare approach him on her own?

No need to worry; no one came in.

When Chase came back, he was on his cell. "I understand. I'll let her know ... She brought some stuff for you ... Uh, okay, bye." He pulled his lips into an apologetic smile. "Sorry. He can't make it. Something about a temperamental actress."

Sheesh. Anyone who is anyone in the industry hasn't used the word actress in years. You'd think a big shot director would know that. Would a female director be called a directress? I don't think so. The word is actor! Why is that so hard to remember? And why does the problem person always have to be a temperamental female?

Chase interrupted her internal tirade and motioned to her storyboard. "Uncle told me I should drop off your folder."

"He did?" She hesitated before she handed him her storyboards. "Please thank him for me and tell him he's made one actress quite happy."

On the way home Gracie mulled things over with Harper. "I'm probably being unreasonable expecting Noble to contact me soon."

"Unless Chase gets the storyboards to him right away."

Gracie was hopeful. "And Noble sees something unique."

"Oh, you're unique, all right." Harper laughed. "Now, since I gave you that tip about *Little Black Lies*, I'm sure you'll do the same for me when Noble calls."

"Maybe—if you behave."

Chapter Twenty-One

Polina Zelenka called Seymour the day she returned to New York. "Shalom! I was so pleased when Simka gave me your message. Now that you're in the city, we must get together."

Seymour could not remember one word he had rehearsed while waiting for her call. "That sounds lovely."

Perhaps when the jitters stop, my mind will clear.

"I have a two o'clock matinee on Wednesday at the Majestic. Would you consider being my guest? I'll leave a ticket at the box office. Perhaps we could have an early supper after?"

He steadied his breathing. "That sounds lovely." *Oy vey, did he not just say that? What a schmoe.*

"We have a date. See you Wednesday."

He was glad Polina hung up when she did, because "that sounds lovely" was about to topple off his tongue again. He flipped his phone shut then panicked. Did Polina say "We have a date"? If so, what did that entail? Figuratively? Literally? Financially? He must be sure to bring enough cash. Did he even have enough cash? What was he to do now?

The answer came swiftly—pray, ponder, and wait.

Seymour took thirty minutes to decide which of his three black suits to wear. Once he eliminated the oldest and the newest, his decision was easy. Choosing an eye patch from his sock drawer was another matter. After prolonged deliberation, he excluded his entire colorful collection, opting for the matte black over the more formal sateen. He doubted that a matinee performance of *The Phantom of the Opera* qualified as formal. Or did it? Oy.

He was so focused on following his detailed directions that the trip to the Majestic at 247 West Forty-fourth went by in a blur. There, standing in line, he tugged on his cuffs, wondering if his sleeves were too short for his jacket. Then he tugged on them again. Now they were too long. Uncertain, he dropped his arms to his side.

Seymour faced the teller at the box office window and cleared his throat. "Do you have a ticket for today's matinee for Seymour Kaufman from Ms. Zelenka?"

The teller reached into a cubby, then handed him an envelope. "Show begins in twenty."

Even though Seymour had tried to familiarize himself with the old theater by visiting their website, the online pictures were inadequate to convey the size and opulence of this landmark building. Considering its age, he expected it to be a bit shabby. Instead, the ornate Spanish design was gilded and glittering.

Nothing like this in Postville, and the nearest thing in Des Moines was the capitol.

An usher led him down the dimly-lit center aisle to the third row, end seat. Seymour thanked him for the program, then went through it to see when Polina would appear in her role as Carlotta, the scheming prima donna. His pulse quickened with every instrument the orchestra tuned and every buzz of the audience. He took a few deep breaths to dispel his anxiety.

A sturdy, plain-faced woman came alongside his seat. Her black shawl, brightened by its magenta and yellow floral design, roused a faded picture of his mother.

"Excuse me, sir. You are Polina's friend, Seymour, *nu*? I am personal assistant, Simka Lonnit."

She leaned in a few inches closer, faint lines visible on her pleasant face. "I am Polina's cousin too."

He was charmed by her Eastern European accent, not for its sound as much as for the memories it evoked. "Such a pleasure to meet you, Mrs. Lonnit."

She waved off his formality. "Simka, please."

"Have you been with Polina long, Simka?"

"Three months. After many years apart, we connect again."

"Did Polina mention that I am a native Moldovan? I was fourteen when my parents died. Soon after, I came to the States to live with my uncle in Iowa."

She tucked a stray hair into her tidy, wheat-colored bun. "Iowa? In middle of America, nu? How then did you meet Polina?"

"Through her family. The first time was at her great nephew's bris, then later at her cousin's bar mitzvah."

"Must be father's side of family. Many children I have not met. Polina's mother and my mother were blood."

Simka was most likely about Polina's age. There was a slight familial resemblance, although her complexion was weathered while Polina's was velvety.

Who am I to think this? What do I know from weather and velvet?

"Relocating can be difficult," he said. "The only person I knew when I moved to New York a month ago, other than my cousin Aaron—and I didn't even know him well—was Polina."

"Now you know me." The corners of her mouth lifted slightly.

At least he thought they did. One of Uncle Jacob's adages came to his mind. *Moldovan women do not give their smiles away on a whim.*

Outside of the few plays he had seen at the Jewish Community Center in Des Moines and at the Farmer's Market Festivals in Postville, this was his first professional production. "I have never heard Polina sing live. I do not want to miss a note."

"Opera is her life." Simka tightened her shawl around her. "One can never forget her voice."

The orchestra fell silent as did the audience. The lights dimmed, and the curtain went up. Seymour's breath caught in his throat when Polina made her entrance in the first scene. He almost didn't recognize her. Wild red hair was piled atop her head with a crown of jewels intertwined. She wore a gaudy gown covered in sequins and sparkles. The bold-colored makeup made her appear harsh—contrary to everything he remembered about her.

Although every performer was superb, Carlotta's character was the one who came to life whenever she entered a scene. Or was it Polina? Her voice—what range, what purity, what power! How could each note give him chills and warm him all over at once?

When the curtain fell, Seymour got so caught up in the standing ovation he did not notice when it ended.

Simka pulled on his coat sleeve. "Sit now until people leave. Polina needs time to change and have drink."

Drink? Seymour had never equated Polina with drinking. "Of course." He sat until the chattering audience exited the theater. By the time he and Simka adjourned to the lobby, Polina was only minutes behind them.

She approached and gave him her hand. "Seymour! What a delight to see you again."

"Shalom. You as well." Seymour could not ignore the softness of her hand. "Thank you for your kind invitation."

He was relieved to see the unruly, garish red hair had been replaced by her natural golden blonde. Swept up to one side, it was held by the same mother-of-pearl comb he remembered from their previous tête-à-têtes in Postville. Her creamy complexion and her green eyes—a shade he longed for in early spring—were free from the heavy makeup. In place of the gigantic dress, she wore charcoal gray slacks, a pale-yellow sweater, and a simple strand of pearls. A trench coat was draped over her arm.

Simka tipped her head toward Seymour. "Cousin, you should see friend here. When play is over, he has bug eyes and tied tongue."

Polina laughed softly as she slipped on her coat. "I hope that means you liked the show."

"I have never enjoyed an event as much! The music was so ... Oh, the costumes were ... And that story!" He took a breath to slow his pace. "Above all, your voice—so lovely."

Embarrassed by all his gushing, he shut his mouth. He worried that Polina might think him a bumpkin. As she should since he was.

"I was so pleased you were able to attend and keep Simka company. She's had to sit through too many of these productions alone." Polina fastened the belt on her coat. "Now, how about the three of us enjoy our supper in a less theatrical setting?"

Seymour bowed slightly. "As you wish, m'ladies." *Oy! Now I am bowing like an English peacock. What is wrong with me?*

"Car service is waiting." Simka pushed open the door and hugged her shawl around her. The stiff autumn breeze had no effect on her heavy, ankle-length skirt.

Seymour waited for Polina to exit.

A shiny black Lincoln was parked at the curb. The closest Seymour had come to being in a fancy car like this was when he had gone to the funeral of Uncle Jacob's lawyer friend in Des Moines.

Chapter Twenty-Two

Once they were seated—Seymour across from the women—Polina gave the driver an address, and the car edged into traffic. He felt awkward facing backward. Or was it because he was toe to toe with Polina?

He tried to relax by making conversation. "I read that *The Phantom of the Opera* has been playing at the Majestic Theatre since 1988. Is that not plenty of time for everyone in New York to have seen it?"

"That's a good question," Polina said. "You see, people come here from all over the country, even the world, for the arts. Many see the same play more than once, especially when a new artist joins the cast."

He said, "I see," but of course he did not. How could the average budget permit it? He was too polite to speak of the price of tickets, especially since he had attended the matinee for free.

Simka settled her handbag on her lap. "Cousin fill in for friend who went on honeymoon. People find out. They come for to hear Polina."

Now *that* he could understand.

"Enough about the opera," Polina said. "I would love to know what you've been doing since your move to New York."

Seymour laughed. "Mainly, learning to navigate the subway system so I can arrive on time for my appointments."

"Any sightseeing? Made any friends?" Polina adjusted her hair comb.

"Not much sightseeing. I did go to Lincoln Center once to …" He stopped before he admitted he had gone there hoping to see her. "Grace, a kind young woman I met at the park, showed me around the plaza."

"Yes, the one who gave Simka your card." Polina tapped her cousin's hand. "Simka has only been in the country a short time, but she's been to more cities here than many Americans. I've done three tours in the last three months. First the East Coast, then the southern states. Before that, it was Seattle, Sacramento, and Austin."

He smiled at Simka. "How exciting for you."

Before she could comment, Polina broke in. "All I do is rehearse and perform, which can be tiresome for my assistants. If I don't want to lose my cousin, I need to give her time to make a life of her own."

Simka eyed Polina. "You do much for me already—it is not necessary. Who will make special juice drink for your vocal chords after performance?"

Special juice drink. Seymour was relieved.

"You can show me how. I managed all by myself in Buffalo last weekend." Polina feigned a scowl. "I am your employer, remember? You have to listen to me and make time for fun!"

After a few more turns, the car pulled to the curb. The driver exited to open the door. Seymour could see no restaurants nearby. When he craned to see the full height of the high rise in front of him, he feared his head would fall off his shoulders.

A uniformed doorman approached them and tipped his hat. "Good evening, Mrs. Lonnit. Good evening, Ms. Zelenka. Did you break another leg this afternoon?"

Polina winked at him. "I did my best, Victor."

Seymour looked from him to Polina's legs and back to the doorman again. He tipped his hat in return. "Seymour Kaufman. A pleasure to meet you, Victor."

"Likewise, Mr. Kaufman." Victor held the main door open. "The caterer arrived some time ago, Ms. Zelenka. The concierge let him in."

Polina touched Victor's arm as she went by. "Dependable, as always."

Seymour followed the ladies across the lobby, into an elevator, then down a hall. He half expected someone to pop out of nowhere to unlock the apartment door, but Polina opened it herself.

"Simka, please make Seymour feel at home while I see about dinner. I shouldn't be long."

Simka hung their coats, then led him into a spacious living room. "Sit. Please. Be comfortable."

One glance around the enormous room told him Polina had exquisite taste. A pair of French Bergères, a Charles X secretary, and quality Persian rugs. Uncle Jacob had been into antiques, so Seymour had learned to recognize them. Of course, recognizing was one thing; owning was quite another.

He sat on an oversized Chesterfield sofa upholstered in pale-blue mohair.

Simka joined him. "My cousin has beautiful things, nu?"

Running his hand along the arm of the sofa, he said, "The classic style suits her."

"Most pieces not Moldovan." Simka pointed out various objets d'art around the room. "That one German, these two Italian, and sculpture on mantle from Poland."

By her tone, Seymour could not tell if she was bragging or apologizing. He found no clue in her expression. "Well, it all fits together nicely."

"Da, fits her." She lifted a small, intricately carved wooden box from the end table. "My father make this. He give to Polina."

He took the box she offered and examined it. "Such detail. Talent and patience is needed to do this kind of work."

Simka nodded. "Da."

Seymour stood when Polina entered the room.

She put one arm through Simka's, the other through his. "I hope you're hungry because dinner is ready."

Every ounce of Seymour's tactile sense was drawn to the crook of his elbow on the short walk to the dining room.

The table was simply set without crystal, china, or fine linen. Only colorful dinnerware on a white cotton tablecloth.

When the caterer brought in the platters, Seymour smelled dishes he hadn't in years. "Is this what I think it is?"

"Depends on what you think it is." Polina winked at him, then unfolded her napkin and placed it on her lap.

His recognition jumped from tureen to platter to bowl. "Mutton stew. Stuffed cabbage. Dumplings."

Simka translated as she pointed to each dish. "*Ghiveci. Sarmale. Borș de burechiușe.* There is *Mămăligă* with cheese and greaves too."

He rubbed his hands together. "I haven't tasted food like this since I left my home in Dobrogea."

"The credit goes to Simka. When I told her about you, she thought it would be nice for us to enjoy a taste of home together."

"You kind ladies know how to make a person feel welcome. Do you mind if I say the blessing?" Seymour was so thankful he burst forth before they could answer. "Blessed are you, Lord our God, King of the Universe, who creates various kinds of tasty sustenance, then gives us family and friends to share them with. Amen."

"Amen!" Polina raised her glass. "*Un toast pentru familia și noi prieteni!*" A toast to family and new friends!" The three of them clinked glasses and drank.

He took another sip of his drink. "What is this delicious concoction?"

Polina smiled. "Simka's special Moldovan recipe made from apples, plums, and cherries. The juice is so soothing to my throat. I believe it helps my voice."

Simka said to Seymour. "Could be you sing like bird tomorrow."

He swallowed quickly. "Then it would be a crow."

Both ladies laughed.

Seymour did not want to waste the entire dinner conversation on food or himself. He wanted to learn all he could about Polina. To do that without slighting her cousin was good manners. "Ladies, please tell me about your lives in the old country and how you came to be in America."

Polina rested her fork on the edge of her plate. "Being only a year apart, Simka and I were very close as children. But our lives took different paths as we got older. I was only sixteen when my first mentor discovered me and brought me to the Chisinau Opera. A year later, I moved to the States to begin my career. Nearly thirty years now."

"A successful career at that," he said. "What is this I hear about a gala honoring you in November—twenty-five years at the Met, I believe?"

Polina sighed. "Excuse me while I speak my mind. These types of events are more about making news and raising money than bestowing honor. They even want me to waltz around in some necklace worth millions. How does that advance the craft?"

"Waltz advance craft of jeweler." Simka giggled at her joke. "Because you love opera, you will wear necklace."

"You're right, I will," Polina said, "but I won't like it. The jeweler even has to come over for a fitting."

Simka's eyes flashed. "Fitting? *Prost!* Silly!"

"I know," Polina said, "but the length and shape must fit the neckline of the gown—which I have not chosen yet."

Seymour wanted to tell her no one would be looking at her jewelry when they could look at her and hear her sing, but he was not so bold. Instead, he continued in his politeness. "And you, Simka? Tell me about your life."

She wiped her mouth, then rested her hands in her lap. "I stayed in homeland, married, and raised my son. Nothing exciting like Polina."

"Are you serious?" Polina put her glass down. "You had a family, a son to be proud of. Tell Seymour about Vânât."

A hint of pride was in Simka's voice. "Vânât is smart. How you say? Entrepreneur. He travels all over."

Seymour nodded. "Impressive. Do you get to see him often?"

"No, he must work. I must understand."

The discussion soon came back to Moldova. How the Jewish settlements with their shoemakers, milkmen, blacksmiths, and furriers contributed to society. How dry mud roads compare to sodden mud roads. How the Russians like to claim Moldovans don't like Romanians, even though the two countries share the same language and history.

"Speaking of language," Polina said, "how is it we don't detect a trace of an accent in you, Seymour? If I remember correctly, when we met back in Postville, you said you were a teenager when you came to the states."

"True. Uncle Jacob made sure I learned to speak English well along with Hebrew. I had formal lessons weekly for years. Unfortunately, I have forgotten much of my mother tongue."

"For me to excel in my field, I had to take courses in elocution in Italian, German, French, Russian, and English. Singing the words made the learning tolerable."

Simka wisecracked, "I think maybe milking goats was easier."

They talked of all this and more until Seymour noticed his politeness had turned to interest, then nostalgia. Once the dessert dishes were cleared, Simka excused herself to finalize things with the caterer.

Polina lowered her voice. "My cousin was widowed nine months ago. I'm ashamed to admit I wasn't even aware her husband had died until she wrote to ask if I could help her find a job in the States. I am so pleased to have family with me after all this time."

"How sad to lose a spouse. However, she is blessed to have a son and a cousin who care."

"With all the traveling I do, Simka hasn't had it easy working for me. I leave for another five-day tour on Monday. I would like to give her that time off."

"A thoughtful gesture on your part."

"I would feel so much better knowing she's not sitting in this apartment alone the whole time." Polina leaned forward a bit. "I was wondering, as a great favor to me, would you mind looking in on her while I'm away?"

Seymour placed his napkin on the table. "I would be honored."

"I don't want her to feel like I've hired a babysitter or a bodyguard. Maybe you could invite her to do some sightseeing or see a movie?"

Seymour sat straight and tall. "Do not worry yourself. I will take care of it."

Even though Seymour had no idea what he would do with Simka or how he would show her around a city he did not know, he would do anything for Polina.

Chapter Twenty-Three

Gracie sensed excitement in Seymour's voice when he phoned to recount his evening with Polina.

"After the play, we went back to her apartment for dinner. Oy! A Moldovan feast, it was! Did I mention that Polina and Simka are cousins? A Chesterfield sofa she has, upholstered in blue. Can you imagine?"

Gracie let him talk, mainly because she had as much chance of interrupting his flow as she did that of Niagara Falls.

"Polina is going on the road, as they say, the day after tomorrow. She asked if I would keep Simka entertained while she is away. That shows an inordinate amount of trust in someone you have only met three times, would you not agree?"

"Perhaps—"

"Of course, being willing and being capable are not the same. When it comes to entertaining others, I lack experience."

"Maybe I could—"

"My research has provided a few possibilities. The Bronx Zoo. The Metropolitan Museum of Art. Brooklyn Bowl. What do you think?"

"Is that *bowl* as in bowling?"

Seymour rushed to answer. "Too prosaic?"

"No, I never thought of you as a bowler, that's all." *And it has nothing to do with being prosaic.*

"*Azoy?* Really? That is right. I never did tell you how I got into that sport, did I?"

"I'm sure I would have remembered."

"A story for another time, perhaps," he said.

"I'll hold you to it." Gracie tucked a lock of hair behind her ear. "So, what's Simka like?"

"Simka? A pleasant woman, funny in a reserved way. Polina told me she was widowed this year so there might be some sadness."

"Sounds like any one of your ideas might work to cheer her. Why not let her choose?"

"A perfect solution! She may even have a suggestion of her own."

"She might."

"Did I mention that Polina's personal driver will be available to convey us?"

"You did."

"Oy! Grace, please excuse me for being such a *zhlub*. I have been ill-mannered. I pray all is going well for you."

"Very well, thank you." She felt dizzy when they hung up.

"Slow down, Marisol," Gracie said. "Start at the beginning." It didn't help that their phone connection was spotty.

Zeke and Eli's nanny repeated herself. "Eli was admitted to Mount Sinai for an evaluation by a pediatric hematologist-oncologist. I should have been watching him closer."

"Listen to me. You're an excellent nanny to those boys and their baby sister. The reason he's in the hospital so soon is probably because you *were* watching him closely. Besides, I hear Mount Sinai is the best. How long will he have to be there?"

"Not sure. Of course, the baby is too young to be aware of what's going on, but Zeke is upset. He and Eli are so close."

"Let me take Zeke after school a few days this week. Being with his buddies might get his mind off his brother for awhile."

"That's so kind." Marisol sounded less panicky. "Zeke would like that."

"And when Eli's well enough for visitors," Gracie said, "maybe I could bring the kids by."

Later that afternoon, Gracie helped Miles and Leighton make cards for Eli. Leighton drew a princess in a castle with a field of flowers. Miles was much more literal. His card depicted a hospital bed with a number of tubes sticking out of the patient.

Leighton added a crown on the princess's head. "I hope my card makes him better."

Miles got right to the point. "Is Eli gonna die?"

Ooh, boy. "Miles, he needs to stay in the hospital until the doctors figure out the right medicine to give him."

"Yeah, but is he gonna die?"

Gracie was direct. "Only God knows when we're going to die, and he never tells us." That satisfied him for the time being.

"I know! Why don't we write a play to perform for Eli when he's ready for visitors?"

"Can I be the star?" Miles asked.

"You can be the leading man, and Leighton can be the leading lady."

"But I'm the star, right?"

In her Minnie Mouse voice, Leighton settled things with her brother. "Milesy, you hafta be the star 'cuz you can't be the princess. That's me."

Miles mumbled something about stupid princesses. But it didn't take long for him to come up with an idea he could work with. "I can be a knight with a sword and a shield—and a horse!"

Gracie spent the rest of the week helping them with the play, which was enough to keep Miles off the topic of dying. She prayed they'd have the opportunity to perform.

Gracie told her grandmother about their idea to put on a play for Eli.

"Phooey!" Tempie said. "Now this is why I wish we lived closer."

"I know. We could use your help."

"Remember all those summers you ran the children's theater, Gracie? You did most of the work by yourself."

"I loved it, probably because the kids looked up to me. Tempie, remember the twin girls from Georgia? We had to rewrite the script to accommodate their thick accents. And the preteen boy with the amazing voice? I wonder where he is now. And those five cousins from upstate New York who danced so well?"

"Your gift with children played a huge part," Tempie said. "That's why it worked well. You'll do fine on your own."

"Maybe. But working with you would be fun, like old times. If only you could come for a few weeks. You'd get to meet Miles and Leighton too."

"I know, dear, but since I don't fly, I'd need someone to drive me there and back. Much too much to ask with everyone working."

Gracie thought quick. "But can't God figure something out if we ask him?"

"Is this *my* Gracie? The one who can't find a church?"

Chapter Twenty-Four

A few days later, Gracie agreed to take Zeke and his baby sister to the park with Miles and Leighton. Since there was an infant involved, she wanted backup. In the past, she might have begged Harper, but she thought Seymour might be more agreeable to the idea.

She left him a voicemail. "The kids have a half day today. Doing anything around one this afternoon? If you're able, please meet me at the park. I could use your help."

Seymour came by as she'd hoped. Leighton ran to him like she would a favorite uncle. Miles did too, dragging his buddy Zeke with him.

"Now who do we have here?" Seymour asked.

"This is Zeke." Then Miles pointed to the stroller. "His baby sister's in there, but she's too young to 'troduce."

Seymour extended his hand to Zeke. "My name is Seymour Kaufman."

Zeke shook his hand, eyeing the hole in Seymour's handshake.

"Such a pleasure to meet you, Zeke. Perhaps I will meet your sister formally another time."

The boy stared, open-mouthed, at Seymour's hand and crocheted eye patch.

Miles nudged him. "Mr. Kaufman is not a stranger. He's our friend."

Zeke opened up. "My brother is Eli. You can't meet him 'cuz he's in the hospital."

Seymour nodded. "Yes, I remember Eli. I am sorry to hear that."

Miles put his arm around Zeke's neck and grinned at Seymour. "We're putting on a play for Eli. Gracie helped us write it. Zeke is the set designer. He draws horses real good."

"And castles," Leighton added.

Seymour clasped his hands together. "How wonderful! Does this play have a name?"

"Yup. *The Battle at Mount Sinai*," Miles said. "We just started rehearsing after school. Eli will be the king. Zeke and I play royal knights."

Zeke wielded an invisible sword. "I'm Sir Cure-all. Miles is Sir Remedy."

Swirling from side to side, Leighton announced, "I'm Princess Patient."

"Gracie is Countess Comfort," Miles said. "We still need somebody to play Lady Malady and Count Contagious."

"Do let me know when it opens," Seymour said. "I will do my best to attend."

Zeke whispered to Miles, who then stepped forward. "Mr. Kaufman, Zeke thinks you'd be perfect for Count Contagious."

Seymour rocked back and forth on his heels. "Is that so?"

Gracie chuckled. "He's right. The part's small but important. You wouldn't have to learn too many lines. Mostly, look ominous."

Miles knit his brows and tapped his chin. "The black eye patch would work better though."

Seymour laughed so hard he lost his breath. In the end, he couldn't resist. "I accept. Let me know the day and time."

The baby started crying right as the children complained they were hungry. Seymour handled snack distribution while Gracie bottle-fed the baby. After devouring granola bars and applesauce, the kids hurried off to play. Twenty minutes later, the infant settled down.

"Oy! What a busy bunch!"

"I told you I needed another set of hands." Gracie overlooked her poor choice of words. "How'd you get to be so good with children anyway?"

"I am not sure. Perhaps because I enjoy them. As a boy, I longed for siblings. Later, I hoped to have children of my own." He joked, "Unless God changes my name to Abraham, I doubt that will happen."

Marisol was on time to pick up Zeke and his sister. "This was such a help, Gracie. Thanks so much. By the way, the doctor said Eli can have visitors in a week or so. Is the Sunday after next too soon for the play? He's so excited."

"Works for us," Gracie said. "What it lacks in professionalism, it will make up in enthusiasm. Is that afternoon okay for you, Seymour?"

"I will confirm, but I am sure it will be fine."

Marisol twisted one of her bracelets. "Uh, I hope you don't mind, but when Eli's parents asked permission to have the play in the small visitor's lounge, the staff asked if you'd mind performing for a larger group."

"You know Miles and me," Gracie said, "the bigger the audience, the better."

"Eli's parents are grateful for all you've done to help Zeke get through this. He's been drawing castles and horses like Pablo Picasso. His white stallion even has five legs."

She winked at Marisol. "Focusing on someone besides myself has been more fun than I thought it would be."

While Miles and Leighton built castles in the sandbox, Gracie sat on a bench to speak with Seymour. "Okay, Mr. Kaufman, I've waited long enough. You never finished telling me the story of your job search in Postville."

"Yes, time ran out that day as I recall." Seymour smoothed his beard. "Where did I leave off?"

"You'd lost out on three jobs—the furrier, meat-packer, and taxidermist—which didn't make any sense at all."

"My dear, Grace, God always makes sense—in the end. When it seems otherwise, we haven't reached the end."

"A Yiddish Yoda!" She laughed. "Come on, weren't you the least bit sad or worried?"

"Not at all. I considered every one of those door-closing experiences a blessing. You see, whenever *my* ideas are rejected, I know God has one better in store."

"So you keep saying," Gracie said. "What *better* thing did God have for you?"

"Well, to celebrate my anticipated blessing, I tried an activity I had never done before. I rented some fancy shoes and bowled a few games at the Postville Ten Pin Alley."

She slumped. "Wow. You're not familiar with the term 'living it up,' are you?"

"Poke fun, if you will, but it changed my life. Although I was unable to figure out their scorekeeping system that first night, I kept throwing balls as long as there were pins to knock down. Half the town of Postville soon discovered I had an unusual affinity for clearing a seven-ten split. Whether it was due to my acute peripheral vision or my unorthodox grip, no one could say."

Gracie examined Seymour's face to make sure he wasn't joking.

"My so-called talent drew crowds. Someone videoed me bowling and put the clip on the internet. When Dimitri Thanos, the bowling alley owner, heard that the video had gone viral, he asked me to return on a regular basis."

Sounded like weird science fiction to her. "Did you?"

"Yes. As only God can provide, within weeks I was gainfully employed as head bowling alley attendant."

She frowned. "That's it? After all you went through, God gave you a job as a bowling alley attendant?"

Seymour's countenance upgraded to glee. "That was not the biggest blessing. On my third day of employment, I received an invitation to perform my very first bris from an itinerant haberdasher who was taking orders for bowling league shirts. Meeting him was the break I needed. Word spread. Often there were two different requests at the rental counter—one for shoes and one for circumcision. The bowling alley job paid the bills, and my mohel practice provided meals and fellowship—and the occasional gratuity."

"Amazing. Since the day I met you—when I hit you in your good eye, in case you forgot—I've never heard you complain about one thing."

"What is there to complain about? We met through that misadventure, did we not?"

She smiled and gave him a shoulder bump. "You're right. I can't argue with that blessing."

Instead, she asked the question she'd been saving for the right time. "Mind telling me how you lost your eye and fingers? You don't have to answer if you don't want to."

"My injuries were sustained in the same car accident that claimed my father and mother. I spent my grief on my parents, not on my eye and fingers." Seymour paused a moment and adjusted his patch. "I don't wear a patch out of vanity. However, I feel most people find it less off-putting than an empty socket."

"Some people have glass eyes." Gracie wanted to slap herself for stating something so obvious.

"Yes, they do. My patch serves as a personal reminder that I cannot fully see without God."

"I get it."

"I always wore a simple, black patch, the kind easily found in any pharmacy." He chuckled. "Until I met Dimitri's wife, Lydia, who had an opinion about it. 'Black is the color of mourning,' she would say. 'When you only have one eye, it makes a person happy to dress the missing one up.'"

They both had a good laugh over that.

"Lydia refused to let a perfectly good bit of yarn go to waste, so she crocheted me a collection of patches in colors only someone with cataracts would find subtle. How she fit lime green, red, orange, and baby-girl-pink all in one small patch was beyond my comprehension."

"*Why?* is the real question."

"At first, I consented to wear her creations only at the bowling alley. When performing a bris, I opted for black. A mohel with one eye and eight fingers was as much as I could expect my clients to accept."

"What made you change your mind?"

"Over time, the colorful patches became a curiosity to the non-Jewish bowling crowd. People asked questions and talked. Word about me and what mohels do reached beyond Postville to the sort of people who homeschooled their children and believed that women should wear long hair and even longer skirts. They were godly people who trusted in midwives and doulas above doctors and drugs.

"These people had come to believe that circumcision was a spiritual event, not merely a surgical procedure. They began requesting me. Everyone paid what they could afford—mostly food and fellowship. The only difference was these believers, who lived like the church in the book of Acts, preferred the colorful eye patches. Furthermore, every mohel has to have one. This one is mine."

Gracie's brow furrowed. "Have one what?"

Seymour winked. "A shtick."

Chapter Twenty-Five

For the past twelve years, the Chief had worked alone. The fewer egos involved, the neater the job. He didn't trust many. Those he did, like Oren, were driven by pride in their work, not greed. Even Specialty Dry Cleaners, operated by Oren's son (whose name he couldn't remember), was a legitimate business that did quality work. He envied their close father and son bond—so unlike his relationship with his own father.

The Chief vetted all his jewelers, fences, and document specialists, only working with those who followed a strict code of discretion. He chose his own marks, performed his own surveillance, and practiced his trade quietly. Even those in his industry didn't rank him as their peer. His motto was "No reputation is the best reputation for a jewel thief."

The heist at the Met would be his one exception to his three hard and fast rules. One, he wouldn't be working alone. Two, this job would definitely make the headlines. Three, he would gross twenty times what he made in an average year.

Why was he doing it? He had a debt to pay. Once it was settled, he'd be free.

In preparing for a heist, anticipation was all part of the total experience. Waiting, watching, and listening had taught him not to rush. He'd gleaned some of his most valuable intel during those weeks at Lincoln Center in disguises handpicked from the local Goodwill stores.

Scoping out jobs as a well-dressed guy in a newsboy cap, he'd eavesdropped on the girl and the diamond-cutter rabbi. As a sailor on leave, he'd sought job advice from the security chief. As the sports fan wearing a Yankees ball cap and Derek Jeter game shirt, he'd flirted with the pretty blonde. As a tradesman in jeans and a hard hat, he'd joked with the Air Tech crew. And he had IDs to back up each persona.

The Chief suspected the young women were chasing stardom, not the necklace, and the young men were chasing the women. The Jew was an oddity in the mix, but he was a mohel, not a diamond cutter, an acquaintance of Polina, but not a close one. He doubted the security chief and his limited team had the experience needed to recognize global thieves—like the two pros the Chief himself had spotted the previous week.

He'd first seen the tall, swarthy man, nicknamed "The Spaniard," lurking inside the Met, surreptitiously checking security cameras. He was smart, quick, and known for his flamboyant style, like scaling buildings, running across rooftops, and riding in on motorcycles. His one major fault—he coveted notoriety, a flaw which trumped his skill.

The Chief would do his best to boost the Spaniard's notoriety *before* the heist.

The tall, frail-looking gentleman with the pure white hair and round, frameless glasses had finesse *and* a decoy. Known as "Mr. Chips," he and his so-called nephew had been taking notes for a full week. They'd shared ice cream and chatted with the docents and shopkeepers. Chips had a reputation in the UK, but the Chief didn't think he was well-known in the States.

A surprise introduction to the appropriate authorities would make a fine welcome for this uncle and nephew duo.

Scanning the plaza, the Chief found a couple of local wannabes. Every heist had them. Grunts working jobs they hated, dreaming about the big score. He'd seen these two before, always on Tuesdays and Sundays, probably their days off.

One was a skinny, ginger-haired man whose signature outfit was loose-fitting khakis and a burgundy Members Only jacket. Ginger Hair paced a lot, alternately jiggling the coins in his pocket and twisting his pants to the side. After a few rounds of this rhythmic move, his fly almost rounded his hip.

His accomplice was a stocky man who chewed on toothpicks like a beaver. He was dressed in cowboy boots, polyester pants, and a camouflage fishing hat, which prompted the odd question—Would this fool a fish?

They were thirty feet apart, talking on twin phones, gesturing to each other, and pointing at the Met as if no one could see them.

Stupid, yes, but Ginger Hair and Cowboy Beaver could be useful.

Then there were the Air Tech workmen covering the place like ants waiting for a picnic. A team of thieves could easily infiltrate this crew. His gut was telling him something. He just hadn't figured out what yet.

Chapter Twenty-Six

Gracie sat at Rachel's kitchen island with a cup of coffee.

Rachel handed her a flyer. "Guess who's leading a workshop at school on Wednesday morning."

She scanned the flyer. "Bennett Noble! Really? Wednesday?" Her mind skittered through her schedule. This was a perfect chance to get to Noble before he got back to her. "The kids will be in school. Can I sit in?"

Rachel lowered her head. "Sorry, the offer is only open to students, instructors, and their assistants."

"Oh." She wished Rachel hadn't told her.

"Only reason I brought the workshop up is because I was wondering if you could do me a favor that day?"

Gracie tried not to sound ungrateful. "Sure. What d'ya need?"

Rachel peered at her over the top of her mug. "Would you consider substituting for my assistant that morning? She needs the time off."

She caught the wicked glint in Rachel's eyes. "You may be my boss, but you could easily pass for a bratty older sister."

"I could, couldn't I?" Rachel grinned. "Does that mean you'll do it?"

"My wardrobe is already strutting across the catwalk of my mind. Hmm. What shall I wear?"

Rachel tapped Gracie's arm. "Keep it casual. There's usually a Q&A session after the workshop, but there's no guarantee you'll get to speak with him privately."

She hugged Rachel. "Thanks so much. You're the best."

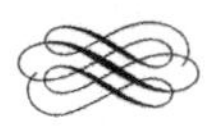

Gracie's goal was to present herself to Bennett Noble as a serious student of drama. To do so, she needed a look that fell somewhere between ingénue and beatnik. Maybe a combination of chiffon and black would work. She didn't want to replicate the style of another actor. No, she wanted Noble to see her for herself.

She chose her black, polished cotton slacks, white eyelet blouse, and black and white tweed jacket. Red suede ankle boots and a matching shade of lipstick provided a flash of color. She nixed her beret and dark glasses—too cliché.

She and Rachel arrived thirty minutes before the start of the workshop. They walked past Illumination Lawn on their way to Juilliard. Harper was seated on the fountain wall. *What is she doing here this time of day?*

"Let me catch up with you, Rache. I want to say hi to Harper."

Rachel snickered. "I'd warn you not to be late, but I doubt I need to."

Gracie jogged over. "Hey! Kind of early for you, isn't it?"

Harper jumped at the sound of her voice. "You scared me." Her eyes swept back and forth across the plaza.

"All I said was *hey*." She tugged on the wire to Harper's earbuds. "What're you listening to?"

Harper grabbed for her earbuds like Gracie was trying to steal them. "Nothing."

"Jumpy, aren't we?" She studied her friend's expression.

"No, just distracted." Harper twisted to crack her spine. "Aren't you supposed to be on nanny duty?"

"I'm filling in for Rachel's teaching assistant today." She bit her lip, hesitating to tell her about the workshop, but figured it was smarter to be upfront than have her find out later. "Bennett Noble is leading a workshop this morning. The only reason I'm allowed to attend is because I'm an acting assistant. Otherwise, I would have called you." Even to Gracie, it sounded like an afterthought.

Harper's shoulders slumped. "That's okay. I've been busy myself."

"Anything exciting?"

"Not really. Mostly, I'm studying the lines for the part I hope to get in *Little Black Lies*." Harper stood. "Well, I'd better get back to it."

"Hey, what are you doing tomorrow night?"

"I'm not sure." Harper glanced around. "My father has this great idea that I should work for him part-time."

"Doing what?"

Harper grimaced. "Anything to prove I'm worthy of the tuition I want for Juilliard."

"Well, call me later."

"Sure."

Gracie walked toward the Juilliard entrance. As she headed down a corridor flanked by a wall of windows, she stopped to look out at her friend. Why was she acting so weird? She leaned in closer to the glass. Wait. Was that Ian heading in Harper's direction? Yes, it was. He didn't look surprised to see her. Like he knew she'd be there. What was going on?

After she'd seen Ian's call come in to Reggie the other night, her text to him had gone unanswered. Now this collusion with Harper. Okay, perhaps *collusion* was a strong word. But was he so distracted by Harper that he'd ignore *her* after they'd been friends for years?

Part of her wanted to smack him. Not hard, but enough to wake him up.

Gracie and Rachel sat off to the right at the front of the large room. No surprise, every seat was taken, and no doubt, the buzz in the room was all about Noble.

Taking in her surroundings, Gracie assessed her privileged place at the head of the class. "Thanks again, Rache. There's no way I would be this close to meeting someone like Noble if not for you."

Rachel got comfortable in her seat. "I passed him in the hall earlier. He should be here soon."

A minute later, a tall, trim man with a mass of gray and black hair and a tangle of matching eyebrows entered. The students erupted in bravos and applause.

Commanding the room with an easy charisma, Noble raised his hands to quiet the crowd. When silence prevailed, he spoke. "The great Russian playwright and practitioner Constantin Stanislavski. The respected German director and dramatist Bertolt Brecht. What do I have in common with these theater greats?"

Gracie couldn't stop herself. She raised her hand and shouted the answer before being called upon. "Storyboards!"

Noble acknowledged Gracie and smiled. "I thought I had a tough one. You've done your homework, I see."

Gracie blushed. Of all the topics for him to cover, he'd chosen storyboards. With her own storyboard in his possession, this had to be another one of those God things.

Noble pointed to her. "As this young woman has discovered, although they are widely used in film and animation, a common misconception is that storyboards are no longer used in the theater. I intend to expound on their value in this workshop. I beg you to keep an open mind."

While the director continued, a young man tiptoed to the front of the hall and handed Rachel a note. She read it, then approached Noble, who stopped in mid-sentence. She whispered something to him. His face registered alarm just before he fled the room.

Gracie sat there stunned. *What just happened? Where's he going? When will he be back?*

Rachel clapped to get everyone's attention. "Mr. Noble has been called away by an emergency. He wanted me to express his regrets."

After the room cleared out, Gracie fussed at Rachel. "Another one of his lame 'temperamental actress' emergencies? This is so not fair!"

Rachel took Gracie by the shoulders. "You're right, Gracie, life is not fair. Especially when a man receives news that his only grandchild has been diagnosed with cancer."

Every selfish bone in Gracie's body ached.

Another sick child? How would she feel if it had been Miles or Leighton? And they weren't even her own.

The only God thing Gracie wished for now was that Bennett Noble's grandchild would be healed.

Chapter Twenty-Seven

Gracie paced around her small (and getting smaller) apartment. Unlike the restless whirring in her head, her place was quiet, too quiet.

She called Harper. "Want to hang out tonight?"

"Can't. Working."

"Working? Where is the Harper who used to like to play?"

"She's working."

"Well, if you get done early, you can find me at the Center by the Revson Fountain."

Gracie arrived shortly after dusk, found a perch, and soaked in the sights. On any given Friday night, as long as the weather cooperated, you could find live entertainment going on—fashion, music, dancing, and drama. She loved bathing in this pool of talent, even if from the sidelines.

As an advertisement for the latest haute couture fashion show, a parade of models dressed in various shades of purple pranced around the fountain which was backlit in hot pink. A shiny-headed actor and his female lead, stars from *The King and*

I, passed her on their way to the Viviane Beaumont Theatre. In the distance, Polina kept pace with the motorized cart of famed conductor George Levinson as they walked to the Met.

Once my career takes off, Gracie thought, I could perform here. Or, at the very least, enjoy inside performances from better seats.

A security officer stopped nearby. "How're you doing tonight? Ms. Camden, is it?"

"Fine." Since he knew her name, she assumed he was one who'd kicked her off the stage. "Did you ever check my references, Officer?"

"Didn't need to. You have a reputation. Name's Dan Favor. Officer's a bit formal, don't you think?"

"Maybe." Gracie glanced at a pretend watch on her wrist. "Don't you ever go home?"

Favor adjusted his hat. "I could say the same about you."

"Not really. I only come here on my days off. Or when I'm helping my boss. Or when guests come to town. Or on an occasional evening."

"And when you're headlining at Alice Tully Hall." He smiled. "This isn't the only attraction in town, you know?"

"I'm not one for libraries and museums filled with old books and dead things. This place is alive! I'm an actor and entertainer, remember?"

"Right. Hope you and your posse aren't planning to break into any theaters tonight." Favor winked at Gracie. "I'd like a quiet shift if you don't mind."

"You're in luck. I'm in the audience tonight, not the cast."

"Then I say that's a shame."

She glanced at Favor to see if he was smirking. He wasn't. "Thanks. Maybe someday."

"I'm sure of it." He tipped his hat. "Have a good evening, Ms. Camden."

"Call me Gracie. You too, Favor."

Gracie's phone beeped. A text from Ian. "First, turtle-boy, now a man in uniform. Fickle one, you are."

She looked around then typed, "Show yourself, coward."

"Can't. Working. Call you later?"

She texted back. "Big of you. I'll be sure to wait up."

"Ouch. I can explain."

"But will you?"

"Later."

Well, he couldn't be working *and* on a date with Harper at the same time. Not that it mattered. What did bug her was that two of her closest friends were keeping things from her. *Why?*

She threw some coins in the fountain, then moved to Illumination Lawn. A flash mob entertained the crowd, dancing to Bruno Mars' song "Marry You" and ending with a real live marriage proposal. Who enjoyed the show more was a toss-up—the bride-to-be or the public.

After sitting for way too long, she walked around the plaza. The memory of Dan Favor's compliment made her smile—and so did the thought of giving Ian grief later. Looking at the time, she headed for the alleyway shortcut between Juilliard and the library to catch the next train home. All in all, it had been a pleasant evening.

Right up until the moment she turned into the alley and saw Reggie Adler kissing Harper Bellamy.

Gracie's stomach clenched. She spun around and raced out of the alley, praying they wouldn't see her. Why? She wasn't the one cheating! She'd introduced Harper to Reggie at Juilliard less than a month ago … on her birthday. How did that innocent introduction become something ugly so fast?

God, how could you let this happen?

Filled with the vision of Harper and Reggie, Gracie's brain was about to burst. By the time she got home, her emotions had run through shock, denial, anger, disappointment, and grief. She had no clue what to do. And if she did anything—like tell Rachel, confront Reggie, or choke Harper—would she make things worse?

When Ian texted, wanting to come by that night, she ignored him. All she could think of was how Reggie could do this to Rachel and his kids. She alternately pounded her pillow and cried until daylight.

Morning broke with Miles and Leighton knocking persistently on her door. She rolled out of bed and let them in.

Miles ran to her. "Wanna see my scab?"

She stretched. "Not exactly what I had in mind first thing this morning."

He sat on the floor and pointed to his wound like he'd earned a Purple Heart.

"Eww! Gross!" Gracie shivered, just as Miles hoped for she knew.

Rachel walked in, scolding them for bothering her on a Saturday morning. "You both know Gracie's place is off limits unless you're invited. Now back downstairs!"

Miles scratched at his sore. "Ouch!"

"Miles! What did Mommy tell you? If you pick at it, you'll make it worse. Now let's go."

Gracie whispered to Rachel, "They can stay for a while. Why don't you and Reggie spend some quality time together?"

"He's still in bed. Been keeping long hours lately."

Right. Keeping long hours.

Rachel drew in a weary breath. "This job is going to kill him."

If you don't do it first.

"By the time he got home, I was already asleep." Rachel sighed. "Might be nice to have a few minutes to ourselves. Are you sure you don't mind?"

"No problem." Gracie tightened the belt on her robe. "Okay, you two, Mom says we can have our coffee together."

Leighton giggled. "Gracie, you know we don't drink coffee. We like chocolate milk."

"Then chocolate milk it is."

Miles gawked at Gracie like he was seeing her for the first time that morning. "Gracie, why are your eyes puffy?"

Rachel followed his eyes. "They do look a little red. Are you feeling okay?"

"Could be allergies." Gracie crouched, ready to pounce. "Or could be because I was woken out of a sound sleep by a couple of silly bears who want to be tickled." She chased them around as they squealed in fear and delight.

"Thanks." Rachel entered the hallway. "But send them down in an hour. They have chores to do."

After the thing between Harper and Reggie, there was no way Gracie could work with her ex-friend. She ignored all Harper's calls and texts filled with details about the *Little Black Lies* audition. Gracie finally sent her a text. "No longer interested."

Harper texted back. "What on earth happened to change your mind?"

She didn't respond.

Chapter Twenty-Eight

Seymour woke up with the overwhelming sense he needed to call Grace. He knew better than to lose time trying to figure out why.

"Good morning, Grace. Seymour here."

"Oh, hi."

She sounded stuffy to him. "I am sorry, did I wake you? Are you well?"

"No, Miles and Leighton paid me an extra early visit, but I'm fine."

Her tone suggested she was not fine, but he would not pry. "I plan to invite Simka to go to the Bronx Zoo today."

"That should be fun."

Without any forethought, he added, "Perhaps you and the children could join us?" He had no idea how Simka would feel about this, but it was too late to take back the invitation.

"The kids would love that. Let me ask Rachel, but I'm sure it'll be okay."

When Seymour called Simka, her voice rose in excitement. "You take me to Bronx Zoo? One zoo we have back home in whole country. In Chisinau. I never go."

"You never went to the zoo?"

"Not to Chisinau at all. Not even to hear Polina at opera. Farming and tending to animals did not allow time."

The woman spent her whole life on a farm caring for animals, and I ask her to see more of them. Was this wise? "Simka, is there something you would rather do?"

"Than go to zoo? Nu! For years I never go. Tell me when? I call driver."

"There is one other thing. I invited my young friend, Grace, and the two children she cares for. Do you mind?"

"Such excitement children add. The car is big. We all fit."

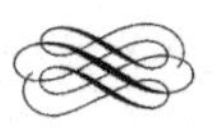

A sunny day greeted Seymour with temperatures in the mid-70s.

He met Gracie and the children at the Adler home, where they waited for Simka. Seymour recognized the driver from the first time he'd heard Polina sing at the Majestic.

He extended his hand. "Hello, again, I do not believe we were ever introduced."

The driver looked over his own shoulder. "*Izvinite.* Excuse me?"

"This is Grace, Miles, and Leighton. Of course, you know Simka. My name is Seymour."

The driver's smile shifted from unsure to sure. "Good to meet you. I am Uri."

Grace and the children sat opposite Seymour and Simka. Once they were settled and belted, Simka whispered to Seymour, "*Uri.* Is Russian name, nu?"

The stability of Russian-Moldovan relations had always been, well, unstable. Not wanting to risk an answer, Seymour mumbled an assortment of syllables.

They kept the destination a surprise for the children, which resulted in one question after another from Miles. "Will it take us long to get there? Is it the planetarium? Is it the Jersey Shore? Are we going to the Lego store? Is Simka a real name or a nickname? If we're good, can we have ice cream?"

Simka laughed and clapped. "Much like my son Vânât! So curious, so smart."

As for Leighton, she seemed more excited about the secret than the destination. She sat with her hands folded in her lap, tittering every so often.

Seymour heard her whisper, "Maybe we're going to a land filled with rainbows."

The Bronx Zoo did not disappoint them. They spent almost three hours watching the sea lions and the penguins, riding real camels and the Wild Asia Monorail from which they viewed red pandas, elephants, and rhinos.

Simka acted as excited as the children. "I learn much watching animals. Each fits best with own kind."

The day was going well. The only one who concerned Seymour was Grace. Often, sadness filled her eyes for no apparent reason.

While Simka and the children rode the big bug carousel, Seymour probed. "Grace, what is bothering you so?"

Tears poured down her cheeks as she sobbed.

Oy, what have I done?

"I'm sorry. Something bad, very bad, happened. I'm not sure what to do about it."

"Is this bad thing beyond God's reach or his healing?"

"No, but I'm afraid it will hurt before it gets better. If it ever does."

"I am often surprised how simply God handles matters we consider impossible." He hesitated, then said, "The Lord has this to say, 'If you pick at it, it will make it worse.'"

Gracie gaped at Seymour. "*What* did you say?"

"I believe God is saying to leave things to him." He put a hand on her shoulder, bowed his head, and prayed. When he finished, Gracie hugged him.

Miles ran toward her. "Gracie, why were you crying?"

"What makes you think I was crying?"

"'Cuz I heard you through the ears of a cute fox."

"Huh?" Gracie was confused.

Simka pointed to a program, which Seymour read aloud. "'In the Animal Senses exhibit, kids can compare their leaps to those of a bullfrog, slide into a turtle shell, see with the eyes of an owl, and hear with the acute ears of a fox.'"

They all laughed, except Miles, who reached for Gracie's hand. "I heard you. Why are you sad?"

Gracie squeezed his hand and smiled. "I didn't think we'd have time for ice cream, but Seymour says we do. What's that song we sing?"

Miles and Leighton shouted, "'I scream, you scream, we all scream for ice cream!'"

Seymour made sure Leighton got hers with rainbow sprinkles.

When the driver pulled away from the Adler home, Simka called out the open window, "*Pa! Pa!* Bye bye, children. You too, Grace."

Seymour was relieved the afternoon had gone so well at the zoo. He was about to comment when Simka's phone rang.

"Is you, Vânât? ... Fine, and you? ... I am in car now with friend Seymour ... Nu, nu, no worry ... Sick? My sister? Is bad? ... Tell her I pray ... You call later? ... Da." Then she hung up.

"I did not mean to eavesdrop, Simka. I am sorry to hear your sister is ill. I hope you did not cut your conversation short because of me?"

"Nu, Vânât always busy. He call later when he learns more about my sister." She turned to him. "Now I insist to take you to diner near cousin's apartment. Best matzo ball soup and cheese blintzes you ever taste. You like?"

"I like. Thank you."

Seymour was amused when Simka gave their Russian driver, Uri, directions in Romanian. Uri must have understood because he drove straight to the right place.

"Do you and Polina come to this restaurant often?" Seymour asked.

She shook her head. "Polina has no time. She is celebrity with obligation to—how you say?—keep image right."

"Surely she can eat wherever she wants?"

"Cousin sacrifice much to be star. Not easy sometimes."

As he and Simka slid into a booth, a feeling akin to wonder—

or was it sadness?—came over him. The idea that Polina had limits on her life had never occurred to him. He had assumed the opposite.

Simka scanned the diner. "The people here remind me of home. Simple but from good stock." She slurped her soup, then laughed loudly. "Good stock like soup."

He grinned at her pun. "Yes, that is how I was raised too—until I moved to Des Moines. Life was somewhat more formal at Uncle Jacob's."

"Do you ever think about returning to Moldova?"

He held his spoon in midair. "I have wondered what it would be like at times, but I never had the opportunity."

"Maybe one day." Simka lifted her bowl and drank the broth. "You could meet our family."

Seymour could not imagine how difficult the move must have been for someone as young as Polina, especially when no family awaited her arrival. "Simka, Polina is returning home on Sunday, correct?"

"Yes, in evening."

"Let us do our best to get her out among simple people. We could even come here again. She deserves good stock too."

Simka toasted him with her juice. "Da. To good stock and Polina!"

Seymour was surprised when Polina called him late Sunday

afternoon.

"Home so soon?"

"Actually, I'm in Minneapolis. One flight was canceled, the other delayed."

"You must be exhausted—even with all those rave reviews I have been reading." Was that too much? Did he sound like a crazy fan?

"I am. But I couldn't go any longer without thanking you for treating my cousin with such kindness. Simka couldn't stop talking about your outing when I called her last night."

"We would have had even more fun if you had been with us." *Oy! Did I say that out loud?* "I, uh, Grace and the children would have enjoyed meeting you."

"And I them. Speaking of that, you know the gala the Met insists on holding in my honor?"

"Yes, we spoke of it."

"I would like to invite you as my guest. Since Simka has to be backstage to assist me with my wardrobe changes, maybe your young friend Grace would like to accompany you?"

"What a privilege. I am sure she will be thrilled. Thank you for thinking of us."

Seymour was well aware of the huge social leap from performing a bris to attending a gala. What would be expected of him—exactly? And what on earth would he wear?

These concerns were minuscule in comparison to the enormity of Polina's personal invitation to him—Seymour Kaufman, formerly of Des Moines, here by way of Postville, Iowa.

Chapter Twenty-Nine

When Gracie arrived home, Ian was sitting at the top of the stairs near her apartment door.

She frowned. "How did you get in?"

"Good to see you too, darlin'."

"No, really, I thought Rachel and the kids were out with her parents today."

"Didn't know that. Your boss Reggie let me in."

Gracie unlocked her door, spun around, then poked her finger into Ian's chest. "Speaking of my boss, how do you know him?"

"How? You introduced us at Juilliard, remember, on your birthday?"

"Nice try. Your name showed up on his caller ID. Of course, he probably told you about it. You guys stick together."

Ian raised his hands in surrender. "Whoa. What have I done to make you so mad?"

"Not you. Him. But never mind. You two are up to no good."

"Can I at least come in?"

Gracie paused before she let him by. "On the condition you tell me what's going on."

He dropped to the love seat and leaned forward, tapping his fingertips together. "Never could keep anything from you."

Gracie handed him a soda. "Spill. And I'm not talking about the drink."

"Okay, but you have to swear you won't tell a soul. Not one single person."

She sat on the edge of her seat. "Why? Are you in some sort of trouble?"

"No, but I *will* be if what I tell you gets out." He leaned in closer. "You have to promise. No friends or family or anyone."

"Okay, okay, I promise."

"Reggie's the guy I'm working for. The senior vice-president of operations for Lincoln Center contracted his security company to update their systems. We've been installing and testing the electronic surveillance equipment my company developed."

"But I thought Reggie worked for some insurance or investment company."

He smirked. "I knew you didn't know what he did for a living."

She swatted his arm.

"This job is sensitive, so to speak. We're not even allowed to discuss specifics between the different subcontractors."

"I'm sure if you'd asked me to keep a secret, I would have."

Ian nodded. "I know, but since you and I are friends, and you and Rachel have become close, Reggie figured it was best to keep this between us two. You know, in case our business arrangement didn't work out."

"Is it working out?"

"Quite well. That's why I'm still in New York, and why I've been too busy to get together."

"But not too busy to hang out with Harper. I saw you two at Lincoln Center last week."

"I'm hanging out, as you put it, with Harper for one reason. She's on the payroll."

"Harper? What does she know about security? She's an unemployed actor. Why would you hire her?"

"I didn't. Reggie did. D'ya know who her father is? He's a vice chair on the Lincoln Center Board of Directors. Before he agrees to pay her tuition to Juilliard, she has to prove she can be responsible. We've got her playing the role of tourist while she does on-site surveillance. I'm one of the few she reports to. With her father on the board, let's just say she didn't have to interview for the job."

"That explains a lot. I actually thought you two were dating." Gracie's jaw tightened. "Until I saw her kissing Reggie."

Ian shot her a look. "What did you say?"

"You didn't know about them?"

"No, I didn't." He shook his head. "This is bad."

"That's an understatement."

He got up and paced. "But he's always going on about his wife and kids. I don't understand. What is he bloody thinking?" He sat back down, fists on his knees.

Gracie noted how Ian's first and last thought was for Rachel and the kids. His every concern reflected his deep-seated sense of decency.

What had happened to Reggie's? And did Harper ever have one?

"The best and only solution is to pray," she said. "God is the only one who can untangle this mess." More and more, she sounded like Tempie and Seymour, mainly because she had no other answers.

Ian crushed his empty soda can. "I don't know if I'll be able to work with the eejit and keep my mouth shut."

Her full attention riveted on him. "If there's a chance for Rachel and Reggie to make it, I'm for it. Our getting in the middle of this problem might make things worse."

He fast-pitched the can into the trash. "I'm Irish, remember? My temper might get the best of me."

"Ian, I have more of an Irish temper than you do, and you know it."

He was smart enough not to agree.

Since Gracie's feelings read like headlines on her face, she'd avoided Reggie since that unthinkable night. But they lived in the same house, and she took care of his kids. She could hide only for so long.

As if on cue, Reggie bumped into her in the front hall as she was leaving to pick up the kids after school. What was he doing home at this hour?

"Hey, stranger! If my children weren't talking so much about the play you three are writing, I might've thought you left us."

"Yes, the play. They want to do it for their sick friend. Even at their age, they know what loyalty means." *Did she really say that?*

"How is Eli, anyway?"

She was surprised he remembered the boy's name with all he had going on. "I haven't heard from his nanny in a few days, so I can't say."

"Anything new with you?"

"Not much." She took a step closer to the door. "Your wife feels bad that you've been keeping such long hours. She's concerned about your health." Guilt might not help, but a little couldn't hurt.

"I know. Just came back for this." Reggie lifted his laptop case. "She doesn't have to worry much longer. Once this job ends, things will change."

Weasel. What exactly is that supposed to mean?

When she arrived at the school for the kids, Harper was waiting outside. Oh great, a twofer day. "What are you doing here?"

"I've been trying to text and call you. What's up with your phone service?"

"Nothing. Been too busy to answer."

Harper grabbed her by the shoulders. "Guess what? I got that role in *Little Black Lies*!"

"Oh."

"Well, aren't you going to congratulate me?"

All Gracie could see was red and her so-called friend's lips on Reggie's. She let the kids get a few steps past the edge of hearing. "Congratulate you? On getting a part in a play that promotes infidelity?"

Harper winced, turned, then walked away without saying another word.

Gracie'd hurt her, but it was the truth. Didn't Harper deserve it? With the kids jabbering at her side, she spent the whole walk home trying to convince herself not to feel bad. But she did feel bad—about the whole stinking thing.

Chapter Thirty

Seymour had been awake for hours, pacing, too nervous to eat breakfast. Finally, he took a deep breath and dialed the number.

Simka answered. "*Alo*. Polina Zelenka's res'dence."

"Good morning, Simka. This is Seymour. Is Polina available?"

"*Nu*. She left early for rehearsing. Can I help?"

"Well, do you recall when you and I talked about convincing Polina to get out among the simple people?"

"Da. On matzo ball soup night."

"Yes, well, I would like to invite her to go bowling."

"Polina? Bowling?" Simka laughed like she couldn't stop. "I must be there to see this."

Seymour had not planned to invite Simka, but now it felt awkward not to. "You are welcome to join us. I had Thursday evening of this week in mind."

"Wait. Let me check calendar ... Da, Polina off Thursday. Is good for her, is good for me. When will you come to us?"

"Does six o'clock work?"

"Yes. I write down."

Seymour had not bowled since his move to New York City. He rummaged for his bowling bag in the only closet he had the use of in his cousin's apartment. Although his belongings were few, the closet was tiny, and Seymour was not.

"Found it." The black vinyl bag held his ball, his thirty-five-dollar Brunswick shoes—a splurge at the time—and his team shirt. His smile widened as he held the customized ball with the blue and orange glow of the Helix Nebula—Eye of God—embedded in the black urethane, a gift from his friends back in Postville. As he put his fingers in the holes, which had been drilled further apart to accommodate his grip, the excitement returned.

He held his scuffed shoes and wrinkled team shirt. The local funeral parlor had been their sponsor. The embroidered logo read: Gransky's Gravediggers. His name was below it in cursive.

"Oy. Perhaps I need to buy new shoes and a shirt if I am to impress Polina." He cringed as soon as his words reached his ears. "Oh, Lord, forgive my pride. You are the one I want to please." He conceded polishing his shoes and washing and ironing his shirt would be sufficient.

With Simka joining them, it occurred to him that a fourth person would allow for two teams. He knew who to call.

"Hello, Grace. Seymour here. Do you mind if we return to the subject of bowling?"

"Uh, guess not."

"I have invited Polina and Simka to go bowling this Thursday. I have a minor dilemma. We need a fourth to make two teams. If you are free, would you care to join us?"

"I might. Whose team will I be on?"

Blushing, he stuttered a few words. He was relieved they were speaking by phone.

She laughed. "I'll take that mumbling to mean Simka will be my teammate?"

He spoke without hesitation. "Yes, that is the plan."

"A plan? Wow, I am totally impressed. Boldness becomes you, Seymour."

On Thursday, Seymour and Grace arrived at Polina's a few minutes before six.

Seymour greeted the doorman. "Good evening, Victor. This is my friend Grace. I believe Ms. Ziesler is expecting us."

Victor tipped his hat and ushered them into the building. "Ms. Z. sure is a busy lady today."

Upstairs, Simka answered the door. "Seymour, Grace. *Intra, intra.*"

Gracie commented on Simka's new hairstyle. "Wow. Very chic."

Simka fiddled with her layered do. "Not too short?"

"Not at all," Grace said. "And that light blue sweater brings out your gray eyes."

Seymour thought she looked different, maybe a little more modern. "Very nice indeed, Simka."

"*Mulțumiri*, thanks." She brushed the sleeve of the sweater. "Polina buy for me." She led them into the great room. "Seeing you is nice surprise tonight."

Seymour's stare pinned Simka with a question. "Surprise? Today is Thursday, is it not? We are going bowling in Brooklyn."

"Da, but bowling is next Thursday, nu?"

"Next Thursday?" Seymour fidgeted with his hat in his hand. "I apologize. I must have gotten the date mixed up."

"Nu worry. I tell Polina you are here. Sit, sit."

He and Grace sat on the edge of the Chesterfield sofa in the great room. When Simka was out of sight, Seymour said, "Grace, I am so embarrassed. I was certain we agreed on this week."

"Mix-ups happen. No biggie." She leaned toward him and jiggled her eyebrows. "Now I get to see how an opera diva lives."

"Polina may be a star, but she is as simple and humble a woman as I have ever met. You will see."

Before he could say another word, Polina swept into the room in a swirling gold ball gown, wearing a necklace which sparkled bright enough to light a whole city.

Seymour stood … and gawked.

Grace muttered for his ears only, "Oh, yeah, real simple."

"Seymour, I am sorry for the misunderstanding," Polina said. "Will you forgive me?" She extended her hand to Grace. "You must be Grace, the helpful young woman who made sure I got Seymour's number."

"A pleasure to meet you, Ms. Zelenka."

"Please, everyone calls me Polina."

Grace smiled. "Polina."

Seymour scanned her appearance. "I should apologize for interrupting your ... your party."

"Party?" Polina remembered her gown. "No, my publicist and stylist are here with the jeweler, fitting me for the gala. The dress has to be a perfect complement to this necklace they insist I wear." She put her hand on the necklace, then scratched around it as if she were wearing poison ivy. "This piece is much too heavy. And a bit much, don't you think?"

"You look lovely," Seymour said before he was distracted by two men in suits, lurking nearby.

Polina whispered, "The jeweler's guards." She touched the necklace again. "This is never out of their sight."

Gracie approached Polina and examined the elaborate diamond and platinum creation. "Wow! The guests in the second balcony will be able to see it."

Simka rearranged the folds in Polina's skirt, which nearly filled a quarter of the room. Then she readjusted the lay of the necklace. "Tsk, tsk. One thousand Moldovan families live and eat for three years on cost of this one piece. Chickens and goats thrown in."

Polina blew out her cheeks. "I know—the inequities of the world. I try to remember the gala is a charity event—in disguise."

Grace circled Polina. "All I know is the whole stage will glow when you walk out in this gorgeous Oscar de la Renta."

Seymour was lost. Who was Oscar and why would he be walking out with Polina?

Polina beamed. "I see you know your designers, Grace."

A dress designer, of course. What was I thinking?

Polina gestured toward the hall with a delicate hand. "The experts have not yet decided on a gown. This is only the second of many I must model. Ralph and Russo, Posen, Marchesa, and more are all waiting in the wings."

Grace stretched her neck, looking past the guards toward the hallway. "Is that true? Really?"

Seymour was sure Grace's eyes could not have opened wider. He took a step toward the foyer. "We should let you get back to your fitting, Polina."

"No, no. Stay awhile. Gracie, I value your opinion on the other gowns." She turned to Simka. "My poor cousin is not having much fun, are you?"

Simka fidgeted. "What do I know from ball dresses? I fit better in bowling alley than ballroom."

"I am so thoughtless," Polina said. "There is no reason you cannot go bowling without me."

Seymour jumped into the conversation before it got away from him. "No, next Thursday is fine. Not to worry. Besides, we need an even number of people for teams."

Polina's face lit up. "I have an idea. Grace can stay with me, and you and Simka can go bowling. Grace? Simka? Does that work for you?"

Seymour's shoulders sagged.

"Are you kidding?" Grace said, "A designer fashion show by an opera star versus bowling?"

Simka shrugged at Seymour. "What we can say to that?"

At a loss, Seymour relented. "If you like."

"Great," Polina said. "Instead of the subway, why not call for a car? My treat for your trouble."

Behind Polina and Simka's back, Grace mouthed "Sorry" to Seymour. The gleam in her eyes made him doubt her sincerity.

After Simka led the way through the foyer, he caught the reflection of his brown and orange bowling shirt alongside Polina's gown of shimmering gold. Polina ... on the subway ... bowling ... in Brooklyn. What was he thinking?

As he and Simka headed for the elevator, his own words came back to him. *Whenever my ideas are rejected, I know God has something better in mind.* Until he knew what that "something better" was, he would make the best of the situation.

He addressed his companion for the evening. "Simka, have you ever been bowling?"

"Ha! Back home, I throw heavy sacks of potatoes into big cart. Rolling ball down lane is piece of pie."

Chapter Thirty-One

The moment Seymour and Simka crossed the threshold of Brooklyn Bowl, he knew he had chosen the wrong place. The sixteen high tech lanes were lit in yellow and green neon. Rock and roll music blared from a live, shirtless, tattooed band on stage. Those who were not bowling were dancing and shouting the lyrics. (He could not classify it as singing.) He was almost certain alcoholic beverages were involved. Apparently, Brooklyn Bowl's motto "Life in the fast lane" was more than witty wordplay.

Under his breath, he said, "To think, I almost brought Polina here. Thank you, Lord, for orchestrating the events of tonight."

Simka's wide opened eyes and mouth told him she felt as out of place as he did.

He had to yell to be heard. "The Postville alleys were not like this. Would you prefer to skip bowling and go to the diner we previously enjoyed?"

"Da." She laughed. "Instead of bowling, we have bowl of borscht."

"Sounds good to me." She was a funny woman and quite agreeable to the simpler things of the city.

The busiest supper hours had passed by the time they reached the diner. Seated in a quiet booth, silliness overtook them after the waitress told them the nightly special was homemade borscht.

Simka waved off the menu the waitress offered. "If gentleman has beet soup, I have same."

"Why not?" Seymour said. "Let us go crazy tonight."

Once they were served and the food had been blessed, Seymour asked, "What do you think Polina would have thought of that bowling alley?"

"She would not stay either. Everything cousin does is under big telescope."

"But even in the public's eye," Seymour said, "I imagine her life has been blessed more than most."

"True, but not in all ways."

"How so?" Seymour buttered a slice of warm bread.

"As the firstborn of girl cousins, Polina was promised in marriage to a man who had much to offer—a house, good farmland, and plenty of livestock. Instead, her talent took her away. She never marry or have children."

"Polina told me you were recently widowed. My sympathy on your loss."

"Almost ten months now, enough time to grieve." Simka dunked her bread in her borscht.

"Do you think Polina regrets not marrying?" He took a bite of his soup.

"She had many chances. Some international stars, most handsome, many rich. She say, 'I married to opera.'"

The borscht soured in the pit of his stomach.

Simka scrutinized Seymour's face. In a hushed voice, she asked, "Are you interested in cousin for more than friendship?"

He stumbled for the right words. "I, uh, only know she is a special woman."

"Da. Even if she refuse rich and famous does not mean she say no to you. After all, you are a mohel, which is servant of God."

If Polina rejected handsome, rich international stars, what chance did he have? He was not ashamed of his position in life, no, but the mismatch between their lifestyles loomed larger than he had originally envisioned. "Simka, when it comes to most women, I am unsure of most everything."

"You not know until you try." Simka chewed and swallowed. "The worse she say is no."

Somehow that did not console him.

"After many years, maybe she ready to give up opera." She took a sip of her drink. "Or you stop being mohel."

Seymour's discomfort increased. "Why would either of us have to do that?"

Simka patted his hand. "Change can be okay."

His stomach rumbled. At that moment, Seymour decided he would never eat borscht again. "Whatever happened to the man to whom she was promised in marriage?"

"As is tradition, he married the cousin next in line. Me. I have Polina to thank for that—and for my son, Vânât."

Chapter Thirty-Two

Guilt nipped at Gracie's heels as she thought of how things had transpired for Seymour. But, since she was having a chance-of-a-lifetime blast, she absolved herself of the sin. Even if she couldn't try on the dresses herself, the private fashion show by Polina was almost as good.

The opera star went through two dozen designer gowns before the stylist, with input from the jeweler and others, decided on a satin gown in silver—the ideal color to celebrate a twenty-fifth anniversary. The fit 'n' flare style complimented her mature curves. Elegant in its simplicity, the portrait neckline did not compete with the diamond and platinum necklace—which, of course, was the point. Even Gracie got that much.

Once the seamstress had pinned the dress for alterations, Polina stepped off the fitting platform.

The jeweler carefully removed the priceless masterpiece and held it up to the light. "Irreplaceable! Nothing like this in all the world." He laid it gently in its velvet-lined black box, the top of which had the Harry Winston signature HW stamped in gold.

"If you don't stop telling me how irreplaceable it is, I might break out in hives the night of the gala." She scratched where the necklace had been.

Yvonne, the publicist with the shrill voice, scolded Polina. "You're not helping." Then to the visibly alarmed jeweler, she said, "Don't be concerned. Ms. Zelenka has never had hives in her life."

Polina soothed the jeweler's nerves. "Sorry. I'm a little crabby after all this fussing."

Yvonne clapped her hands. "People! Remember, Polina's official sitting with the photographer is tomorrow afternoon at the Met. Both the dress and the necklace must be there."

"Who's the photographer?" Polina asked. When Yvonne told her, Polina moaned. "Isn't he the one who takes forever?"

Yvonne's jaw tightened. "We needed those posters of you up yesterday. He was available."

As the entourage gathered the gowns and jewels in preparation to leave, Gracie's kneejerk thought was *Harper will never believe …*

The scene between Harper and Reggie replayed in her mind. Her heart sank deeper. She refocused, choosing instead to enjoy the time she had left at Polina's.

When the parade of experts and handlers finally vacated the apartment, Polina excused herself to change clothes.

Gracie wandered around the living room, admiring Polina's taste in furnishings and art. She doubted she'd ever be as successful in her acting career as Polina was in the opera, but that was fine with her. She could do without the exhausting demands this woman endured, demands that seemed to overtake any personal life she might otherwise have.

Every so often Gracie added to her boilerplate prayer. This was one of those times. "God, I still want success and the respect of my peers as an actor—but not at the expense of a personal life. One more thing. Please, please get Harper out of the middle of Rachel and Reggie's marriage. Thank you. Amen."

Her hostess returned dressed in corduroy slacks and a cozy fleece, carrying a tray which she placed on the table in front of the sofa. "Coffee?"

"Thanks." Gracie accepted a cup.

"Phew. That took longer than I thought it would. I'm exhausted. And when the designer and the jeweler went back and forth ad nauseam—"Shall it be the warm gray or the platinum-silver?"—I was thrilled when you spoke up. The silver Versace is my favorite too."

"I'm glad I could help. This evening was work for you, but a treat for me."

Polina scooted further back on the sofa. "Now, in addition to being a connoisseur of fashion, I hear you're an actor."

"Yes, since I was a child, mostly in community theater. A few months after I moved to Manhattan, I got a role in a small production. Nothing since then." Gracie sipped the strong brew. "Are you excited about the gala?"

"More obligated than excited, I think. But I do hope you'll use the extra ticket I gave Seymour and attend with him. I'll include backstage passes, too, so we can go to the after-party together."

"What fun! Thank you."

Polina checked the clock on the mantle. "Speaking of fun, I wonder how Simka and Seymour are doing. My cousin hasn't had it easy with her husband's passing and with her son galloping around the globe. Seymour is such a mensch to spend time with her."

"'Mensch'?"

"That's Yiddish for a good, all-around guy."

Gracie wondered how she could let Polina know about Seymour's feelings for her without coming right out and telling her.

"You know Seymour," Polina said. "Do you think something more could come of his and Simka's friendship?"

Gracie's cup rattled in its saucer. "I, uh …" Before she could gather enough words to form a sentence, Simka and Seymour walked in.

Polina sat forward and smiled. "How was the bowling, you two?"

They glanced at each other and broke out laughing.

"Let us say," he said, "that Brooklyn Bowl is not exactly how I had imagined it."

Simka covered her mouth with her hand and giggled. "Da, he did not want to get tattoo and sing with rock band, so we go to Jewish diner."

Polina and Gracie exchanged puzzled glances.

Seymour remained standing. "Allow me to make a long story short. The diner suited us better."

Wanting to give Seymour some time with Polina, Gracie suggested the two join them for coffee. When that didn't work, she changed the topic by picking up a small, carved wooden box from the end table. "This is lovely, Polina. Where did you find such craftsmanship?"

Simka walked over and gently lifted the box from Gracie's hand and proceeded to demonstrate how it came apart to reveal secret drawers. "As child, I watch my father carve and put together. Beautiful, nu?"

Gracie agreed.

"A true work of art," Polina said. "But I treasure the box more for the sentiment it represents."

"Da, he gave to Polina as parting gift when she go to Chisinau." Simka set it back in its place on the table.

Seymour turned his hat over in his hand. "Well, Grace, the hour is getting on. I think we have taken enough of the ladies' time."

When Polina failed to convince him to stay longer, she insisted they use her car service to return home. "After all, you entertained my cousin and left Grace here to help me."

A disappointment to Gracie, Seymour declined politely yet firmly.

Once they were in a cab, she said, "You sure were in a hurry to leave."

"Not at all. I did not want to outstay my welcome." He clicked his seatbelt. "Did you enjoy your time with Polina?"

Her guilt grew heavy. "Seymour, I'm really sorry things didn't go the way you'd planned."

He sighed. "That is often the problem with man's plans. They are seldom the same as God's."

She thought of her recently revamped prayer but didn't take time to dwell on it. "Did you at least have a good time?"

"Yes, it was quite pleasant." Seymour smiled. "That woman has an engaging sense of humor."

Seymour got twisted up in his sheets that night. *Why?* He usually had no trouble finding sleep. Was it embarrassment at having gotten the bowling date mixed-up? Or was it disappointment at having his initial plans with Polina pirated away? He had enjoyed the evening with Simka more than he thought he would. Then, what was gnawing at him? He had sought the Lord about his plans, had he not? Of course, he had.

A still, quiet voice spoke to his spirit. "You did not seek my will."

Shame overtook him. The Lord was right. He had presented *his* plans to the Lord to be blessed. He had tried to manipulate circumstances to his advantage to be with Polina, like partnering Gracie with Simka. Telling the women they needed teams was a lie. Even his choice of activity—bowling—was a prideful attempt to show off for Polina.

He moaned his apology. "Lord, I have done exactly what I have advised Grace not to do. Please forgive me. You alone know what is best for me."

He waited on God until the Lord gave him peace and sleep.

Chapter Thirty-Three

As soon as Tempie appeared on her monitor, Gracie said, "Guess what?"

Her grandmother rested her chin in her hands. "I'm too old for guessing games, dear. Why don't you just tell me?"

"*Love and Waffles* is reopening off Broadway at Stage 2! The old Little Shubert. The notice said they're holding general auditions. I applied online and got a spot!"

Tempie seemed to perk up. "And Noble is directing?"

"Yes!" Gracie pumped her fist. "Can you believe it?"

"I can." Her grandmother smiled. "What monologues are you preparing?"

"I was thinking of Kat Hamilton's last scenes from acts 2 and 3."

Tempie pursed her lips. "You didn't read the fine print on the notice, did you? In general auditions, actors never perform monologues from the play being cast."

"That doesn't make any sense. Why can't I do …"

Her grandmother frowned. "You mean why can't *you* do what you want to do? Because rules apply to you as well, Miss Too-Big-for-Your-Britches."

She slumped. "Now what?"

Tempie tapped her upper lip. "Simple. We choose lines they haven't heard a million times."

"What about something from that old monologue book you gave me?"

"*Old* is the operative word. Throw it out. Trite might be fine for local theater, but this is New York." Tempie paused for a moment. "I've got it! One of those hilarious scenes you had in *Powerless to Pump* would be perfect. Since so few people are familiar with the play, it'll sound fresh. Then, you offset it with a dramatic monologue. Maybe from a lesser-known Neil Simon play."

"I like it. And if I choose a Simon play I know, I won't have to memorize anything new."

"Gracie, just because you *knew* the lines, doesn't mean you still do. Memory is a fickle friend. You need to rehearse."

"Okay, what else?"

"Don't underact in your audition. A lot of beginners make that mistake." Tempie repositioned herself in her chair. "And wear business casual with a touch of personality. You're good at that. Then, if and when you get a callback, wear the same outfit. They'll be more apt to remember you."

Gracie glanced at her bedroom door where the waitress dress and apron she'd washed and ironed hung in preparation for her Kat Hamilton scenes. "I should have called you first."

"If you hadn't, I bet you would've shown up in that waitress costume you absconded with the day the BCP burned down.

Only an amateur would do that."

How did her grandmother know?

"Before we sign off," Tempie said, "I've got one more tip for you, more valuable than all the others."

Gracie leaned closer to the monitor. "What?"

"Plant yourself in a good church and grow."

She sunk lower in her seat. "I should've seen that coming."

"And?"

"I will, Tempie, after the audition."

"I'll hold you to it." Her grandmother wagged a finger. "Remember, dear, the competition is stiff in your corner of the world. Don't expect to be a shoo-in."

But Gracie *did* expect to get the part. She'd already missed her chance with Noble twice—first at Starbucks with Chase, then at the Juilliard workshop with Rachel. This had to be God, which would only be fair.

All that week Gracie rehearsed her monologues, one from *Powerless* and the other from *Mile Marker 4*. Originally, she'd planned on using a scene from Neil Simon's *Barefoot in the Park*, but when she'd read the *Mile Marker 4* monologue, she knew she should do that one. Since she *felt* every word, memorizing came easy. To be safe, she'd gotten Tempie's approval.

The theater where *Powerless* had played held sixty people. The capacity of Stage 2 was 499—the maximum seating to still be labeled off Broadway. Considering that most theaters in this category had room for fewer than two hundred and that this play and its director were well respected in the industry, Gracie knew this was huge.

She arrived an hour early with her completed audition form, résumé, and glossy headshot. There was a line at the registration table, which could mean either casting was running late, or the actors were early or both. With some actors in and out in a few minutes, you never knew when your turn would come up. Theater auditions ran by their own clocks.

On looks alone, Gracie evaluated her potential Kat competitors. She immediately eliminated the three girls in the waitress uniforms and the one reciting lines from *Love and Waffles*. Her self-confidence grew … until the line grew longer.

When her turn came, she was led into the audition space. A group of five sat in front of a long table. The only one she recognized was Bennett Noble. She stood on her mark.

One of the men said, "Ms. Camden, is it? What do you have for us today?"

Phew. I passed 'the look' test.

"Yes, Grace Camden. I'll be performing a monologue from *Powerless to Pump* written by Jocelyn Ulbricht."

She paused a few seconds, then jumped in, trying not to underact as Tempie had advised. Her rhythm was good, the words flowed. When the decision-makers laughed in all the right places, she knew she'd killed the recitation.

One of them spoke, "Anything else for us today, Ms. Camden?"

They wanted more, a good sign.

"I do." She announced the play and author and began the dramatic *Mile Marker 4* monologue as if she'd written the words herself. She spent her best on this one.

As she floated out of the audition room, she overheard one of the men at the table, "How many more auditions for Kat do we have? We've whittled it down to thirty so far."

Thirty? So far?

By the time she'd schlepped to the subway, Gracie's self-confidence had slid down a few rungs on her ladder to success.

Chapter Thirty-Four

When Gracie checked her voice mail a few days later, she heard, "This is the casting director for *Love and Waffles* with your official callback. If you're still available, be at Stage 2 a week from Tuesday at two in the afternoon. No need to return my call."

Tuesday. Her day off. Perfect! She had ten days to hone her performance and go through the *Love and Waffles* script.

She left a voicemail for her grandmother, who called her right back.

"Screening your calls, Tempie?"

"No. Not as fast as I used to be. You'll understand someday. What's up, dear?"

"Got the callback! I'm halfway there."

"Wonderful! But don't get all puffed up yet. A callback is not the halfway mark."

"Yes, ma'am." Gracie teased her grandmother. "That's all you've got for me today? No advice about planting myself in a good church?"

"Now that would be nagging, dear, wouldn't it?"

"Oh, and you never nag." *Right.*

After their call, Gracie crisscrossed her apartment like a cougar on catnip. Who else could she tell? She hadn't won a Tony Award or anything, but it *was* a callback for a Bennett Noble play in Manhattan!

She tried three times before she completed a text to Ian. "Guess who got a callback for L&W?"

His message read, "U! Had no doubt."

She typed. "Can u celebrate later?"

"7 ok?"

"See you at my place."

Once again, Harper intruded upon her thoughts. Gracie missed what they'd shared together—love of the theater, celebrity-watching, and the ups and downs and hopes and dreams of this peculiar business. If it hadn't been for Harper putting her onto Backstage.com, she might not have known about the *Love and Waffles* audition. Perhaps she should call to thank her.

Right. And thank her for stealing Rachel's husband too. No way.

If she hurried, she'd have time to go downstairs and tell Rachel and the kids her news before Reggie got home.

Miles fist-bumped her. "You already played that part, so it's gonna be a cinch to do it again."

"I'm not sure I *have* the part. A callback is when you get a chance to audition again."

"A do-over?" Miles scrunched his face. "Didn't you get it right the first time?"

Rachel stifled a laugh. "Miles, in New York, there are so many good actors that choosing only one is hard for casting directors."

"Simple. They should choose Gracie 'cuz she's the best."

Gracie kissed his cheek. "Ever think about becoming an agent, Miles? I'd hire you."

"Stay for dinner?" Rachel plated a stick of butter. "We're having Reggie's favorite—lasagna. He's picking up Leighton at a friend's. They'll be home soon."

Bleh. Reggie's favorite. "Actually, Ian's coming by. In fact, I should get going—"

Reggie walked in with Leighton. "Hey, stranger! Staying for dinner?" He held up a bag. "I even stopped at the bakery for Italian bread. Still warm."

Leighton took hold of her hand. "Please, Gracie, please."

"You can celebrate two times," Miles said. "With us first and Ian after."

Reggie handed Rachel the bread. "What are we celebrating?"

Miles answered. "Gracie got a do-over audition."

"For *Love and Waffles*? Congratulations!" He high-fived her.

Not responding would have been awkward.

"Stay until Ian arrives," Rachel said.

She couldn't refuse. "Sure."

Now put on a good performance and be sociable to Reggie.

Reggie hung his and Leighton's jackets. "Did Rache mention our Thanksgiving vacation plans?"

"No, she didn't." She hoped they wouldn't ask her to come along.

Rachel handed Gracie a stack of placemats and went back to the stove. "We're thinking about taking the kids to Plimoth Plantation when we visit Reggie's parents on the Cape. You lived in the area, what's your opinion?"

Gracie set the placemats around the table. "Good choice, a bit pricey, but something for everyone. History, pilgrims, and Native Americans. Miles, you'll love it."

Miles's eyes held a question but not for long. "Are the Native Americans real?"

Gracie said, "Yes. Mostly from the Wampanoag tribe."

He yanked at his mother's arm. "Can we go? Please?"

Before Rachel could answer, the doorbell rang.

Reggie stood. "I'll get it." He came back with Ian. "I convinced this guy to stay for dinner, so you've lost your excuse, Gracie."

Miles and Leighton cheered. Gracie glared at Ian.

He rubbed his hands together. "What Irishman can resist lasagna?"

"Good thing," Rachel said, "because I made enough to feed Little Italy."

Gracie maneuvered Ian into a seat near Reggie. She sat next to Rachel at the opposite end of the table. Every glance at Rachel made her feel sad. She couldn't look at Reggie without replaying the scene with Harper. While everyone else raved about dinner, Gracie's appetite waned.

How could anyone find a happy ending in this mess?

As long as Miles and Leighton were present, talking about hatchets, headdresses, rain dances, and 'poopooses'—Leighton's word for papoose—the conversation remained light and kept flowing. Once the kids were dismissed to watch a movie, the air got heavy, and talk dragged to a stop.

What did Gracie expect with all these secrets? She and Rachel weren't supposed to know Ian worked for Reggie. Reggie wasn't supposed to know Ian told her about it. And Reggie and Rachel didn't know what she and Ian knew about Reggie and Harper.

Her stomach turned inside out.

"Okay, this is way too weird," Reggie said. "I have to clear my conscience."

What did he say?

"Gracie," he continued, "I know Ian better than you think. I contracted his company over a month ago. But due to your personal relationship with him and mine with you, I kept it quiet in case we weren't a good fit. I only told Rachel because I can never keep a secret from her."

I bet.

Ian put his drink down. "Truth is, Gracie dragged it out of me last week—but she promised not to say a word to anyone." He turned to her. "Right?"

Rachel raised three fingers, her thumb crossing her pinkie. "Girl Scouts' honor, Gracie and I never mentioned it to each other, did we?"

Gracie cringed at the word *honor*. "Nope."

"While we're confessing, Reggie," Ian said in an even tone, "I also told Gracie you hired Harper as part of the surveillance team."

Gracie watched Reggie's expressions and body language for clues.

"*Had* to hire her, you mean." He took a sip of his coffee. "Her father's on the Center's board of directors. I know she's your friend, Gracie, but that girl's a loose cannon."

Rachel started laughing.

"Quit your hee-hawing over there," Reggie said. "It's not that funny."

"Yes, it is," Rachel choked out, "and it gets funnier every time I think of it."

What did all this have to do with Harper?

Rachel was trying to catch her breath. "Oh, just tell them, Reggie."

"Do I have a choice?" Reggie's complexion was a shade somewhere between red and purple. "A few Fridays back, your friend Harper and I were discussing a couple of characters she'd noticed skulking around. The next thing I know, she was swallowing my lips."

Gracie's hand trembled as she picked up her water. "Why would she do that?"

"That's what I asked her. She said she was trying to protect our *cover*. Our protocol prohibits various security teams from being seen talking to one another."

Rachel cracked, "But apparently she's fine with kissing."

"As I was saying," Reggie scowled, "the only warning I had was her whispering in my ear, 'Quick! Someone's coming. Play along.'" That's when she grabbed me and kissed me. I'm still not sure about her—"

"In the alley?" Gracie took a sip of her water. "The one between Juilliard and the library?"

Reggie's forehead puckered. "She told you already?"

Ian gave her the go-ahead nod.

Gracie fiddled with her flatware. "Well, um, those footsteps Harper heard in the alley that night, uh, were mine."

Reggie focused on Gracie then Ian. He pointed at Rachel. "I told you something was going on with these two! Ian's been giving me daggers all week, and Gracie's been avoiding me even longer."

"I'm sorry, Reggie," Gracie said. "I was so shocked and upset I didn't know what to do."

"Well, if you ever see him kissing another woman again,"—

Rachel tapped her finger on the table—"tell me, *I'll* know what to do."

Gracie asked, "Rache, what *did* you do when he told you about the kiss?"

"I know my husband too well." She smiled at Reggie. "He's no Casanova. If he had a family crest, loyalty would be at the center."

Seymour's words about God came back to Gracie. *I am often surprised how simply he handles matters we consider impossible.* Tears filled her eyes. *Thank you, Lord, for being the God of the impossible and the fixer of misunderstandings.*

Once the air and the table were cleared, Gracie and Ian took a walk.

"Mind my asking what you're going to do about Harper now?" he said.

"This requires a face-to-face apology. A text or a call won't do."

Ian put his arm around her shoulder and squeezed. "That's my girl."

More like your fool.

Chapter Thirty-Five

The next day, Gracie found out where Harper was having lunch at the Center and approached her.

Harper picked at her salad. "What are you doing here? Come to gloat, have you?"

"Gloat?" Gracie was confused. "You mean about my callback?"

"What callback?"

"For the role of Kat Hamilton in the revival of *Love and Waffles*."

Harper kept her eyes on her plate. "Didn't know about it."

Gracie pulled out a chair and sat. "The reason I'm here is to apologize."

Harper looked up. "Apologize?"

"Yes. I'm sorry for what I said about your part in *Little Black Lies* and everything else. The reason I went ballistic is that I saw you kissing Reggie in the alley. Apparently, mine were the footsteps you heard."

Harper blinked twice. "You actually thought I was romantically involved with Reggie? What kind of person do you think I am?"

"I think you're a pretty good actor. You sure fooled me."

"Is that why he's been avoiding me?" Harper chuckled. "I made him that nervous, huh?"

"Yeah, but he'll get over it. Now, if you didn't know about my callback, then why am I gloating?"

Harper's shoulders slumped. "My part in *Little Black Lies* was almost as offensive as its director. I quit when he made a move on me the first day of rehearsals. What a pig!"

Gracie reached over and touched her friend's hand. "That's awful. I didn't know."

"I would have told you, but I was too embarrassed."

She kept a straight face. "And I wasn't talking to you anyway."

"There was that," Harper said, faking a frown.

"Are we okay now?"

"I think so." Harper tapped her cheek with one finger. "I can't recall making out with anyone else you know."

"Good. I've missed you. When it comes to the arts, nobody understands like you do."

Harper drummed her fingers on the table. "About this *Love and Waffles* callback, when is it?"

They spent the next half hour plotting ways to maximize Gracie's chances of winning the role. Before she left, she enlisted Harper's help with the children's hospital play.

"*The Battle at Mount Sinai* is the title. We still have the role of Lady Malady to fill, which can be yours if you want it."

"Depends. What's the director like?"

"He's charming and bossy, but have no fear—he's only seven years old. By the way, you have less than two weeks to learn your lines. Dress rehearsal is a week from Saturday at Mount Sinai, and the play's on Sunday."

She sped off before Harper could change her mind.

Ian's early morning text read. "IMPORTANT. What time will you be home this afternoon?"

Gracie answered. "By four. Why?"

"Secret."

Why did he insist on driving her crazy? His methods worked. She was home by 3:45.

Minutes later, he knocked on her door. "Anyone home?"

How did he get to her floor without her hearing him clomp up two flights? She swung the door open. "So what's so import—Tempie!"

Ian grinned. "I drove to the Cape this morning and look who I found."

Gracie wrapped her arms around her grandmother. "Come in!"

"I hope my coming is okay, dear," Tempie said. "Ian made me promise not to tell."

"Your being here is way more than okay. Do the Adlers know yet?"

"Let me catch my breath." She lowered herself onto the love seat. "They were in on it from the start. When I spoke with Rachel—what a sweet person!—she invited me to use their guest room during my stay. I believe they kept it from the children though, afraid they'd spill the beans."

"Wise decision." Gracie sat next to her grandmother and held her hand. "I still can't believe you're here!"

"I might not be if it weren't for the elevator. How do you manage those stairs every day?"

"Up and down is good cardio, Tempie. No one uses the elevator."

"Well, someone will while I'm here." Tempie rubbed her hands together. "Now, when do I meet those children?"

"I can answer that," Ian said. "Rachel expects us all for dinner at six thirty."

"A cup of tea before you get settled in your room?" Gracie asked. "You might want to rest before dinner. Miles and Leighton will run you ragged before the night's over—mentally and physically."

Tempie winked at Gracie, then pointed to Ian. "My nerves could use some calming after driving five hours with Mario Andretti over there."

"Be nice," Ian warned, "or I'll have Mr. Magoo drive you back."

"If you're going to spar with me, young man, you will lose." Tempie followed Gracie to the kitchen table.

"I even have your favorite blend—valerian." Gracie hugged her again. "I always hoped you'd visit."

After some tea and talk, Gracie showed Tempie to her room. When she got back upstairs to Ian, she hugged him too. "Who would have guessed that God could use an Irishman to answer my prayer?" Gracie played it straight. "But if he can use a donkey to speak to a prophet, I suppose anything is possible."

Ian laughed. "A fine way to thank me."

"Seriously, you're the best, Quinn."

"Now enjoy one another, darlin'. I'll drive Tempie back to the Cape whenever she's ready."

There was no lack of conversation around the Adler table that evening.

"You're Gracie's bubbe?" Miles said. "The one who taught her to act?"

"Yes, I am. But my friends call me Tempie."

Seated next to Tempie, Leighton spoke softly, "If you want, I can be your friend."

"I'd like that, sweetie. Miles, how about you? Want to be my friend too?"

"Sure." Miles hesitated like he was trying to formulate his next thought. "Know what? Sometimes friends work together."

Tempie nodded. "That can happen. What did you have in mind for us?"

Miles wiggled in his seat. "Well, you see, we're working on a play—*The Battle of Mount Sinai.* I'm the director. Gracie was gonna help me, but she's doing a bunch of other stuff, so I can't ask her. Do you wanna be my AD?"

"AD? As in Assistant Director?" Tempie tried a poker face, but she couldn't conceal the mirth in her eyes.

Ian teased Grace. "The boy's throwing you out with the bathwater, he is."

Gracie pretended to pout. "Miles, is that right? You don't need me anymore?"

"No, that's not what I meant." He squirmed again. "Just that old people like your bubbe know more."

"Miles,"—Reggie sighed—"calling people old is not polite"

Tempie disguised a chuckle with a cough.

"Sorry," Miles said. "Can I say *older*?"

Rachel ignored his question. "Miles, Gracie and her grandmother may have plans to do other things while she's visiting."

"You can do that too." He turned serious as he reasoned with Tempie, his hands doing most of the talking. "The play won't take long, and this will make things easier for Gracie."

Reggie pinched the bridge of his nose. "Oh, yes, that's my boy, always putting others first."

Gracie eyed her grandmother. "I didn't exaggerate about Miles, did I?"

Rachel rested her hand on Tempie's arm. "Please don't let my children coerce you."

"On the contrary," Tempie said, "I'd love to be Miles's AD. I've pretty much done everything in the theater. Maybe I can help finish up the costumes."

Joining his sister, Miles rushed to Tempie's side of the table. "Yay!"

Rachel intervened, "Children, at least let our guests finish their meal."

"I'm well satisfied with your delicious cooking," Tempie said. "If you'll excuse us, perhaps I can show the children the cloaks and hooded capes I've been working on? They may come in handy for the play."

Leighton protested, “But princesses wear ball gowns and crowns, not hoods.”

“They do indeed!” Tempie answered. “We’ll make sure your costume is princess-worthy.”

“Can we have a castle?” Leighton asked, wide-eyed.

“We do need one, don’t we?” Tempie tapped the table. “And I have some other ideas about set design too.”

“Awesome! ’Cuz all Zeke can draw good is horses.” Miles’s eyes bugged out. “Mom, can we go now?”

True, the children charmed her grandmother. But Tempie seemed more excited than she had in months.

Chapter Thirty-Six

Gracie set out their evening tea and toast while her grandmother thumbed through *The Battle at Mount Sinai* script.

"Come on, Tempie, put that aside. We can work on changes with Miles later."

"You're right, dear." She laid the script down. "This will be fun. I was just getting my old stride back when the Andersons decided to turn their company name—We'll Always Have Paris—into a reality. They won't be back from France for three weeks."

"Good for them. Now back to you. What would you like to see while you're here?"

Before Tempie could answer, a list of landmarks flew out of Gracie's mouth. "Broadway? Lincoln Center? World Trade Tower? Empire State Building? Statue of Liberty?"

"Hold your horses! And I'm not talking about the ones pulling carriages around Central Park." Tempie put her teacup down. "Being here with you, meeting the family you live with and the friends you've made, that's what's important to me."

Gracie scoffed, "I know you. You'll spend all your energy working on the play and forget to take time for yourself."

Tempie spread preserves on her toast. "Gracie, I'm eighty-two. At my age, taking time for myself means doing whatever I want."

Gracie shook her head. "You're incorrigible. How about this? Tomorrow, Rachel's parents are picking up the kids after school and keeping them for supper. We can take a tour bus. That way we can see a lot without hopping from subway to subway or walking all over the place."

"Perfect, because my hopper isn't what it used to be."

"Ha! I'll have trouble keeping pace with you. I'll see if Harper and Seymour can join us for lunch somewhere near Lincoln Center, which is one of the few places Seymour knows how to find."

"Now tell me again how you met this Seymour?"

"On the subway, and then at the park. You'll love him. Is nine o'clock okay?"

"I'll be ready." Tempie pushed herself up and took her dishes to the sink. "There is one thing I'd like to do Sunday. Attend service at St. Luke's, which is on Amsterdam Avenue, I believe. One of my old friends goes there."

Good. Tempie had a church lined up already. No way did Gracie want to be responsible for crossing her grandmother's conservative line of worship. "I'm sure we can find it."

"About church," Tempie said, "you'll feel more comfortable if you wear a dress."

Of course, I would. Gracie suspected Sunday was all part of her grandmother's scheme to "plant" her in a good church.

Gracie and Tempie compromised and caught the hop-on hop-off bus tour at Times Square and Seventh. She let her grandmother decide when and where to get off.

One of the tour guides, a bowed-back, reed-thin, elderly man, fancied himself an entertainer. He also flirted like crazy with the ladies—especially Tempie—who was not impressed. "With stale lines like that, his tip from me will be where to find new writers."

"Shh, he'll hear you," Gracie scolded. "This is the Lincoln Center stop. Let's get off here before he kicks us off."

"Humph. I'd like to see that measly squirt try."

The picture of these two octogenarians scuffling in the aisle gave Gracie the giggles.

Tempie had her signature made-you-laugh twinkle in her eye.

Gracie hugged her just because.

With a half hour left before they were to meet Seymour, the two strolled arm-in-arm across the Center's expanse. They peeked into Alice Tully Hall and took a mini tour of the Met before they went on to the restaurant.

Seated facing the window, Tempie stared out at the city. "I used to wonder if I'd bemoan what might have been if I ever visited New York City."

"Are you bemoaning?"

"No." Tempie paused. "My role at the BCP was my 'little cup of water' to those God put before me. Maybe some people—like your parents—found it difficult to comprehend, but it gave me joy and a purpose. I wasn't only content, I was grateful."

"And that makes me glad." Gracie wondered if she'd ever find that same contentment in her career. Her mind wandered to Miles and Leighton. She might not have her name in lights, but those two young stars kept her busy—for now.

"Is that your friend the mohel?" Tempie asked, nodding to Seymour.

"That's him." Gracie waved him over.

He removed his hat and bowed slightly. "What a pleasure it is to meet you, Mrs. Camden."

"Oh please, call me Tempie, and I'll call you Seymour."

He sat down. "My, my, we have only met and have managed to settle two issues already. Just think what we could do if given a day."

Tempie cupped her ear. "Did you say 'if given a *play*?'"

Seymour caught on. "A play will do."

"You may not know this, but I'm Miles's new assistant director. Your role as Count Contagious may change by a grunt or two."

He chuckled. "Such a difference a grunt or two will make?"

"My goodness, yes," Tempie said, "the difference between the audience imagining tight shoes or the bird flu."

He feigned shock. "Oh my, we cannot have that. I will be diligent in timing my grunts as directed."

When Seymour asked Tempie what she thought of the city, she said, "You know those chestnuts they sing about, the ones roasting on an open fire?"

He nodded. "Yes, I am familiar with them."

"I think they stink."

Seymour held his nose. "They do."

"But the crowds ..." Tempie folded her hands on the table. "... they're ripe for the harvest, wouldn't you say?"

"A field awaits us, does it not?"

That's how it went between Tempie and Seymour. One sentence and one laugh led to another. Gracie didn't have a chance to speak for a full ten minutes. She was pleased her grandmother got along so well with her friend. Like they belonged to the same secret club.

Harper swung by after her shift to meet Tempie and Seymour, arriving in time for dessert.

Tempie patted the empty chair next to her for Harper. "You're the beautiful Lady Malady I've heard so much about. Meet your costar Seymour Kaufman, otherwise known as Count Contagious."

Harper and Seymour exchanged greetings and chatted about their roles. Gracie was sure Harper was checking to see if his role was the greater.

"Harper, you and my granddaughter are blessed to have each other," Tempie said. "This industry can be tough on a person going it alone."

"Got that right," Harper said. "Did Gracie tell you about our failed attempt to meet with Bennett Noble at Starbucks?"

"Yes," Tempie said, "but something else will come along."

Harper grumbled. "I hope that 'something else' is not like my horrible experience with *Little Black—*"

Gracie jumped in. "Dresses. Little black dresses." She kicked Harper under the table. "No one needs to hear about your wardrobe malfunctions."

Despite her confused expression, Harper kept silent.

Since Gracie never did audition for Dupris's play, she thought mentioning it now would only prompt a lecture.

Seymour snuck in his motto, "When things don't work out, God always has a better plan for you. Perhaps you'll discover it in *The Battle of Mount Sinai?*"

Tempie's smile warmed the room. "Could be, Seymour, could be."

Chapter Thirty-Seven

The Chief had been conned a few times himself when he'd first started out. Even now, years later, he wasn't smug enough to think it couldn't happen again. Fear is what gave him an edge and what made him take a closer look at Grace Camden and her gang of misfits.

The longer he watched, the more he realized she was the hub in the wheel, the others were spokes. Although she was connected to everyone, they weren't necessarily connected to each other.

One of her bosses was a Juilliard instructor. The other was responsible for security systems at the Center. Then there was the almost-rabbi. How did a plain-looking man like him worm his way into the life of a glamorous opera star? The Irishman and the blonde were always hanging around. And he'd seen Favor, chief of security, chatting with Camden on a few occasions.

Was she simply a nanny and wannabe actress? Or was she a thief with a clever cover? Could the Jew be a mole instead of a mohel? Or maybe a diamond cutter after all? If they were up to something, what use could they possibly have for the nerd?

He'd stick as close as he could without being noticed. There were too many coincidences, too many variables, and too many connections for him to ignore. Some of them quite recent—like the old lady showing up. What was he missing? Maybe nothing. But he wasn't willing to take that chance.

Chapter Thirty-Eight

Gracie was surprised to get Chase's call. Though nothing to do with his uncle, the news was another kind of good. He offered to purchase costumes for all the kids involved in the play—both cast and patients. Before he had a chance to change his mind, Gracie asked if they could meet that afternoon.

She left Tempie and the kids painting four-panel screens which Reggie had put together out of old bi-fold doors. Tempie had employed this idea for scenery many times before.

Gracie waited for Chase outside the Disney Store in Times Square. When she'd suggested one of the less costly Halloween shops that always crop up in the fall, he'd responded, "Oh, no. Mother insists on the quality of Disney."

She couldn't miss him, half-running toward her, tripping over his slacks that still needed shortening.

"Ciao, Gracie! Mother told me not to buy a thing without you."

Gracie pulled the door open. "I'm sure you would've done fine." *Not really, but it was the nice thing to say.*

He pushed his square glasses back up his nose until his hair covered half the frames. "Knowing what to do for sick children is hard. This seems like a good thing."

"And quite generous of you too." Gracie unfolded her list. "According to my count, we need costumes for fourteen princesses and eleven knights and princes. That covers the patients who have permission to attend and the kids in the cast. I have all the sizes."

He raised his hand. "I've also been ordered to purchase eight more princess costumes because Mother promised to outfit my niece and her friends for her seventh birthday party. In case I forget, remind me to get one Cinderella costume for the guest of honor."

Did her taco-truck date have any idea how much this would run him? How would they carry them all? "Maybe we should ask the clerk if they can ship the costumes directly to our homes."

"That would work for my niece's birthday which is a month away, but do we want to chance shipping delays with your costumes?"

"No, maybe you're right."

They rambled down the well-stocked medieval aisle and managed to find almost every Disney princess, prince, and knight costume ever created, all in various colors.

"Boys are easy," she said. "They'll be happy with a sword and a shield. To feel like a true princess, a girl needs it all—a crown, some jewels, a wand."

At her comment, Chase piled more royal accessories into their cart.

"Are you sure you want to do that?"

"I don't ever want to look back on the play and think it wasn't a success because I was chintzy."

Wow. There was a big heart under his tight, buttoned-up polyester shirt. She was glad she'd had the chance to discover it.

After they unloaded their purchases at the Adlers', Gracie prompted Miles. "Remember what we talked about?"

He chewed on his bottom lip, then said, "Thank you for the costumes, Chase."

Chase ruffled his hair. "No problem."

Miles rushed off, patting his hair back into place. Gracie caught Miles scowling in Chase's direction.

Had something she said about Chase contributed to Miles's intense dislike of this man? Or was it the way *she'd* behaved? She needed to be a better example to these kids.

Chapter Thirty-Nine

Knowing full well Tempie would want to be early for Sunday service, Gracie was ready by nine. She'd chosen one of her most conservative dresses. The high neckline and low hem of this beige jersey wrap-around would meet with her grandmother's approval.

"Rise and shine!" Tempie called out as she burst through Gracie's door.

Gracie's mouth dropped open. *Yikes.* Her grandmother stood before her in a red and white chevron-patterned suit and matching purse and shoes. She'd finished the ensemble with a bucket-shaped hat with a huge bow.

This from an old Cape Codder? Where did my grandmother go?

Tempie commented on Gracie's dress. "Are you wearing that? Rather bland, don't you think? Maybe a bright scarf or brooch would help."

"I've never seen you go to church in anything but bland—except at Easter when you wear pastels. What's with the suit and hat? Are we meeting the Queen of England?"

"To paraphrase the apostle Paul, 'To the New Yorkers I became like a New Yorker ...'" Tempie checked her hat in the mirror. "I've taken a cue from you, dear, and dressed the part."

"What part? I thought we were going to church?"

"We are. Dressing up is fun for a change." Tempie started toward the door. "Get a scarf and come along. We don't want to be late."

The taxi dropped them off in front of a large, redbrick church on Amsterdam Avenue in Harlem. They entered the gathering of smiling black congregants. Like Tempie, most of the women wore colorful outfits and ornate hats.

Gracie was the one who stood out. Not because she was white—but because she was boring and beige.

The organist played like a professional. No sour notes like Gracie had heard from the organist at Tempie's church. He accompanied the choir with plenty of heart and soul. The choir members, dressed in white but for a single red flower, swayed, clapped, and sang their way down the center aisle to the dais.

Tempie whispered to Gracie, "Now this is going to be worship!"

All Gracie could visualize was her grandmother's small, white clapboard building with a steeple on the hill, where clapping and loud music were frowned upon. As the worship continued, she recognized some traditional hymns she'd heard at Tempie's church, but they definitely were not sung in the same funereal manner. These people were alive.

The preacher didn't hold back his words, but held his Bible high, reciting verses from memory. The congregation responded with shouts of "Amen" and "Tell it, brother!" As a child, she'd always been shushed in the pew. Not here—where celebration was proportional to solemnity.

She had to admit, she kinda liked it.

When the service ended, instead of filing out with the others, Tempie stayed put. "I'm waiting for my friend. He'll be here soon."

The organist, built like a football defenseman, rushed over to them before the sanctuary emptied. He hugged Tempie, gently lifting her a foot off the floor. "Miss Tempie, when you called to say you were coming to New York, I could not believe it. After all these years."

"Neither could I," Tempie said. "Cedric, you're still as talented a musician as ever. I think the angels trained you."

"One of them did." He smiled large at Tempie.

"Don't try to flatter me, you old rascal. Cedric, this is my granddaughter, Gracie. She's the one doing the play I told you about."

"Miss Gracie, what a pleasure to meet you. Now, how may I help?"

"Help?" Gracie had no idea what he was talking about.

Tempie patted Gracie's hands. "Now, Cedric, I didn't mention anything to Gracie because I didn't want to disappoint her if you weren't available."

"My calendar is clear!" he said like he'd been given the chance of a lifetime.

Gracie still had no clue. "Uh, available for what?"

"Your grandmother said you need incidental music for your play."

"You'd be willing to do that?" Gracie's pulse quickened. "Um, without pay?"

"I would be blessed to help you …" Cedric's smile stretched the width of his face. "… and honored to work with your grandmother again."

Tempie put her arm around Gracie. "I hope you don't mind, dear. Cedric's live music will be so much better than canned, don't you agree?"

"How could I not?" Gracie's smile was almost as broad as Cedric's.

The Battle of Mount Sinai dress rehearsal was scheduled for the day before the play, mainly so the cast wouldn't forget their lines. The members of the cast and crew—Miles, Leighton, Zeke, Harper, Seymour, Tempie, Ian, and Gracie—were joined by Cedric who brought his electronic organ and sound equipment.

While Gracie and Harper helped the children into their costumes, Tempie produced three long, hooded capes for the adults. She'd chosen shades to match their characters. Lady Malady's was the color of week-old pea soup. Count Contagious's was a brownish-rust. And Countess Comfort's was a healthy shade of pink. "Capes are adaptable," she said. "We'll have the bad guys wear their hoods up, and the good guys wear them down."

"Zeke and Miles were right, Seymour," Gracie said. "That cloak combined with the patch does make you look ominous."

Seymour pulled his hood up. "Between this robe and my lines consisting of grunts and growls, I am sure the desired effect will be achieved."

Harper examined her cape and made a stink-face. "Is this all you have? This color is ugly."

Tempie spoke up. "We'll have to depend on your acting prowess to portray the character of Lady Malady effectively—not the robe. Gracie already told me there isn't a color you can't pull off, and I agree."

Harper put the cape on and examined her reflection in the glass door. "I see what you mean."

Gracie whispered, "Smooth, Tempie."

She nudged Gracie. "All part of the AD's job."

"I had no problem memorizing my four *short* lines," Harper said. "I'm guessing with Miles in charge, his part is more substantial."

Gracie adjusted the hood on her robe. "Correct. But he put everything he had into this play—not for himself, but for Eli and Zeke. I'm proud of him."

Since Eli was their main inspiration for the show, they'd given him the title of King and allowed him to handpick his Queen. Eli had chosen Alyssa York, an engaging six-year-old with big, amber-colored eyes and a shining-star smile.

The rehearsal went as Gracie expected. Most of the cast were more interested in their costumes and props than their lines. Miles as director, with Tempie as backup, managed to calm the kids down long enough to run through the twenty-minute production a few times. Cedric's background music and sound effects made the play so much better.

They were as ready as they'd ever be.

On Sunday, Gracie's heart cracked as the Mount Sinai staff wheeled in the audience, aka Royal Subjects, to be positioned behind King Eli and Queen Alyssa's makeshift thrones. Hospital beds lined the back row, wheelchairs the next. Twenty-two patients in all—most of them pale and puffy, many of them with no hair. Some were connected to IVs. Most wore protective masks.

What had Gracie expected? She was ashamed to admit she'd been so preoccupied with the play and its trappings she'd almost forgotten the reason they were performing. She fought back the tears as she looked from one child to the next, all of them robed in royal costumes—and joy.

Parents, grandparents, and friends, Rachel and Reggie included, were seated in a semicircle facing the children. The painted screens were set to the side to maintain an unobstructed view of the production. After a brief welcome by Gracie, the play began.

The Royal Knights of Mount Sinai, Miles as Sir Remedy and Zeke as Sir Cure-all, clippity-clopped on stick horses in full armor, battling their enemies. Lady Malady schemed with Count Contagious, their evil goal to thwart the efforts of Countess Comfort. Leighton, as Princess Patient, stood on a balcony, waiting to be cured—or *rescued*—as she corrected them more than once. Miles filled in lines others forgot, and Cedric accompanied the action with music and sound effects as if he'd been rehearsing for months.

After the final scene and the initial applause, Gracie introduced the cast. She made sure to give Zeke extra credit as set designer, Miles as playwright and director, and Tempie as his assistant.

When the time came to present their special guest stars, Harper wheeled Eli out while Gracie followed with Alyssa. King Eli extended his scepter to the audience, and Queen Alyssa gave the crowd the royal wave.

Most of the audience lost it when Miles, in the middle of a round of applause for the cast, did a one-eighty and faced the patients, clapping even louder for them. The whole room joined in.

Before the applause ended, Miles ran over to Gracie, crying. "We-e did it! We ma-ade them feel good for a whi-ile, didn't we?"

"We sure did, sweetie." She put her hand over his heart and talked around the lump in her throat. "Because in here is a heart that cares."

On their way out of the hospital, Gracie whispered to Reggie and Rachel, "That applause for the patients? Not scripted. That was all your son."

Rachel dabbed at the corners of her eyes. "Thanks for telling me. Just when we think he couldn't get any more full of himself . . ."

Gracie nodded. "I know. He *gets* it."

On the way home, Tempie took hold of Gracie's hand and kissed it. "I'm so proud of you. You did a wonderful thing tonight."

"We *all* did." Gracie patted her grandmother's hand. "Hope we didn't wear you out."

"Well, I might need some time to recuperate before I head back to the Cape. Tell Mario I'll be ready in a few days.

Chapter Forty

Seymour found himself on the end of a panicky phone call from Grace.

"You do realize we only have weeks before Polina's gala?"

"Yes, Grace." He did not understand what that had to do with them. "I am sure Polina and her people have everything well in hand."

"Of course, they do. But we don't."

He was still lost. "What do you mean? I received the tickets and backstage passes from Polina days ago."

"Yes, I know. But we need to find you a proper tuxedo. You can't wear one of your work suits. You'd stand out. And you don't want to stand out on Polina's night, do you?"

"I had not considered that." But now he considered what little he knew about buying a tuxedo.

"Are you free tomorrow?"

He pulled out his pocket calendar. "I am open, but—"

"Good. We can rent everything you need at Baldwyn Formals on West Forty-fifth—even your shoes."

He breathed a sigh of relief. Renting sounded much more sensible than buying. He could swing that.

Swing that. Listen to yourself, Seymour. Such a man about town—attending the opera, taking ladies out, performing in plays, renting formal wear, going to galas, attending after-parties. What will be next? A parade?

Seymour held the tuxedo shop door open for Gracie.

She stepped inside. "This place is famous for its great selection of designers."

"Good, good." What did he know from designers? Surprised by the many different styles on display, he fingered a mint-green jacket worn by a blond, bewigged mannequin. He conceded Grace might know more about formal wear than he did, but he would have to put his foot down if she chose this one.

A tall, thin gentleman with deep-set eyes and short, crimped silver hair greeted them. His eyeglasses, attached to a chain, were perched on the end of his slightly hooked nose.

"Good morning. My name is Norris. How may I be of assistance?"

Once Gracie explained what they needed, the clerk led them past the prom section to a rack of black suits.

Seymour felt more comfortable already.

Norris attended them well. "We have quite a selection appropriate for this type of occasion." After taking Seymour's measurements, he said, "We'll find one that best compliments your stature. Of course, in the right shade of black to go with your skin tone and fawn-colored hair."

Who knew there were shades of black? Apparently, the clerk did. And when did his hair become fawn-colored? He had always been told it was mouse-brown.

Seymour tried on a total of three tuxedos. Grace and Norris agreed on the first one, a Ralph Lauren classic fit, in a soft shade of black called *bistre.*

Grace studied Seymour from his head to his shiny shoes. "Hmm, I wonder if they have an eye patch in bistre."

Norris said, "Of course. I shall be right back." He entered a stock room through a pair of velvet drapes.

Seymour whispered to Grace, "Is he serious?"

She fluttered her lashes. "Why not? They have everything else in this place."

When the clerk returned, he directed Seymour to a dressing room, where a new patch, in bistre, lay atop tissue paper inside a small box.

"When you're ready," Norris said, "let us see how it agrees with the Lauren."

How agreeable can an eye patch be?

Seymour compared the patches. True, his patch was a few shades darker. As instructed, he put the new one on and exited the dressing room.

Smiling, the clerk led Seymour to a three-paneled, full-length mirror.

Seymour, not prone to fussing about his personal appearance, was taken aback by his reflection. "Grace, perhaps we should rethink this."

Grace's face fell. "Why? You look dashing!"

He tried unsuccessfully to hide his mischief. "I know, but I thought the whole point was *not* to stand out on Polina's special night."

"Well, listen to Mr. Comedian. I was going to buy you lunch, but now I don't know—"

"Lunch? Perhaps at a nice Jewish deli?"

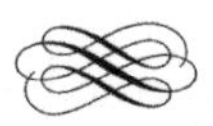

Seymour's mouth watered as he read the menu. He made up his mind fast. "I would like the corned beef on rye with Swiss and spicy mustard and a side of sauerkraut. Please, may I have a few extra sour pickles?"

"Make that two—minus the sauerkraut and extra pickles," Grace said.

"Comin' right up." The seasoned waitress shoved her pad and pen back into her pocket.

"Thank you for your help this morning," Seymour said. "I had never thought about looking out of place at the gala."

"If you've never been to a gala, how would you know what to wear?"

"You are too kind, Grace."

"Hey, you helped me with *Mount Sinai.* I helped you with your tux."

"Speaking of the play, what a blessing for those young children. A success, was it not?"

"I'd say so. Not everyone would jump in to help like you did. I appreciate it."

"Grace, when I said I was honored to be asked, I meant it."

"I have to confess," she said, "God taught me a lesson in humility at that hospital."

Seymour tilted his head. "Oh. What might that be?"

"That there are more important things in life than my acting career. I'll never make that mistake again."

Seymour bobbed his head. "The word *never* is one I do my best to avoid. Every time I use it, God teaches me another lesson."

"You? I thought you were like King Solomon with all your wisdom."

Seymour burst out laughing. "Yes, that would be me. Remember the bowling date I planned without first consulting God? You saw how that turned out."

"I'm so sorry. I didn't mean for—"

"Again, no apology necessary." Seymour cleared his throat. "My point is that our good intentions, unless directed by God, are only good intentions, which have nothing to do with his will."

"I don't get it."

"Instead of seeking God's perfect will and timing in the situation, I made my plans, then assumed God would bless them."

"I think you're making too much of it. Anyway, didn't you tell me you had a good time with Simka?"

"That I did. But that was God's grace, not my planning."

"God's grace? How well *did* things go with Simka that night? What about Polina?"

Seymour sighed. "I know even less about women than I did before. Reading people—women in particular—has never been one of my gifts. I will wait on the Lord."

"Don't wait too long. I believe when God gives us talents or *other* opportunities, he expects us to use 'em or lose 'em. I don't intend to miss out by overthinking everything."

"Overthinking is not the issue here, Grace. Surrendering your will to God is."

"I know, but I have a feeling things are going to go my way soon."

His way, Grace, his way.

Chapter Forty-One

After Grace left to retrieve the children, Seymour elected to tour part of Midtown Manhattan. Navigating was difficult since many of the streets had more than one name. The official name of Sixth Avenue was Avenue of the Americas. Forty-seventh Street was also known as Diamond Jewelry Way. The street lamps there had jewel-shaped globes. Large red letters on the building on the corner read Diamond Center. Seymour chuckled to himself, thinking this must be where Grace had thought he worked.

He passed places he had read about and heard about on the news—NBC Studios, Radio City Music Hall, Rockefeller Center, and the Time & Life Building. As far as he could determine, there was more of everything in New York—skyscrapers, restaurants, traffic, storefronts filled with all manner of goods, food carts and their aromas—some not so pleasing. He could hardly take it all in and wasn't sure he wanted to.

So many people in a hurry, so much noise, yet so little peace and joy.

He remembered what Gracie's grandmother had said, "Ripe for the harvest." *Lord, where would you have me begin?*

A young tattooed girl passing by shoved a flyer at him for a show at The Museum of Modern Art located a few blocks up on Fifty-third Street. His attitude brightened. The museum might be a welcome respite.

Even amid the cacophony of sounds and confusion, Seymour jumped when his phone rang. Had he forgotten an appointment? Was Grace all right? Did Aaron need him?

The caller ID read "Polina Zelenka." With no time to deliberate over a witty greeting, he decided on "Hello."

"Seymour, this is Polina."

"Yes. How are you?" *Yes. How are you?* Could he be more ordinary?

"I'm well, thank you. I was wondering …"

A cab went by and honked at a truck. Both drivers exploded in angry words.

"Please excuse me, Polina. The noise here is a bit deafening."

"Where are you?"

He read the street sign. "Not far from The Museum of Modern Art. I think."

"Are you free to meet at the museum? I'm at Harry Winston's on Fifth Avenue. I can be there in ten."

"That would be lovely." *That would be lovely? Oy, had he regressed to that again?*

He increased his speed. Once he reached the museum, he hoped his heart rate would be near normal by the time Polina arrived. But he doubted seeing her would help slow its pace.

Polina exited her car and greeted him with a smile. "Mind if we sit in the café instead of touring the museum?"

"My feet would be forever grateful." He laughed. "I must confess, I don't really understand modern art."

Polina put her arm through his. "Neither do I, but I love their café."

A young receptionist greeted them. "Go right in, Ms. Zelenka. I'll put you down for one guest."

Seymour tried not to stare. Half the girl's head was shaved; the other half was dyed blue. Her dress was one big Campbell's tomato soup label.

"Thank you," Polina said. "Let me guess. There's an Andy Warhol exhibit today? Love the dress."

The girl grinned. "If you want, I'll let you borrow it for your gala."

"If I'd only known …" Polina rested a hand on her hip. "… I would never have committed to the Versace."

They left the girl giggling.

Seymour marveled at the ease with which Polina interacted with others. Just as she had with him the first time they met.

After taking the elevator to the second-floor café, Polina chose a table away from the entrance. "Now, Mr. Kaufman, what brought you to Midtown this afternoon? Sightseeing or service?"

"You did, indirectly. Grace accompanied me to a tuxedo shop this morning, so I might be properly attired for your gala." He paused at her grin. "After we parted company, I took a stroll."

She fingered a petal in the small vase of fresh flowers. "And what did you discover about this great city?"

"That people do not *stroll*." He chuckled. "I was in everyone's way."

She laughed, which pleased him.

He muddled over his next words. "*Meh.* I mean no offense, but I have observed more frowns than smiles. To find such sadness on the countenances of so many grieves me."

Polina nodded. "I felt the same way when I first arrived. This city tends to drive people at a frantic pace, like a powerful engine without its brakes. You can see it and feel it."

He looked out the window at the street, teeming with traffic and people, thankful for the glass that kept the sounds out. "How did you avoid getting caught up in it?"

"My singing kept me grounded. I was blessed to have talented people willing to mentor me. They taught me how to appreciate much of what New York has to offer—the art, the beauty, the energy, the talent. Over time, I didn't see the harshness as much as I did the kindnesses. There are many, you know. I call them flowers among the weeds."

Of which you are one, Seymour dared not say.

Polina removed her scarf and tied it around her handbag.

His eye was drawn to her neck, red and chafed.

She pulled her shirt collar up. "You noticed my awful rash?"

He was mortified at being caught. "I did not mean—I am sorry. Is it painful?"

"No, but quite itchy. I saw my doctor this morning. He said it'll be gone in a few days."

"Harry Winston is your doctor?"

She smiled. "No, remember, Harry Winston is the jeweler, but there is a connection. I was there because ..." She waved her explanation away. "... it's a boring story." She steered the conversation in another direction. "Seymour, I called you because I wanted to ask you something."

"Of course. What is it?"

"The other night at my home, did you refuse to let my driver take you and Grace home because you were upset with me?"

"Upset? Why would I be upset with you?"

"Well, you seemed somewhat down when you left, although Simka said you two had had fun."

"Yes, she spoke rightly." He set his palms down flat on the table, giving himself a moment to examine his thoughts. Up until now, he had not admitted, even to himself, the real reason he had declined her offer. "I am an old-fashioned man, Polina. One not used to having women pay my way into the theater and send drivers back and forth for me."

She leaned forward. "Surely, you would do the same for me if the situation were reversed?"

"Of course." He had backed himself into a corner.

"I believe when the grace of God blesses one person financially, it blesses others in different ways. As members of the same family, don't you think we should share our variety and abundance with each other?"

Seymour could not argue. "When you put it that way—"

"I do. To give when you have a surplus is easy. Receiving and being thankful is noble."

"Ouch. A well-deserved hit to my ego."

She smiled even wider. "Are we all right now?"

"Yes, more than all right."

"Good," Polina said. "Then may my driver take you home after our visit?"

"I would be delighted." Seymour cupped his ear. "Did you hear that? My toes just did the dance of King David with all their might."

Polina's melodic laugh became the musical score for the rest of his day.

Chapter Forty-Two

Gracie was on her way to Stage 2 for her *Love and Waffles* callback. Although this theater wasn't nearly as ornate as some, its intimacy kept the ticket cost down and attendance up. Appearing here was a great start for any actor.

She'd asked Harper to come along for moral support.

Harper hurried beside her. "Are you nervous? You're fast-walking again."

"Sorry. Actually, I'm quite calm." Mainly because she was sure her confidence in God would pay off this time. But she couldn't tell Harper that.

"Calm or not, a second audition for a Bennett Noble play is an honor."

"I guess." Gracie didn't guess. She knew.

As they reached West Forty-second Street and neared Stage 2, Gracie tried not to be obvious about sizing up the competition milling about. One girl could've passed for Meryl Streep's daughter. Another looked like a twenty-something Viola Davis. A third had a near-perfect look for the role.

Gracie reminded herself that none of that mattered with God on her side.

"Make sure your phone is off," Harper said. "If it rings, that could cost you the role."

"Not a problem. I forgot to charge it after Tempie and I video chatted last night."

"Your grandmother video chats? Amazing." Harper pointed to the door. "Now go! Act! Make it worthy of a Tony."

"Thanks," Gracie said, "but it won't happen in this theater. There's a five-hundred-seat minimum required for Tony eligibility."

"Who cares? Quit stalling." Harper opened the door and shoved her toward the line to the check-in table. "I'll be waiting outside."

After standing in the line of about twenty or so, Gracie finally reached the table where a pretty, middle-aged redhead sat. Her nametag read Konnie Viner, Assistant Casting Director.

"Name." Ms. Viner didn't look up.

"Grace Camden."

The woman ran her pencil down her list. "Your last name again?"

"Camden. With a C."

She scanned the sheet again. "No Camden here." She pursed her lips. "This has been tried before, you know, and it never works."

Gracie tried not to panic. "No, the assistant casting director left me a voicemail. Maybe I'm listed under "G" for Grace."

The woman checked again. "No."

"I would have confirmed," Gracie said, "but he said it wasn't necessary."

"I can only go by the final list. Sorry, you'll have to leave."

She was being dismissed? How could that be? She wanted to argue but didn't know how.

"Next!" the woman shouted.

Gracie struggled against the tide to the exit. *Really? Are you kidding me, God?*

As she stumbled out the door, Harper raced over to her. "What's going on?"

"They don't have my name on their callback list."

"Well, that's crazy," Harper said. "Who's in charge?"

Still in shock, Gracie muttered, "Apparently, Konnie Viner, the redhead."

Falling back against the closed door, Gracie tried to think. She could prove her callback by her voicemail … if only her stupid phone weren't dead. What else could she do?

Nada. Nihil. Nothing.

Chapter Forty-Three

A brisk wind whipped Gracie's hair around as she propped herself up against the Stage 2 entrance. Her bragging about her "confidence in God finally paying off" haunted her.

What on earth are you doing, God?

"Are you okay, miss?" An older man with a Mets ball cap and oversized, dark glasses addressed her.

"Excuse me?" She wiped her eyes and scanned the area. *Where did Harper go?*

"Are you lost?"

"Maybe I am." She shook off the self-pity, then noticed she was standing between him and the door. "I'm sorry. Am I in your way?" She moved a few inches to the side.

The man tugged at his cap. "Do I know you?"

Gracie wondered if he was a creep with a line of clichés. "I doubt it." *And the way my career is going, you never will.* Great. Self-pity was back.

Harper came flying out the door, almost knocking the two of them down. "That witch! You won't believe what I heard."

Gracie grabbed her arm. "What do you mean?"

"That Viner woman. When I went in to vouch for you, I overheard her whisper to the next girl in line that she 'owed her big time for eliminating Camden as her only serious competition.'"

The man took a step closer to them. "Excuse me. What did you say?"

Harper scanned him from head to toe. "Who are you?"

He took a step closer. "Humor me, please, and repeat what you told your friend here."

His gruffness must have caught Harper off guard because she did as he asked.

Walking around them, he opened the door. "You two, come with me."

Gracie and Harper shrugged simultaneously, then followed him into the theater.

The man motioned for them to stand off to the side. "Wait here."

Whatever his plan, it was better than anything Gracie could think of.

He approached Konnie Viner and removed his ball cap and sunglasses.

Gracie and Harper gasped at Bennett Noble's trademark wiry hair and bushy eyebrows.

"May I speak with you a moment, Ms. Viner?"

"Director! I wasn't expecting you so early." She called out to the actors waiting to check in. "Ladies, take a few steps back to give Mr. Noble and me some privacy."

Noble spoke barely loud enough for Gracie to hear. "Just between you and me, Ms. Viner ..." He winked. "... is there anyone on this list I should pay special attention to?"

Konnie pursed her lips and put a star by a single name. "This is the one you want, sir."

"Good," he said. "I'd like you to add one more name." He waved Gracie over. "Ms. Camden, is it?"

Gracie nodded. "Grace Camden."

"Of course." Konnie's hand trembled as she wrote Gracie's name.

Noble swept the area. "Ms. Viner, I don't see my casting director. Is he here?"

"Yes. He's in the audition room. I offered to handle the sign-in for him."

"That won't be necessary now ..." He placed both hands on the table and leaned in to make eye contact. "... because you're fired."

Bug-eyed, she stammered some questions and excuses with little effect. Finally, she gathered her things and skulked out.

Noble cautioned Gracie. "You've got your audition, but I can't promise any more than that."

"Yes, sir. Thank you. I'll give you my best." When it was Gracie's turn, she did exactly that.

Two hours dragged by before the casting director announced, "Thank you all for coming. I know this is tough, but if I don't call your name that means you can go."

He called two names. Gracie's was not one of them. Her heart sank but rose again when he offered the two women minor roles. Both said yes immediately. He called three more names and cast them as customers in the restaurant scene.

When Noble himself called out the name "Phoebe Ogden," Gracie figured she'd lost her chance.

"Ms. Ogden," he said, "I want you for the lead's understudy." Then he pointed to Gracie. "You're my Kat Hamilton."

Gracie heard someone say, "Thank you," then realized she had spoken.

"Don't thank me," Noble said. "Just work hard, 'cause Ms. Ogden is good."

So you did have a plan, Lord?

Noble announced that three weeks of day-long rehearsals would start in two days. Opening night would be after Thanksgiving. Gracie was thankful the play wouldn't conflict with her attending Polina's gala.

Before she left, she stopped by the table for a rehearsal schedule.

Noble raised his head. "Questions, Ms. Camden?"

"I do have one. I'm curious. Did your nephew ever give you my storyboard bio?"

"Hmm. I would have remembered a storyboard bio. Perhaps it got misplaced." His eyebrows shot up. "Ah-ah! Now I know why you looked familiar."

"Oh?" She guessed perhaps from the Juilliard workshop he never got to give.

"I was in the audience for *The Battle of Mount Sinai*."

"You were?" She wanted to ask why.

"Yes. Queen Alyssa is my granddaughter."

"I had no idea. What a beautiful outlook that sweet girl has. How's she doing?"

He smiled. "They've seen a marked improvement in her recent tests."

"I'm so glad. I'll keep praying."

"Please do." He leaned back in his seat and locked his fingers behind his head. "What you did for those kids displayed good character …" He jiggled his bushy brows. "… which makes my selection for lead even sweeter."

Gracie called Ian. "I got the role!"

"I knew it. Tempie must've done a backflip."

"She doesn't know yet."

"You told *me* before your grandmother?"

"We're scheduled to video chat in an hour. Seriously, Ian, this was a God thing. I'll tell you about it tonight."

"What's tonight?"

"A bunch of us are getting together to celebrate. Please tell me you can make it."

"Wouldn't miss it. One thing, how're Reggie and Rachel going to feel about their nanny hiring a babysitter to take care of their wee ones while she's off rehearsing?"

"Rachel and I have discussed this possibility before. We've had a contingency plan in place for some time. We only have to find coverage for the three weeks of rehearsals, and after that, for the matinees. Uh, and who do you think is throwing the party?"

"I'm guessin' it'd be the Adlers?"

"You're quick, if not pretty."

"Aw, how can you say that, Gracie? I'm a sight for sore eyes, I am."

"Speaking of that, don't bring a date. This is a small affair, only close friends. Miles and Leighton will be there, so no bimbos allowed."

"You say that to me after you dated turtle-boy?"

"Again, I didn't *date* Chase. But since you brought him up, I had to invite him tonight because he bought all the costumes for the kids' play."

Ian shot back, "That's the story you're going with, is it?"

"I'm going with the truth. Be here at eight and don't be late."

Gracie had one more person to call. "Hey, Seymour, doing anything tonight? Want to help me celebrate?"

"Praise God! You won the role."

"I did. Now, how about it?"

"Oy, Polina is out of town. I promised her I would keep Simka company this evening."

"Bring her along. We're meeting at the Adlers's home. Nothing fancy. Rachel told me to invite anyone I wanted. Simka might enjoy seeing Miles and Leighton again."

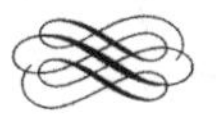

That night, Ian, Harper, Seymour, Simka, and Chase joined the Adler family to commemorate Gracie's milestone. The children seemed happy to see Seymour, but more than once Gracie caught Miles skewering Chase with a sharp glare. She pulled him aside to reassure him that Chase was only her friend.

"I know that." He crossed his spindly arms. "But he's weird, and he smells like fish."

Turtles, most likely. She couldn't scold him for being honest—mainly because she agreed about the weird part.

Like a chipmunk remembering an acorn, Miles said, "And why is one of his eyebrows like Zaide's?"

"Zaide's? Like your grandfather's? What d'ya mean?"

He demonstrated on his own brow. "Brown here, white on the end."

So it wasn't toothpaste Gracie had seen at Starbuck's. "Sometimes people have white hair like others have birthmarks. They don't need to be old."

Miles seemed satisfied for the moment.

After a number of toasts in Gracie's honor, Ian sidled up alongside her. "Enjoying the limelight, are you?"

Gracie couldn't tell if he was being facetious. "Tempie's been quoting Zechariah 4:10 to me for years, something about not despising the day of small beginnings."

"The humble actor is quoting Scripture." Ian's eyes lit up. "Should I tell your grandmother you've also found a church?"

Now she knew he was being a wise guy. "Go away, brat."

He winked at her then headed for the dessert table.

Gracie surveyed the room. Chase and Simka stood together in front of the floor-to-ceiling windows, staring off at the city lights. What could this odd duo be chatting about? Before she could speculate, Simka turned to Chase and wagged a finger. By the frown on the older woman's face, Gracie sensed one or the other of them might need rescuing.

Gracie approached them. "Excuse me, Chase. Would you mind if I stole Simka away?"

"Not at all." He patted his hair down then pushed up his eyeglasses. "Ciao, Mrs. Lonnit. Nice meeting you."

"Şi tu," Simka took Gracie's arm.

When she and Simka were out of Chase's earshot, Gracie apologized. "I hope he didn't go on about his turtles or his mother."

"Da, he spoke much of them." She folded her arms and grunted. "I scold him for to put turtles before mama."

She chuckled. "You do speak your mind, don't you?"

Simka's eyes searched Gracie's. "Is impropriu? How you say? Not polite?"

Gracie patted her shoulder. "Don't worry, Simka. Honesty is always the best policy."

Chapter Forty-Four

Dressed in loose-fitting jeans, a green quilted vest, a striped knit hat, and low-profile skate shoes, the Chief ambled into Lincoln Center from Amsterdam Avenue, carrying a used performance skateboard. He almost bumped into the Spaniard who was standing at the corner of the Koch Theater, squinting in the direction of the Met.

Think quick.

The Chief called out to two skaters loping through Hearst Plaza. "D-d-dudes! W-w-wait u-up!" Once he reached them, he engaged them in conversation by admiring their boards until all three of them exited on West Sixty-sixth.

Too close. The Chief needed to rid himself of his competition before they caught on to him. And he knew just the dolts who could help him.

Sunday morning, the Chief dressed in a navy polyester suit, cheap white shirt, red tie, and vintage gray fedora. He slicked his hair back, glued on a Van Dyke beard and moustache, and added a pair of *Men in Black* sunglasses. Armed with an Interpol ID and dossiers good enough to fool Ginger Hair and Cowboy Beaver, he took a cab to Lincoln Center.

He found them near a grove of trees and flashed his ID. "William Mason, Interpol. Can we talk privately?"

Except for Ginger Hair jangling his coins and Cowboy Beaver gnawing on a toothpick, the two didn't move.

He'd have to be gentle, or they'd wet their pants. The Chief whispered, "Not sure if you're private security or bounty hunters—great disguises by the way—but I need your help closing a case."

A few seconds passed before Ginger Hair spoke. "Uh, what case?"

The Chief looked around cautiously before pulling out the fake documents—redacted for authenticity's sake. "These three men are international jewel thieves." He pointed to a photo of Chips and the nephew. "These two work in tandem." He switched to a mug shot of the Spaniard. "This guy works alone."

His two marks read the documents and looked at the photos.

"I've been watching them for weeks," the Chief said. "The thing is, without official sanction, the FBI can't know Interpol was here. That's where you two come in."

Cowboy said, "What's in it for us?"

"Interpol policy prevents agents from accepting reward money—so the fifty grand would go to whoever reports them to the FBI—provided they're caught, that is."

Ginger eyed his partner, then said to the Chief, "Give us a minute, okay?"

"No problem."

They walked about ten feet away—close enough for the Chief to read their lips—for the most part.

Ginger grumbled. "... necklace ... worth more ... fifty grand."

Cowboy removed the toothpick from his mouth. "What chance against ... The last thing we stole ... three lengths ... copper piping ... fixer-upper in Queens."

Ginger jangled his coins. "... suppose fifty grand is fifty grand."

"And ... guaranteed. Most ... ever made."

They walked back to the Chief.

"We're in," Ginger Hair said. "What do we do next?"

"Go to the local FBI field office at Federal Plaza. Today, preferably." He exchanged the fake dossiers for a half dozen candid photos of the thieves. "Tell them the men in these pictures have been casing the Met. They're wanted across the globe. They'll take it from there."

Cowboy Beaver chawed down on a fresh toothpick. "You don't want us to mention you at all?"

"Not unless you want Interpol to take the credit and return the reward to their slush fund." The Chief shook their hands. "Thanks for getting me out of a jam. Look me up if you're ever in Berlin."

Chapter Forty-Five

This was Gracie's first time working with a world-famous director. Everyone had been warned about Bennett Noble's rule—three times tardy and you're out. She factored in possible transportation tie-ups and left earlier than necessary for her first day of rehearsals.

When she arrived, Noble was already there. True to his style, a number of storyboards were lined up in front of the stage. She was glad she knew her lines already—and everyone else's.

Once the rest of the cast and crew were there, the assistant director made some general announcements. "People, we only have a few weeks to learn our lines, get comfortable in our roles, and find that elusive chemistry." He waved a copy of the script. "I want all actors with speaking parts on stage with their scripts. The director wants to start with a simple read-through this morning."

Noble explained, "Every time I redo one of my plays, I have to tweak some lines to reflect the times. We'll start at the beginning and read straight through. I'll make notes along the way. You're first, Ms. Camden."

At the Barnstable Community Playhouse, they'd always gone right into a full rehearsal. Other than when she was home alone, Gracie had never done a simple read-through. She wasn't sure how much acting to put into it—so she gave it her all.

The AD raised his hand. "Stop. This isn't an audition, Ms. Camden. You've got the part already. A simple reading will do."

She started over.

The AD stopped her again. "A monotone voice won't help us here either. More feeling, please."

When she finally found her voice and rhythm, he called her out on volume.

At Noble's direction, the AD either slowed or increased the pace of the reading, allowing the director to jot notes and scribble on his storyboards. At the end of the first rehearsal, Noble announced, "I'll make the changes tonight. Your new script will be ready tomorrow."

New script? But I know the other one by heart. Could it change that much?

The next day she realized it could—and it did. Especially her part. Learning was one thing. Unlearning was quite another.

Noble announced, "Consider this your first official rehearsal. You can use your scripts, but I want to see some acting."

Kat Hamilton had the opening lines. "Their love is as cold as these frozen waffles! And you can't convince me it will ever thaw."

The actor playing Kat's love interest, Noah Parmenter, responded. "Why would I try to convince you otherwise? Truth is, I agree with you."

Kat. "You do? Finally. A man with some common sense."

The AD yelled, "Stop! Camden, you're chewing up the scenery. I know you're used to carrying your small-town productions all by your lonesome. You don't have to do that here. We've got more than one professional in the house, so tone it down a bit."

Not once did Noble raise his head.

In a flash of frustration, she tried harder. Even she could tell her performance was worse. Drained of every ounce of self-confidence at the day's end, she promised herself that tomorrow would be better.

But it wasn't. Neither was the rest of the week.

Doubting everything she'd ever learned about acting, she challenged God. "What about that big plan you had for me? What happened to my gifts—the ones that were supposed to bring you all that glory?"

Gracie called her grandmother for advice ... and to complain. Before she could get a word out, Tempie announced, "Guess what? I've got a new gig!"

"A new gig? Where?"

"The Andersons are back from Paris. We'll be at the Southridge Retirement Center in Dennisport tomorrow, performing a scene from *Sabrina*. The 1954 version. I'm playing Humphrey Bogart's mother."

"That's wonderful!"

"I know these venues aren't *real* theater, but the mini performances will keep me occupied until the playhouse is rebuilt—which will take forever since three commissions and multiple egos have gotten involved. How're your rehearsals going? Knocking 'em dead, are you?"

"Yeah, dead." Gracie decided not to whine. And asking for advice was tantamount to the same.

Her grandmother ended their conversation as she often did. "Planted yourself in a good church yet, dear?"

Gracie sighed silently. “Not yet.”

“Then how do you expect to grow?”

She didn’t dare roll her yes. Even without video, her grandmother would know.

Chapter Forty-Six

On Friday evening, Seymour was waiting for Grace outside the theater when she finished rehearsal.

"Seymour! What are you doing here?"

"This is where the Lord led me."

"I'm glad he's leading someone 'cause he sure isn't leading me." Grace's eyes welled up. "Rehearsals have been dreadful. No, *I've* been dreadful. Forgetting lines. Losing my pace. Getting confused. Like I've never acted before. I feel like an author with writer's block or a batter in a slump."

"Is that phenomenon common in your profession as well?"

"Common or not, this kind of stuff has never happened to me."

"Let's walk." Seymour slipped his arm through hers. "Have you spoken with the director about it?"

"And give him a reason to replace me? No way. My understudy is waiting in the wings, rubbing her hands and licking her acting chops. No, I'll get myself together over the weekend, refocus, then try harder on Monday."

"Perhaps we should pray, Grace?"

"Sure. I've got one. 'God, why give me the part to begin with if all you're going do is let me fail?'"

Seymour discerned Grace was not ready to hear God's answer. "How about we go for a nice bowl of chicken soup?" He winked. "I hear it is good for the soul."

Grace gave him a half-hearted smile but groused all the way to the restaurant while he prayed silently.

Once seated, Seymour opened with a topic he hoped might interest Grace. "Have you chosen your dress for Polina's gala yet?"

She folded her hands on the table. "I think I'm going with my midnight blue Vera Wangish sheath with the bateau neckline."

"Sounds lovely." Seymour had no idea who Vera Wangish was or what *bat toe* meant.

"In the end, it'll depend on my mood. If my rehearsals don't improve, I might show up in the Count Contagious cape."

Seymour hesitated, then spoke the words Grace had used to convince him he needed to wear a tuxedo. "Then it will be *you* who stands out. And you don't want to stand out on Polina's night, do you?" He tried to be serious, but his eye belied him.

She smirked. "Touché, Mr. Kaufman."

"You spoke the truth to me, I simply return the favor. Furthermore, God has taught me that acting solely upon my mood is often in opposition to his truth."

She sighed. "What *is* God's truth?"

"His Word, of course."

"No, I mean, how do I fix what I'm doing wrong if I don't know what it is?"

"I see. The Lord reveals things in many ways. Sometimes his Word jumps off the pages of the Bible, speaking to me as I read it. Other times his Spirit guides me through conviction or simply gives me peace. Often, my circumstances will confirm his leading."

"Like when you moved to New York?"

"Yes. However, I confess I am still not sure why that was. I keep putting one foot and one prayer in front of another because I know God's best is ahead of me."

"Tempie has been telling me all my life that God blessed me with a natural talent to act. Others have thought so too. If that's true, then why am I having such a hard time?"

"The Lord works in ways we do not fully understand, at least this side of heaven. For me, it was often a matter of timing. There were also occasions when I was not using my gifts in a manner he preferred. I know one thing, when the Lord wants to get my attention he knows how to do it. Quite uncomfortable at times."

"Uncomfortable? This is downright painful."

Seymour leaned in. "Grace, have you found a home church where you can be mentored in your faith?"

Grace dipped her head. "Are you sure you haven't been talking to my grandmother?"

Chapter Forty-Seven

"Shalom, Simka. With the gala coming up, I wanted to see how Polina was doing." Thinking it might sound too personal, Seymour did not mention Polina's rash.

Simka laughed. "She wishes whole thing was over."

"Is she available to come to the phone?"

"Agent is here and publicist person. I see if she can talk."

"No, please do not interrupt them." He did not want Simka to hear the disappointment in his voice. "You must find this whole event exciting. I imagine having a member of your family receive an award of this magnitude does not happen often."

"Da. I want gala to be special for her. I can never repay her for all she has done for me."

"I am sure having you there will mean more to her than the award itself."

"I hope so. Wait, I think they leave now. Polina will be glad. Agent and publicist argue much. Agent say publicist has no class—like cheap, rented tuxedo."

Cheap rented tuxedo? Is that what they will think of me? "On second thought, Simka, do not bother Polina now. I will speak with her later."

"Okey-doke."

Seymour sat on the corner of his bed, facing a bare wall. "Lord, why am I here? It is clear I do not fit with Polina's lifestyle." He was tempted to let his mood overtake him until his words to Grace resurfaced. *God has taught me that acting based on my mood is often in opposition to his truth.*

Bowing his head, he prayed. "What is your truth, Lord? Could it be you have something better in store for me?"

For a second, his mind flashed to Simka.

Chapter Forty-Eight

Gracie video chatted with Tempie on Sunday. Staring into her grandmother's discerning eyes, she was unable to hide how bad rehearsals had gone. "I've been horrible. I don't know what's wrong."

"The list of actors who've experienced stage fright and given less than perfect performances is as long as the membership of the Actors' Equity." Tempie paused. "The most famous one I know of is Sir Laurence Olivier. One time, his manager had to push him out on stage. Singers suffer bouts too. Renée Fleming. Barbara Streisand. Polina Zelenka."

"Why does knowing this not make me feel better?"

Tempie poured her nightly cup of tea. "You tell me."

Gracie thought a moment and didn't like the answer she arrived at. "Because I think I'm above it all?"

"Well, do you?" Tempie took a sip.

"Maybe. I guess I assumed when God *called* someone to a career, he'd work out the details."

Tempie chuckled. "Oh, you're a funny one. At the risk of repeating myself, dear, plant yourself in a good church and grow. Before you know it, God will put your gifts and talents to good use."

"Think so?"

"I do. But the Lord might surprise you with the when, where, and how of it. Now say good-night, Gracie. I'm off to bed."

"So early?"

"Got a busy day tomorrow. And the tea did its job."

"Okay, love you."

Her grandmother smiled. "Love you back."

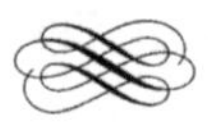

After a fitful night, Gracie overslept by an hour, catapulting her into panic mode. Of all mornings. She'd hoped to have time to relax and breathe before the second week of rehearsals began.

The more she rushed, the worse things went. She washed her hair with conditioner instead of shampoo, brushed brown eye shadow onto her cheeks instead of pink blush, and smeared a glob of toothpaste onto her cashmere sweater. She changed outfits but could only find one of her matching shoes. Even skipping her normal coffee stop didn't help her catch the train. When the second train was delayed, she had a hissy fit.

Like a stealth operative, she snuck into the theater late, hoping no one would notice. They were too busy watching her understudy playing *her* role. She sat where the director could see her, hoping he'd let her take over. He didn't.

Her fear allied with self-pity. When lunch break was over, she wanted to cry. By late afternoon, it was obvious they weren't going to call her. Not able to take any more, she left the theater before rehearsal ended and walked to the train through a torrential downpour.

Perfect.

Well into her trip home, she got a text from the AD. "Director's rules. One strike for being late. Two strikes for leaving rehearsal early."

Pluperfect.

Her phone rang as she climbed the stairs to her apartment. *Her parents.* In no mood for familial advice, she let it go to voicemail. She kicked her shoes off and threw herself onto her bed.

She awoke an hour later. When the brain fog cleared, she remembered every rotten thing about the day. Mostly that her understudy's portrayal of Kat Hamilton had been good.

Could things get any worse?

Thunder boomed and lightning struck close enough to scare her. *God, I meant that as a rhetorical question.*

She grabbed some hummus and pita chips, fell onto the love seat, and covered her legs with her quilt.

Her phone beeped, indicating a text. "Please call us as soon as you get this."

Gracie growled. "What does my mother want now?" She couldn't put them off forever … could she? She steeled herself for their nagging questions and called.

Her mother answered. "Honey, I'm afraid we have some bad news. Tempie had a heart attack last night and …"

"What? How is she?" Gracie threw her quilt off and jumped to her feet. "What hospital is she in? I'll take the first flight out.

Not sure what time." Gracie was furious with herself for not answering their earlier call.

Her dad's tone changed. "Honey, hear what we're saying. Tempie didn't make it. I found her still in bed when I stopped by for lunch. The medical examiner soon determined the cause."

Every part of Gracie went numb. She held the phone but didn't feel it. Her parents talked, but she didn't respond.

"Gracie, listen to me," her dad said. "We were able to reach your friend Ian earlier. He's agreed to drive you home tomorrow rather than have you fly."

She whispered, "Okay."

No sooner had she hung up than there was a knock at the door. Without waiting for her to answer, Ian entered and crossed the room. He didn't say a word, but just held her. She wanted to thank him but couldn't. Not yet but someday.

"If we leave now, darlin', we can be there in five hours. There's no sense waiting, you won't be able to sleep anyway."

Unable to process the simplest things, Gracie nodded and let Ian help her pack. They stopped to tell Rachel and Reggie on their way out. Gracie remembered their hugs, not much else.

They'd been driving silently through heavy rain for over an hour. Ian turned the radio on to catch the news. The meteorologist said the storm's direction was the same as theirs—Cape Cod. Their five-hour trip might take them six or more.

Gracie finally spoke. "Ian, can we go straight to Tempie's? I don't think I can deal with my parents right now."

"Sure. Still have your key?"

Gracie checked her keychain. "I do." The feel of Tempie's key in her hand unlocked a dam of tears. She hugged her knees, faced the side window and let them flow.

The rain was still heavy when they pulled in Tempie's driveway shortly after two in the morning. The small, three-bedroom ranch was in total darkness, not even a nightlight. Gracie wondered if her father and uncles were already trying to save money on the electric bill. She scolded herself for being unkind. Tempie would not have been pleased with that thought.

Once the house was well-lighted and the heat turned on, Gracie searched for signs of her grandmother. No teacup in the sink. No scripts on the ottoman. No dust on the mahogany furniture. Her mother had definitely "tidied up." Why couldn't she have left things as she'd found them?

When Gracie clicked on Tempie's mouse, the monitor lit up, showing the video chat logo, evidence of their last conversation. A sticky note on the cover of a journal read, "Tell Gracie about my next role as Christina Drayton—Katharine Hepburn—in *Guess Who's Coming to Dinner.*"

Ian interrupted her meandering. "Whaddya want me to do? I can stay or leave. Whatever you feel is best."

Gracie wanted to be alone but didn't want to seem ungrateful. "Where would you go at this hour?"

"I texted a buddy before we left the city. He said I could crash at his place. Is that what you want?"

She nodded. "Thanks for understanding."

Once he left, Gracie walked down the hallway to her grandmother's bedroom. The bed had been made. Her mother again. She turned down the covers on Tempie's side and sat where her grandmother had fallen asleep for the last time. Laying her head on the pillow, the scent of Jean Naté wafted over her. She pulled the covers over her and wept.

God, why did you have to take her so soon?

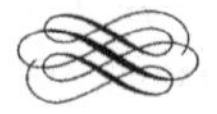

Even after a sleep pummeled by bouts of grief, Gracie got up early, knowing she had calls to make.

"Hi, Dad. How're you holding up?"

"I'm okay. How about you, honey? Are you on the road yet?"

"Actually, Ian and I left soon after you called. I had him bring me to Tempie's since it was the middle of the night."

"Is he there now? Do you want me to come get you?"

"I need some time here, Dad, understand? And I don't want Mom doing any more *straightening*. She's done enough." Even to herself, her tone sounded sharp.

Her father sighed. "That's just your mother's way of helping, sweetie."

"I know." But Gracie knew her mother. Her cleaning and straightening were more about her being embarrassed to have anyone see her mother-in-law's cluttered house.

"How 'bout I come get you around noon? You can help us with the arrangements."

She was surprised her mother hadn't already planned the whole service. Gracie managed not to say what she was thinking.

"You know your grandmother." Her dad chuckled. "She wants us to honor some nontraditional requests."

Gracie smiled, the first time since she'd heard the news. "Okay, Dad. Later then."

The next call was to Bennett Noble. "Mr. Noble, this is Grace Camden."

"Hello, Grace."

She bit her lip so she wouldn't break down. "My grandmother passed away unexpectedly yesterday. I'm on the Cape right now. We have to …" Words stuck in her throat as a sob escaped.

"I'm so sorry to hear that and, of course, to lose you for this run of *Love and Waffles*. I understand your place is with family right now."

"Thank you." Gracie thought of his granddaughter. "How is your Alyssa doing?"

"Thank you for asking. The doctors are amazed at her progress. You know, she still talks about her role in your play."

"I'm glad." Gracie could still see Alyssa's smile when she'd been crowned queen.

"You take care now, Grace. We'll see each other when you get back to New York."

Would they?

She couldn't think about that now.

Chapter Forty-Nine

Though she didn't much care for it, Gracie made a pot of valerian tea in honor of her grandmother. In a surreal way, she felt closer to Tempie. She sat at the small, green enamel-topped table positioned in the sunniest spot in the kitchen. Once, when Gracie had referred to the table as *vintage*, Tempie had scoffed, "Vintage is just a fancy word for old."

A bounty was set before her—bottles of vitamins and prescription medications, stacks of mail, mostly from charities, and a basket overflowing with free address labels and notepads—enough to last all nine lives of nine cats. A semicircle of framed family photos stood in the forefront, leaving enough room for the plastic Holy Land place mat.

Gracie could still hear her grandmother's words: "I eat every meal with my wonderful family—whether they join me in person or not." She reached for the picture she'd sent Tempie—a selfie taken on her first visit to Broadway—then held the photo against her heart.

After she rinsed her cup and saucer, she wandered down the hall to the bedroom which had been converted into a sewing room years ago. The closet was still filled with costumes from plays long past. The sewing machine was out and threaded. A dress pattern lay pinned to green poplin fabric on the cutting table.

Could it be the dress for her role in *Guess Who's Coming to Dinner?*

That reminded Gracie. She would have to call the Andersons. She doubted her parents or uncles would know to inform them—or if they even knew Tempie was working with them. Gracie was privy to most of what went on in her grandmother's life. As for the rest of the family, Tempie would wink and say, "My little secrets do well to stop the flow of their little opinions."

Gracie smiled, then cried at all they had shared, all she would miss.

The third bedroom, known as "Gracie's room," hadn't changed since she was a teen. Anyone was welcome to stay there, but no one else ever did. The black and pink Parisian scene wallpaper was covered with posters of Gracie's favorite movies, plays, and actors. The shelves held awards, certificates, and memorabilia from both Tempie's and her years at the BCP.

She moved on to Tempie's bedroom and picked up her Bible. The leather cover was supple and worn, the pages well-marked in different colors of ink. Gracie flipped to the ribbon bookmark. Psalm 16. Tempie's favorite. She had highlighted some verses.

> I have set the Lord always before me;
> Because He is at my right hand I shall not be moved.
> Therefore my heart is glad, and my glory rejoices;
> My flesh also will rest in hope.

For You will not leave my soul in Sheol,
Nor will You allow Your Holy One to see corruption.
You will show me the path of life;
In Your presence is fullness of joy;
At Your right hand are pleasures forevermore.

She smiled, trying to imagine her grandmother's first encounter with Jesus.

Four large hatboxes were piled on the shelf in the closet. Outside of playing a role, her grandmother didn't often wear hats—except on Easter and when she'd visited Gracie in New York. She reached for the box closest to her, which was filled with letters and cards. She removed the other three boxes, which held more of the same.

The mail was saved chronologically, more or less, by decades. The box farthest back held love letters written to and from her grandfather who'd died before Gracie had been old enough to know him. A half century of birthday and Mother's Day cards were jammed in too.

She took the boxes to the living room and sat in Tempie's script-reading chair, thumbing through the notes and letters. The correspondence wasn't all from family, but from people Tempie had mentored through the years.

Words scrawled on a postcard card shouted, "Thanks, Tempie! You were right. He did want to marry me. Hope you can make the wedding. Much love, Fay."

The message inside a peony-flowered note card said, "Even though we both knew acting wasn't my gift, you showed me that nursing was. I will always be grateful. Love, Teresa."

A letter written on church letterhead read, "Thank you for

having faith in me when no one else did. If it weren't for the summers I spent with you and your friends as a Fresh Air Kid, I'd be in jail instead of leading worship for the glory of God. If you're ever in Harlem, Miss Tempie, please call. Fondly, Cedric Washington."

Tempie had never forgotten Cedric's invitation. His was the church they'd visited, and Cedric was the one who provided the music and background sounds for the kids' play.

Gracie picked up a pack of letters tied with a blue ribbon. She opened the one on top which was dated May 18, 1985. "As a fifteen-year-old boy, I dreaded spending summers on the Cape with my maiden aunt—until I got involved with the Barnstable Community Playhouse. I never would have worked so hard to reach my goals if it hadn't been for your patience and tutelage." The letter was signed Benny, as were the others in the pack. In every one she read, he'd sought Tempie's advice.

She wept as she thought of the many lives her grandmother had touched. She was ashamed when she recalled the times she'd asked Tempie if she ever felt bad about "not making it big."

Gracie finally understood Matthew 10:42, the verse Tempie would often quote: *And whoever gives one of these little ones only a cup of cold water in the name of a disciple, assuredly, I say to you, he shall by no means lose his reward.*

Her grandmother had spent her whole life giving to others without a thought for herself. That was her secret to success.

Or was it *the* secret to success?

Ian called around ten. "I didn't want to wake you. Did you get some rest?"

"Some. Thanks for driving me. Being here helped."

"I hope you don't mind, but I spoke with a few people. Harper sends her love, and Will and Elizabeth Anderson plan to see you at the service."

"That's fine, Ian. The less I have to say she's gone out loud, the better."

"Can I do anything else for you?"

"No, my father's picking me up in a few hours to go over the arrangements with family."

"Okay. Love you, darlin'. Text if you need me."

"Thanks. I will." Gracie held her silent phone. What would she have done without Ian?

She called Seymour next, knowing she'd be encouraged after they spoke.

"Oy, Grace, I am torn between sorrow for you and joy for your grandmother."

"Wanting her back feels selfish." She bit her lower lip to stave off the tears.

"God understands. Imagining her first encounter with Yeshua might help."

She choked back a sob. "I did imagine that, and you're right, it helped."

"Grief is most difficult early on. Over time, your joy will increase, not for you necessarily, but for your grandmother."

"I like knowing that."

"Shalom, Grace. Call me upon your return."

She went back to the treasures in Tempie's hat boxes. After an hour, she'd made a small dent—enough to confirm what she already knew. Tempie was well loved by many.

When her dad arrived, she hugged him tightly. He grabbed a paper towel and wiped his eyes. "Let's sit for awhile before we head back to the house."

"Sure." Watching a parent cry was something she hadn't thought much about before now. Her heart broke all over again.

"Wait until you hear the plan *your* grandmother has hatched for her funeral ... uh, I mean her Celebration of Life service." He shook his head and smiled. "My mother is a pip, she is."

Gracie was glad her father talked about Tempie like she was still alive. She wasn't ready for the past tense.

He pulled some papers out of his jacket pocket. "Tempie left us a script of sorts. You've got the biggest part, of course, the eulogy."

"What about the rest of the family?"

"Your two uncles and their sons can't handle the stress of public speaking. Besides you giving the eulogy and me doing a reading, her favorite BCP director and her pastor will share a few words." He flipped over a page. "Get this. In addition to specific hymns, she wants us to play the Sha Na Na version of 'Goodnight Sweetheart' from some old movie, while people walk down the aisle on their way out the doors."

Gracie laughed. "*Holiday in Mexico* was one of her favorites."

"See. I told your mother you'd know it." Her father put his hand on hers. "Can you handle giving the eulogy?"

"I'm honored she asked me."

"Well, she didn't exactly *ask*." Her father cracked up as he pointed to the papers. "She wrote you in."

Gracie's smile turned to tears again. "I loved her so much, Dad."

"I know, honey. She felt the same about you."

She leaned on him while they wept together.

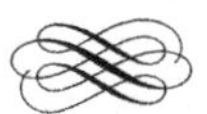

Between her dad and herself and the other speakers, there were more laughs and funny stories than sadness at the Celebration of Life service for Temperance Camden. Much of Gracie's eulogy spoke of Tempie's legacy of relationships revealed in the cards and letters she'd treasured over her lifetime.

Tempie's last wish was granted. When the sounds of "Goodnight Sweetheart" rang out, those who knew her best strolled down the aisle, smiling. Tempie would have loved it. Then again, she'd written the script.

Gracie spent the next ten days on the Cape going through Tempie's house and distributing her belongings to family, friends, and charities. Her parents offered to store the things she wanted for herself. The only items she planned to take back with her were Tempie's Bible, journal, hat boxes, and the tweed shawl Ian had bought Tempie in Ireland.

Becoming a child again under her parents' roof felt weird. To them, it seemed normal. She would always be "their little girl." Gracie had matured enough to understand that sentiment. But she still needed to go home.

And home was Manhattan.

Chapter Fifty

Gracie took a cab home from JFK Airport. Ian would've come if she'd asked him. But with the Lincoln Center gala only a week away and the security systems having to be in place and tested, she didn't want to bother him.

Her arrival was as she'd planned—Rachel and Reggie were at work and Miles and Leighton in school. Unlocking the door, she climbed the stairs, her suitcase thumping behind her. She needed time to settle in before she dealt with more sympathy and sad faces. Mostly, she didn't want to fall apart in front of the kids.

By the time she heard the family come in, Gracie had unpacked, showered, and dressed in comfy clothes. She cracked the door, wondering if they knew she was home. She'd missed them more than she'd expected.

Miles's voice carried through the foyer. "Mom, can we go see Gracie now?"

Before Rachel could answer, Gracie called down, "Send those two silly bears up here. I need someone to tickle!"

They giggled all the way up, then ran into her arms.

Leighton pointed to Gracie. "What took you so wong to come home?"

Miles nudged her with his arm. "Mommy told you, 'member? Gracie's bubbe went to heaven."

Leighton bounced her fingers together. "But when's she coming back?"

Miles blew out his cheeks.

Gracie intervened. "Leighton, when someone goes to heaven they can't come back, and they don't want to. Tempie is happy to wait for family and friends to join her one day."

Leighton's face filled with worry. "Are you going there too?"

"Someday. But right now I'm very glad to stay here with you." She tickled them until they cried "uncle!"

Rachel joined them upstairs. After a big hug, she insisted Gracie join them for dinner.

She consented. Dinner might be a good way to slip back into normal, as normal as grief would allow.

Miles hung back when Leighton went down to help her mother. He joined her on the love seat. "I'm sad Tempie died. She was really fun. I liked her a lot."

"She liked you too." One of Gracie's most satisfying memories was that her grandmother got to meet the Adlers and see New York. "Tempie is the one who made me and others fall in love with acting."

"Was she famous?"

Gracie thought about the accolades at her funeral. "Not like some people. She was famous for helping people feel better about themselves."

"Like we did when we put on *The Battle of Mount Sinai*?"

As usual, this boy was wise beyond his years. "Exactly."

Miles stood and faced her, leaving one knee propped on the couch. "That brings me to my point."

Gracie hid her smile. "And what point might that be?"

"When we made people feel better, we felt better too. Why did we stop?"

"What do you mean?" Gracie sat forward. "Our goal was to write and perform a play for Eli, and we did what we set out to do and more. We made a whole bunch of kids feel better."

"Then why did we stop? There are other sick kids in other hospitals all around New York. Daddy said so."

"I know, but we can't do everything. You and Leighton have school. And helping your Mom and Dad and going to auditions takes most of my time."

"Uh, well, I was thinking, now, um, that you don't have to be in that dumb *Love and Waffles*, it would give us something important to do. We could write more plays and go around to different hospitals. Anyway, kids like seeing the same play over again."

Unbelievable. Where did this boy get his chutzpah?

Gracie was glad when Leighton yelled up the stairs. "Milesy, Mommy says to come wash your hands for dinner."

She walked him to the door. "You're a thoughtful young man with an interesting proposition. Let's take some time to think it over, okay?"

"Okay." Miles stepped into the hallway but popped his head back in. "Don't take too long to decide—" He grinned.—"'cuz I can always ask Harper."

"You little stinker!" Gracie chased him until they reached the top of the stairs. "Miles, stop."

"Why?"

"Because I need another hug."

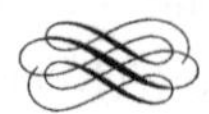

Dinner was full of chatter and energy. Once or twice, a quiet, grief-conscious moment appeared, but the Adler family seamlessly filled in the silence. The company, the meal, and being home were all good.

Seated next to Miles, Gracie whispered, "Have you mentioned your idea to your parents?"

"Yup. At breakfast yesterday," he said, "but they weren't listening."

"What idea is that, son?" Reggie reached for the basket of rolls.

Miles put his fork down. "Writing and performing plays for sick children." He leaned toward Gracie and mumbled, "Told you they weren't listening."

"Miles, that play for Eli was a great idea. Your father and I were very proud of you."

"Mom's right," Reggie said. "Now will someone please pass me the butter."

Gracie handed it to him.

"Thanks," Reggie said. "By the way, I've been meaning to tell you, your friend, Ian—what a find! He's done an excellent job, getting everything in place on time. Only a few minor details left. Of course, we'll need him to stick around for awhile after the big event to train our guys."

Gracie put her fork down. "I never thought to ask you two, are you attending Polina's gala?"

"No, Reggie will be working throughout the night, so I passed." Rachel flirted with her husband. "And going to the Met is no fun without a handsome escort."

Miles pushed his chair back. "May I be excused?" After his parents gave him permission, he whispered to Gracie, "We can talk later."

She smiled. He wouldn't give in without a chance to present his case in full. She couldn't wait to hear his closing arguments.

Later, alone in her room, Gracie pulled out the last of her grandmother's hat boxes and began where she'd left off. They held over sixty years of praises and appreciation from people all over the country for a woman she knew as *her* Tempie.

If I were to live to eighty-two, what would my legacy be?

Chapter Fifty-One

Seymour was surprised to hear Polina's voice.

"I was searching my caller ID for my manicurist's number. I noticed you called my landline last week but didn't leave a message."

"I spoke with Simka. She told me you were busy with your agent and publicist. I did not want to interrupt."

"Oh? She must have forgotten to tell me. All this gala hoopla is distracting."

"How is your rash?" Oy! Seymour regretted the question—one you should never ask a lady—the minute the words were out of his mouth.

"All gone, thank you, and ready to flash all those jewels. Unless I faint from the weight of them."

"I am certain you will triumph over this minor adversity. Besides, that wig you wore in *Phantom of the Opera* must have weighed even more."

Polina's laugh gave him goose bumps.

"You're right." She paused. "I don't know why this bothers me so much. I've worn other items to advertise a designer or to please a benefactor in the past."

"The necklace is not the draw for the guests. *You* are the draw. If all they wanted was to see the fancy jewelry, they could visit your Mr. Winston." Seymour couldn't believe his boldness—yet he was glad for it.

"Thank you. Your opinion means a lot to me."

"The truth is not my opinion."

Polina was silent long enough for Seymour to wonder if their call had been disconnected.

She cleared her throat. "May I confess? The embarrassment I feel over all this praise and honor may have something to do with Simka."

"Simka?"

"Yes, her life in Moldova was rich in a simpler, yet profound way. My cousin was married for over thirty years to a hardworking man who loved her. They had a son who made them proud." Polina sighed. "Compared to her lifetime achievements, sometimes mine seem shallow."

"One thing I know, God created us all unique for a reason—his reason. He is the potter, we are the clay. He loves us as we are."

"Yes, but does he want us to stay that way?"

Was there a specific reason behind Polina's question? He wasn't sure how to answer, so he said what he would say to anyone else. "Regeneration is the Lord's work. He is continuously changing us from the inside out."

"You're right, my friend. Enough of my doubts. Now tell me, are you and Grace still planning to meet us backstage to attend the gala after-party?"

"We are. Our response has been sealed and delivered. It is too late to rescind your invitation even if you want to."

Long after they hung up, he could still hear her laughter.

More than once, since he had first met Polina six months ago in Postville, he had imagined what life would be like with someone like her. No. Not someone *like* her, with Polina herself. After he moved to New York and saw her life up close, it had given him pause.

Was he attracted to Polina like people were attracted to sparkling jewels? He wondered if a simpler relationship with someone as kind, practical, and amusing as Simka might be better. Did he connect with Simka because he could relate to a less polished stone? Do opposites attract? Does like attract like? Which, if either, was true?

What pride and nonsense. Who did he think he was, deliberating between two women, both of whom had only shown him friendship? Did he think he was buying livestock? Would he be checking their teeth next?

Seymour bowed his head and repented of his pride. "Lord, my future is yours to determine. Keep me open and humble. I will follow you even if I must travel this earthly road alone."

Seymour called Grace early Saturday morning. "The weather service predicted a mild and sunny afternoon today. Are you and the children in the mood for an adventure?"

"The park?"

"Actually," Seymour said, "I was thinking of The Big Apple Circus at the Guggenheim Bandshell at Lincoln Center."

"I've tried to take the kids to see that show before. There was always a schedule conflict. Let me talk to Rachel."

"The show starts around noon and sounds like an hour and a half of fun."

"I could use some fun about now—and a bit of your wisdom."

Seymour chuckled. "Ironic. Wisdom is what I was hoping to receive from you."

Gracie was pleased with Seymour's suggestion. The Big Apple Circus Grand Tour had everything kids and kids-at-heart could hope for—animal tricks, clowns, jugglers, acrobats, and aerialists—each made even more dramatic by their live band's accompaniment.

Miles and Seymour were in awe the whole time, cheering and clapping through act after act. Miss Leighton was another matter. Most of the time, she huddled with Gracie, hands covering her eyes. Even so, when the show was over, Leighton denied missing a second.

At Gracie's direction, they took the diagonal route across the Center toward the same restaurant where she and Seymour had dined with Tempie—mainly because it had a kids' menu.

When they reached the Revson Fountain, Miles called out, "Hey, there's Harper!"

If Harper was working undercover, her cover was blown now.

Harper waved. "Well, if it isn't my fellow cast members. What're you guys doing here?"

Miles and Leighton tripped over each other telling her all about the circus.

Gracie finally got a word in. "Are you, uh, on duty?"

"My shift ends in ..." Harper looked at her watch. "... thirty seconds. How're you doing?"

"Better, thanks." Gracie gave her a quick headshake, hoping to stem the flow of sympathy. Today had been so uplifting she didn't want to spoil it. "Want to join us for lunch?"

"I've got to okay it with Ian first." Harper craned her neck. "Who is heading this way as we speak."

Ian did high fives with the kids, shook Seymour's hand, and gave Gracie a big hug. "You feeling better, darlin'?"

"We had a great time at the circus, and we're on our way to lunch." Before he let her go, she warned him in a whisper, "Don't give me that sad face. I don't want to cry in front of the kids."

"Gotcha. I'll take my hug back then."

He could always make her smile. "Are you still on the clock?"

"I am, but I'll call you later."

Once they placed their meal order, Miles stood. "Since most of the cast is here, I'd like to talk about my idea."

Seymour leaned in. "What idea is that, young man?"

Harper chuckled. "Taking the show on the road, are you?"

"Sorta." Miles went on to explain his plan to Harper and Seymour as seriously as he had to Gracie.

Gracie sat back and let him have at it. *He'll make a successful producer—or lawyer—one day.*

When he was done, Harper said to Gracie, "Did you put him up to this?"

"Nope. This was all him. Isn't that right, Miles?"

"Right." Miles sat down. "I'm not even sure Gracie's on board yet."

On board? What shows has this kid been watching?

Miles opened his hands to plead his case. "These kids need us. We don't even have to be real good to make them happy. Think about it, okay?"

"Let me take a look at my calendar," Harper said.

Seymour rubbed his beard. "Miles, I can see you've given this idea a lot of thought. I most certainly will consider it in prayer."

Gracie didn't think either of them was anxious to stomp on a seven-year-old's dream to help sick children.

Miles sat back down. "I don't need an answer today. But let's keep the dialog going."

The dialog going? Who was this old man in this young boy's body?

Even after Gracie and the children were home, Miles bounced more ideas off her. "Whaddya think about Eli and Alyssa having parts in the next play?"

His enthusiasm was contagious. Gracie got sucked in, adding to his plans. "Well, their parents and doctors would have to approve. But it would give them a chance to give back and have fun at the same time."

Miles crossed his arms over his chest and nodded like a corporate decision-maker. "I think you're the best person to ask the doctors for permission. You did it last time."

"Actually, I think Eli's parents asked."

"I remember now. But you would be even better."

She laughed. "Quit your schmoozing. I'm still not sure I have the time."

He shifted to another angle. "What about Mr. Kaufman and Harper?"

"If and when this happens, they'll have to decide for themselves."

He smiled. "I think they'll say yes if you do."

Leighton raised her hand, "Milesy, can I still be a princess?"

He covered his face with his hands and mumbled through them. "Okay, okay, Leighton, you can still be a princess."

Chapter Fifty-Two

The Chief walked the half block to Specialty Dry Cleaners. He looked around for the crazy old woman and her cop friend from last time. *Nope*. When he entered, the clerk slid him the key without a word.

Once inside the small, cluttered room, adjusting to the low-level light took a few seconds. The bright spot over the jeweler's head almost resembled a halo.

Oren greeted him with a grunt, then continued what he was doing.

The Chief smiled at the empty express packaging piled on a long bench in the corner, evidence of their successful relationship. "If I didn't know better, Oren, I'd think you were sentimental."

Oren raised his head. "What?"

He gestured to the bench with his thumb. "How many years have I been sending you work?"

The jeweler rubbed his white whiskers. "Almost nine." Then he snarled, "Six months after the new manager at Harry Winston's told me my services were no longer required after forty-seven years."

The Chief smiled. "Like I always say, their loss was our gain." He walked over to Oren's desk. "Let's see what you have for me."

Proud as any reputable artisan, Oren laid the elaborate necklace on the black velvet pad and handed the him a loupe.

Under the high-powered lens, the Chief could see how Oren had added slight flaws to the Moissanite stones to replicate real diamonds. And the facets were sharp not rolled like imitations. He teased his jeweler. "Are you sure you didn't just lift the original?"

Oren's eyes cut to the Chief. "I create, I do not steal."

"Let's not forget, I steal so you can create." The Chief admired his workmanship again. "No one will suspect a thing for days."

Oren removed a trench coat hanging on a clothes rack. He carefully inserted the necklace into a hidden pocket sewn into the woolen lining. After covering the coat with a plastic garment bag, he handed it to the Chief. "Now I take a vacation."

"A well-deserved one at that. I'll wire the final payment to your off-shore account per usual. May take some time."

Oren said, "You have my trust."

They shook hands to seal the deal.

Carrying the bag over his arm, the Chief walked past the clothes conveyor, rounded the corner, and bumped right into the cop.

"Whaddya know? You're the reason I'm here." The cop rested his hands on his thick black belt.

"Don't you love a coincidence?" The Chief tossed the garment bag over his shoulder.

"Yep, I thought of you when I had to use the head." He laughed at his own joke. "I figured I'd try your pit stop for a change of scenery."

The Chief obliged him with a chuckle before he tossed the key to the clerk. "Wrong key. And with my condition, good thing the door was unlocked. Still is."

"Sir, my apologies," the clerk said. Then to the cop, "The restroom's down on the right, officer."

As they passed each other, the Chief saluted the cop one last time. "Good seeing you again, officer."

Chapter Fifty-Three

Harper inspected her fresh manicure. "I hear Noble's running a full-dress rehearsal this afternoon. Want to sneak in? You might feel better watching your understudy's amateur performance."

Gracie consented, but only after she convinced herself it was more out of professional curiosity than pettiness.

They reached the Little Schubert and found the side door unlocked. She and Harper peeked in. Their timing was perfect—right in the middle of the pre-dress rehearsal rushing and ranting. When they didn't see Bennett Noble or his AD, they scurried to the back and sat in the dark.

Harper whispered, "Be truthful. When you chose this field, did you think it'd be this difficult?"

"Probably not." A deep line formed across Gracie's brow. "Maybe because I grew up believing this field had chosen *me*. Acting is all I ever knew, all I ever wanted to do."

Harper mumbled. "Sometimes I think the only reason I want to succeed is to get my father's approval. How dumb is that?"

Gracie took her friend's hand. "Wanting parental approval is normal, not dumb."

When the noise settled down, so did Gracie and Harper. After a few commands from the directors and cues from stagehands, the curtain rose on act 1, scene 1. Phoebe Ogden, Gracie's understudy, was front and center as Kat Hamilton, playing off the male lead as Noah Parmenter.

Gracie, in hyper-critical mode, waited to pounce. What would come first? Missed lines? Insincere dialogue? Overacting? Weak projection? Awkward physicality? Lack of chemistry?

She waited. Through every scene. Until she forgot what she was hoping to find. Phoebe's portrayal of Kat—although unlike the way Gracie would have played her—was spot on.

She and Harper were silent as they snuck out into the cold.

Harper spoke first. "She wasn't *that* good, was she?"

"Better." Shame and humility fell over Gracie. Silently, she prayed for God to forgive her. If he really did have a perfect plan for her, she hoped she hadn't ruined her chances.

"How 'bout we do something tomorrow," Harper suggested, "completely unrelated to the theater?"

"Can't. With only a few days before Polina's gala, I have a lot to do."

"You? What? Other than get dressed and go?"

"I'm pretty sure I'll be hand-holding Seymour. He's a wreck."

Harper chuckled. "You certainly have some unlikely friendships."

Gracie raised one eyebrow. "Like ours, you mean?"

"Come to think of it, you are kind of odd." Harper chuckled at her own wisecrack. "Speaking of odd, have you heard from Chase since you returned from the Cape?"

Gracie deadpanned, "No. He's probably still fretting over his sick turtle."

"What about his mother? Can't she babysit the turtle when he goes out?"

"To quote Chase, 'Caring for my turtles is all too much for Mother to handle.'" Gracie gave way to a giggle.

Harper shuddered. "I'm sorry I ever felt bad for that guy. What he needs is a backbone."

The next day, Gracie ran into Marisol while waiting for the kids to be dismissed from school.

Marisol's face brightened when she saw Gracie. "Hi! Miles told Zeke and Eli about the theater group you're putting together. What a wonderful idea."

"Correction. The idea belongs to Miles."

"Really? But you're going to do it, right?"

Gracie rubbed her forehead. "Miles is way out ahead of me on this one. I don't know how I'd find the time."

Marisol frowned. "The boys will be so disappointed, especially Eli. Now that he's better, he wanted to be part of the cast. Well, I guess you can only do what you can do."

Why did Gracie feel like a villain? She tried to reinforce her reasoning. "There're just so many days in a week. For instance, the gala for Polina Zelenka is this Sunday, and I'm escorting my friend, Seymour."

"Rubbing elbows with the rich and famous again, huh?"

Instead of the sick. Is that what Marisol was thinking?

"The only reason I'm going is that Polina personally invited Seymour and me. I couldn't refuse."

"Oh, I see."

Why didn't Marisol believe her?

Gracie heard from Seymour Thursday evening.

"When do we pick up the tuxedo? Will it need to be ironed?"

"We will—"

"What about a hat? Oy! My overcoat is still at the dry cleaners. What if it is not ready?"

Gracie spoke softly. "Take a breath. We'll get everything done tomorrow after your appointment at the men's salon."

"A salon sounds kind of fancy to me. And expensive."

Her shoulders sagged. "Again, Seymour, what have we said about you standing out on Polina's night?"

"That I don't want to?"

"Yes, a good haircut and a more structured shape to your beard will help you blend in with the opera crowd."

"Oy, Grace, does not all this fussing seem prideful to you?"

"No, it seems like you think enough about Polina to look your best. I'm a woman. Take my word for it."

When they left the salon, Gracie knew Seymour was pleased by the way he walked. There was no schlepping.

"Thank you for insisting, Grace. I feel more presentable."

His overcoat was ready. She even talked him into buying a new black fedora. Next stop the tuxedo shop.

As they entered, Norris greeted them in a tizzy. "I am so sorry. We will fix it. I don't know how it happened. We're doing our best to find it."

Seymour spoke slowly, "Find what?"

His hands clasped tight below his chin, Norris spoke at a frantic pace. "Your order. Our new clerk either misplaced it or gave it to someone else."

Seymour wrung his hands. "You do know the gala is tomorrow?"

"Yes, Mr. Kaufman, and I've been so careful. I never should have hired him, my sister's youngest. He's never been responsible. But I'm on top of it."

Seymour glared, "How are you on top of it, sir?"

This was the first time Gracie had ever seen Seymour upset.

"I'm checking with all our customers." Norris pivoted in a circle making one call after another.

"I apologize, sir, but could you please check the ticket."

"You say he's out for the evening and wearing the tux?"

"I'm so pleased you're so pleased, sir."

"You ordered the powder blue one. That's right. Sorry to be a bother."

After he pocketed his phone, Norris said, "I promise, Mr. Kaufman, we'll do our best to locate your order. When we do, I will personally deliver it to your home."

Gracie didn't want to exacerbate the situation. "Seymour, the worst thing that can happen is you can wear one of your black suits."

"The *worst* thing?" Seymour drew in a long breath.

"What I mean," Gracie said, "is that you can wear your *best* black suit. At least you'll have your new shirt and tie, shoes, and—"

Norris hung his head. "I apologize. Everything—tuxedo, shirt and bowtie, shoes, and eye patch—were packaged together."

Gracie sucked in her breath. "I promise it will work out. Now let's see if we can do something about your nerves."

Seymour was quiet for a few moments, then said. "You are right. I let God's peace get away from me. Time alone with him this evening is what I need."

Seymour might calm down, but Gracie was fuming.

Chapter Fifty-Four

Later that afternoon, Seymour got a call from Simka. "Please, I need help. My younger sister, she is ill. Can you tell me what should I do?"

She was crying, that's all he knew. "Where is Polina?"

"Rehearsal." Simka sniffled into the phone. "Please do not call her."

Rather than question Simka and upset her further, he promised to get to Polina's apartment as soon as he could. "We will figure this out together."

What they would figure out he had no idea.

Simka opened the door and collapsed in tears into Seymour's arms. Once she calmed down a bit, he walked her over to the sofa. "Now tell me what is wrong."

"My sister in Moldova—doctors say she could die. I must go to her."

"Of course, you must. Do you need me to make flight reservations?"

"Nu." She wiped her tears and blew her nose. "Vânât bought me ticket, but flight is tomorrow night." Her voice quivered. "If I go, I cannot help Polina after performance when she needs me most."

"Breathe in, breathe out." He held her hand. "That is what you are worried about? Surely, Polina will understand."

"If I leave without proper notice, I fear she not take me back."

"I cannot imagine any circumstances under which your cousin would not want you back—especially these. Why would you even think that?"

Simka lowered her head and took her time speaking. "Maybe being Polina's friend is not same as being personal assistant. Some tell me assistant before me was let go because she wanted to go to daughter's wedding."

Seymour didn't believe it. "Would you like me to speak to Polina for you?"

"Would you? If you explain, she might forgive me."

"If working for Polina is not ideal, and your sister needs you back home, perhaps you can find work there."

"Moldova is bankrupt. I have nothing there but poor family. If I have no job here, I cannot send money home to them. Vânât can help, but I am not kind of mother who wants to burden my child."

When Simka calmed down, he rose to leave. She caught him off guard when she kissed him on both cheeks. "You are hero."

Seymour's face flushed. He left quickly, not wanting to show further embarrassment. On the way home, he admitted it felt good to help a woman, even if it was somewhat uncomfortable. As a grown man, he could count on one hand—the hand missing the two fingers—the times he had been blessed with that honor.

Hero or not, an hour after he was home, Seymour was still troubled by their conversation. The idea that Polina could be unsympathetic had never entered his mind. Could it be that Simka had heard gossip or misconstrued her cousin's words or actions? If not, how could he have missed that character defect in Polina? And why had the Lord not revealed it to him?

Or were Simka's concerns meant to be that revelation?

He prayed before he called Polina. Her outgoing greeting sounded like the woman he knew—cheery, kind, confident. He left her a brief message to call him back.

She returned his call soon after. "Seymour Kaufman, you'd better not be backing out on tomorrow."

He sensed humor in her tone—did he not? "No, I would not do that. I am relaying a message for Simka. She was too upset to tell you herself." Was that a lie? No, it was not.

He told Polina the whole story about Simka's sister—except the part about Simka being afraid she would be dismissed.

"Poor Simka. I had no idea her sister's illness was serious. When's her flight?"

"Her son booked a late flight from LaGuardia tomorrow night. The trip will be long, the best he could do on short notice. A stop in Boston, then London, with a bus ride between airports, before her flight to Chisinau. He is with his aunt now, but he plans to meet his mother's flight." Seymour cleared his throat. "Simka's other concern is not being around to assist you after the gala since she has to be at the airport two hours before her flight."

"Nonsense. Getting to her sister is more important. I only wish they had better medical facilities in Moldova. People in this country have no idea how blessed they are."

She sounded like her caring self to him. "Simka will bring her luggage with her. Vânât scheduled a cab to come for her as soon as the curtain comes down. Does that work for you, Polina?"

"Yes, but it might be better if she used the time to pack and rest. I can get ready on my own—or perhaps my stylist could attend me."

Seymour surmised Simka might take either of those suggestions as a sign—and not a good one. "She was upset enough to think she was leaving you in the lurch. This way she is kept busy and not left on her own to fret."

"Maybe you're right. I'm glad she had your calming influence."

Calming? Seymour reddened at the thought of his behavior at the tuxedo shop.

"Okay, then, here's the plan," Polina said. "Uri will drop Simka and me off at the Met a few hours early. He'll come by around six for you and Grace. That will give you an hour to get situated before the show begins."

"We will be ready."

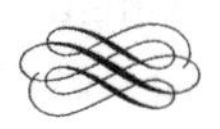

With Simka's anxiety neutralized, he turned to his own dilemma—preparing his second-choice clothes for the gala. He washed and bleached his newest white shirt, trying unsuccessfully to remove the ink stain from the front pocket.

Perhaps I will not have to remove my jacket?

As he polished and buffed his worn black shoes, the creases

filled, and a dull sheen appeared. He ran a damp cloth over his sateen eye patch.

His best black suit was the problem. Mainly because the last place he had performed a bris had been home to four white Persian cats. He tried the same damp cloth method as he had on his patch, but it only matted the hairs into the suit's fibers. After a run to the drugstore, he returned with a lint roller, as sold on TV. The gadget was not the miracle it claimed to be, but it would have to do.

Seymour was not happy.

He went to his room to sit in his communion chair—his name for the rocker-recliner where he conversed with God. His investment portfolio on the nightstand caught his eye. He reached for it.

Years ago, while attending a free dinner and talk given by a financial advisor, Seymour learned the importance of "diversifying investments." *How* Seymour diversified was not quite what the advisor had suggested. Instead of stocks and bonds, Seymour had invested in orphanages, specifically those in Moldova. By diversifying his giving, if something were to happen to him, the orphanages would only have to replace a small share of their income. He wanted those who ran the orphanages to depend on God, not him.

He opened his portfolio to pray for each investment. Despite their lack and their lifestyle, the faces of the children and their guardians always smiled up at him. Once again, the Lord used their joy and gratefulness to convict him.

"Lord, I ask your forgiveness, especially for my attitude with the clerk at the tuxedo shop. The gala is not about me and my fancy tuxedo, but about honoring Polina for using the gifts you bestowed upon her. Please, Lord, show me what you want me to see, teach me what you want me to learn, and help me to do your will. Amen."

As was his end-of-day practice, he read a chapter from the Bible. In Matthew 6, he came to verse 28: *So why do you worry about clothing? Consider the lilies of the field, how they grow: they neither toil nor spin.*

He chuckled. "Perfect timing coupled with a keen sense of humor—could it be, Lord?"

That night, sweet sleep fell upon him.

Seymour was awakened abruptly at seven-thirty by a pounding on the front door. He jumped out of bed, rubbed his eye, and called out, "One moment, please." He put on his robe and prayed it was not a woman.

Mr. Big Shot, how many women have ever knocked on your door that you should worry? None. That is right.

Norris stood on the front step, relief plastered all over his face, holding a garment bag and boxes. "Your tuxedo, Mr. Kaufman, along with your shirt, tie, shoes, and patch."

"You found them! Norris, please accept my apologies for my behavior." Seymour took the items from him. "I hope you were not too hard on your nephew."

"I owe you a confession." Norris chortled in an adenoidal tone. "I didn't trust my nephew, so I stored your items myself for fear he would misplace them. In my haste to blame him, I forgot what I'd done. While tossing and turning in my bed, I remembered. I've learned a hard lesson about trust, Mr. Kaufman."

"We all have, Norris."

He laid out his clothes for the gala. Humbled by the grace of God, he prayed, "You care about all things, Lord, big and little. Thank you for letting the light shine on Polina, not on my shabby clothes."

Chapter Fifty-Five

Gracie removed her silk shantung sheath from the Sax Fifth Avenue garment bag. She'd purchased it during an off-season clearance sale. Her reason—some might say *excuse*—was simple. No gown was ever truly out of season, was it? The only time she'd worn the dress was to model for Rachel and Leighton.

She ironed a few wrinkles out of the skirt, then did her hair and makeup, taking extra time to add smoke and drama to her eyes. She was attending the opera, after all. The midnight blue dress contrasted well with her light complexion. The antique gold filigree earrings and brooch she'd inherited from Tempie brought out the gold flecks in her irises.

Before going downstairs, Gracie examined herself from all angles in her three-paneled mirror. She was pleased.

I wonder if I'll see Ian or Dan tonight.

Her conscience teased her. *Don't you mean you wonder if they will see you?*

No difference.

If you say so. Her conscience again.

Gracie admitted nothing—except that it would be nice to get the attention of a man—especially when you'd gone to all this trouble. And, as much as she cared for him, Seymour didn't count. Even in his tuxedo.

When six o'clock arrived, she was waiting in the foyer with her long, black wool coat over her arm. She'd bought the wrap on sale to go with the dress—the one she didn't know she would ever wear. A woman had to be ready after all.

Uri was on time, and Seymour came to the door with his hat in his hand. "How pretty you are, Grace."

"Thank you." Though she'd seen Seymour in each separate stage of his transformation, now that he was all put together, the word *debonair* came to mind. But she didn't dare tell him. She knew him well enough to know he'd feel self-conscious. Instead, she said, "And you, sir, will fit right in at the opera."

"Thanks to you and the Lord—and the perseverance of Norris."

They arrived at the Met forty minutes later. Gracie was glad for no rain on this chilly November evening. A light snow might have added to the ambiance, but New York snow got dirty fast. No, this crisp, dry air was perfect. She was certain the stars were out—even if she couldn't see them for the city's glow.

Outside, strings of tiny white lights filled Lincoln Center, many more than usual. All promotional banners in the windows (which patrons had complained obscured the view of the murals and chandeliers) had been removed for the occasion.

Though Gracie had never been to an opera, she'd been around the theater enough to feel that palpable charge. The travertine plaza was abuzz with onlookers, jostling for a better view. Celebrities exchanged pleasantries. Some gawked in awe like non-famous fans. Others hugged like family. A few seemed aloof to it all.

Gracie tried to stall their entrance, knowing once she and Seymour were seated, her view of the rich and famous would be obstructed. She had no choice when the wave of people carried them forward. As they intermingled with the utmost fashionable, Gracie recognized some of the designer gowns—Karan, Packham, Givenchy. She hadn't seen this much fur in one place since she'd visited the Bronx Zoo with Seymour and Simka. Perfume filled the air, none to be mistaken for Tempie's drugstore brand.

Gracie was well aware of her non-status in her chosen field, more so in this environment.

God, when will it be my turn? What good was her so-called talent if her stage was a milk crate in her nanny suite, used for the amusement of a couple children? A verse Tempie had often recited and made Gracie memorize came to mind—I Peter 4:10: *As each one has received a special gift, employ it in serving one another as good stewards of the manifold grace of God.*

But that's what I'm trying to do, Lord. What am I doing wrong?

Gracie caught herself in the mid-whine. *Give it a rest, Camden. Tonight is not about you.*

At the portico, Ian and Dan Favor were deep in conversation. Gracie doubted they'd notice her. She was wrong. Ian grinned and winked. Favor gave her a thumbs-up. A minute later, the two men went in opposite directions. Ian's job for Reggie climaxed with this event. She wouldn't do anything to distract him.

Inside, the Met shimmered like the jewels Polina would be wearing. The general opera-inspired art display had been exchanged for productions in which Polina had starred.

Right in the middle of it all, Gracie took Seymour's arm and smiled. "Thank you."

His brow creased. "Why are you thanking *me*?"

"I wouldn't be here if it weren't for your crush on Polina."

Seymour cleared his throat. "I am not sure I would use that exact word. But from what I know at present, Polina is a lovely person."

Gracie winked. "Yes, she is." Then she swept her arm around the full, rich scene before them. "So, what do you think of all this?"

He took in the crowd. "I think I am way out of my league."

"Mr. Kaufman, art belongs to the people, even the opera. Erase the thought of leagues from your mind right now."

He saluted crisply. "Yes, ma'am, Ms. Camden."

Chapter Fifty-Six

On the morning of the gala, the Chief had conducted his last recon mission of Lincoln Center, posing as a deputy chief inspector from the FDNY Bureau of Fire Prevention. With his final check completed, he returned to his hotel to take a long hot bath and a nap.

Four hours later, he joined the crowd congregating near the Met. He adjusted his bowtie and ran his hand through his slicked-back hair. Although his nature was drawn to a less conservative designer, he'd chosen the Armani from his collection because it suited the opera best. This was business not personal.

Or perhaps a little of both.

Some of his possible conspirators were in the crowd. He snickered. The mohel looked good, too good. He doubted Gracie and her comrades would pose much of a threat. All the better if they caused a distraction.

The Chief meandered through the affluent opera fans, conversing effortlessly yet not lingering long enough to leave a lasting impression. He likened it to social media friends—not that he had any. His most used line: "I see my companions have arrived. Please excuse me. Perhaps we'll see each other inside."

Despite these pompous fools tempting him with their expensive baubles, he would keep his hands in his own pockets tonight. With cameras in hundreds of locations and undercover security personnel probably crawling over the place, he must show restraint. The payoff would be worth it.

Something niggled at him. What was it? He thought back on his walkabout that morning. He'd seen Air Tech vehicles on every street abutting the Center. He scanned the area around the Met. Uniformed Air Tech workers were everywhere.

Ha! How had he missed it? The Air Tech people *were* the undercover personnel.

He sent one last text before the show began.

Chapter Fifty-Seven

Gracie and Seymour entered the auditorium. An usher escorted them to the red velvet, front row seats in the Grand Tier.

Before Gracie could take her seat, Seymour protested. "The front row? Excuse me, sir, there must be some mistake."

The usher handed them each a program then smiled. "Apparently, Ms. Zelenka thinks otherwise."

Gracie counted the crystal chandeliers at the level of the Grand Tier. Twelve. They made a gentle tinkling noise as they rose toward the famous twenty-three-carat gilded ceiling.

She peeked up and down their row and a few behind them. "I recognize some of the artists from their photos on the marquee posters," she whispered, "but I don't recall any of their names."

Seymour glanced around. "Most people here look as comfortable as I feel at the bowling alley."

Grace's tone was flat. "Then pretend you're at the bowling alley."

He chuckled at her remark. As the orchestra warmed up, he read the program. "Polina will perform arias from three operas.

Mozart's *Le nozze di Figaro*, Dvořák's *Rusalka*, and Massenet's *Manon*. He flipped the program over. "How will we know what the lyrics mean?"

"They say," Grace whispered, "the secret to understanding opera is to let your emotions act as the interpreter."

"You are right. When I heard Polina sing in *The Phantom of the Opera*, the understanding came from her tone and movement more than the words."

"Feel better now?"

The gala commenced with a welcome from the Met's general manager, serving as the master of ceremonies. "We've come together this evening to honor Polina Zelenka on her twenty-fifth anniversary with the Metropolitan Opera. Quite an achievement, wouldn't you say?"

The audience applauded like they'd been waiting for this day forever.

He continued, "Ms. Zelenka, or *Polina* as she prefers, is known as 'The People's Diva.'" He paused then smiled. "I have only one question. How is it, in all these United States of America, the 'People's Diva' comes to us from a small, eastern European country called Moldova?"

As the audience laughed politely, Gracie elbowed Seymour. "That's your homeland. You should be proud."

Did he just sit up straighter?

The MC went on. "Polina will thrill us tonight, performing arias from three of our best-loved operas. She'll literally shine like the star she is, wearing the amazing diamond and platinum creation on loan from Harry Winston. And, if that's not enough, we have even more surprises for you."

After a rustling of programs, both Gracie and Seymour's included, the MC joked, "Why are you searching your programs? What kind of surprises would they be if we told you ahead of time?"

Once the tittering from the audience subsided, the MC said, "Without further ado, please welcome our beloved music director and conductor George Levinson, who will share a few of his experiences working with Polina for these many years."

The conductor motored out in his customized cart to a hearty round of applause and cheers of "Maestro! Maestro!" His words were full of praise for Polina. He choked up more than once when he spoke of their special bond, one made even stronger when he'd struggled with health issues.

Conductor Levinson took a few seconds to compose himself before he introduced the guest of honor. "I am privileged to present my friend and fellow opera lover, Polina Zelenka."

Gracie was nervous for Polina. Her palms dampened when the curtain rose on the softly playing orchestra. Seconds later, Polina floated across the stage like a platinum goddess. The audience rose and applauded. The Versace gown fit perfectly, and the diamond necklace wowed with its brilliance.

Gracie whispered to Seymour, "They could have skipped the French chandeliers and just gone with the light reflected from those stones."

He didn't respond, his attention riveted to the stage. Gracie doubted he'd even heard her.

She enjoyed Seymour's reaction almost as much as Polina's voice. Gracie wasn't sure if he'd become a fan of the opera in general or of Polina, specifically. She suspected a little of one, a lot of the other. During one of Polina's longer notes, she was sure he had stopped breathing.

In between Polina's arias, opera notables who'd performed with her through the years paid special tribute to her in songs and speeches. Although not previously familiar with many of them, Gracie was now.

As the event neared its conclusion, the MC took Polina by her hand and led her to center stage. A page handed him a large glass sculpture. "On behalf of the Metropolitan Opera and its faithful patrons, it is my great honor and pleasure to present our own Polina Zelenka with the Lifetime Achievement Award on her twenty-fifth anniversary with the Met."

Polina accepted the award with a royal curtsey. The audience would not stop cheering. At one point, she wiped at her eyes with the edge of a finger, and her voice cracked a few times during her acceptance speech.

Once the guest of honor had left the stage and the curtain had dropped, Gracie whispered to Seymour, "I know Polina said this event was more about fundraising than her talent, but those accolades sounded pretty sincere."

Seymour beamed. "The admiration in the hall was so tangible, almost as if I could touch it."

The two of them descended the grand staircase amid the crowd. When they veered down the hall in the direction of the stars' dressing rooms, a security guard stopped them. Once they presented the backstage passes Polina had provided, he let them by.

The Chief smirked after the mohel and his lovely date brushed by him.

Right on cue.

Chapter Fifty-Eight

Within feet of Polina's dressing room, Seymour and Grace heard Simka scream, "Nu, nu! Cousin! What is wrong?"

Seymour didn't wait to knock, but rushed in, almost felling the two Harry Winston guards.

Holding Polina under her arms, Simka yelled, "*Ajuta-ma!* Help me!"

Seymour reached Polina just as her legs gave out and her eyes rolled back. He carried her over to the chaise lounge and laid her down.

Simka put a pillow under Polina's head and fanned her with a program. She shouted to the guards. "Too many people. She needs air. Go to hallway!"

The stern-faced guard spoke. "Sorry, ma'am, but we can't leave without the necklace." He opened a velvet case.

Simka spat. "You care only about necklace!" She felt Polina's forehead. "Grace, please, get cool, wet cloth. Seymour, in small ice box, maybe get water bottle."

Seymour found the water. Gracie returned from the bathroom with a damp hand towel.

Simka placed the cloth on Polina's forehead and patted her cheeks, trying to revive her.

At Seymour's suggestion, Gracie called 911.

While Stern-face texted someone, his bald counterpart said, "We're ready, ma'am. The necklace, please."

Seymour thought Simka would bite the man if he got any closer. Instead, she held her tongue and entreated Seymour, "Please lift cousin's head enough so I can undo clasp. I need both hands."

Once she had the necklace, Stern-face stepped forward and took it from her.

Simka snarled. "Now get out, you and your stupid *colier*!"

Together, the guards placed the necklace in the velvet-covered box, then locked the box in a stainless steel briefcase. After a series of quick knocks on the dressing room door, Stern-face opened the door and passed the case off to someone in the hall. Seymour didn't see who. Without so much as a backward glance, the two guards left.

Seymour sat on the edge of the chaise, adjusting the cold cloth on Polina's forehead. "I think she's coming around."

"Did I faint?" Polina asked in a weak voice. "I haven't done that in years."

"Cousin, take sip of water." Simka held the bottle to her lips.

Seymour stepped closer. "Rest until the EMTs arrive."

"EMTs? I only fainted." Polina tried to sit up. "Simka, you need to go. You have a plane to catch."

"I cannot go now." Simka gave her another sip. "You need me."

The EMTs arrived before Polina could respond to her cousin.

Seymour stepped aside to let them through. "My, you are fast."

"On the premises for the event." One of the EMTs walked over to the chaise.

Polina raised herself on one elbow. "Sir, tell my cousin that fainting is not serious."

The EMT shooed everyone back. "Ms. Zelenka, fainting can be serious. Let's check you out first." He took her vital signs, shined a light in her pupils, and asked her some questions. "But I don't think we have anything to worry about in this case."

"What if it happens again? I cannot go." Simka's phone rang. "Da?" Uncertainty covered her face as she hung up. "Car is outside to take me to airport."

"Simka, go!" Polina said. "Give your sister my love and tell her I'll be praying."

Seymour grabbed Simka's bags, took her by the elbow, and escorted her to the rear exit. "I will make sure everything is fine and ready for you when you return." He comforted her with a hug.

She held onto his arm. "Thank you. You understand me best."

Seymour pushed open the door and stepped aside. "Now hurry! Your sister needs you."

Chapter Fifty-Nine

An alarm sounded. Gracie kept Polina still. Seconds later, Ian, Reggie, and Favor converged on the dressing room.

Thinking they'd come to check on Polina's condition, Gracie interceded. "She's fine. The EMTs confirmed it was a simple fainting spell. Did you really need to sound an alarm?"

"Wasn't us. A smoke bomb went off in the foyer. Pretty sure the mini explosion was meant to be diversion. Just in case, the Met's on lockdown." Reggie addressed Polina. "Are you sure you're all right, Ms. Zelenka?"

"More embarrassed than anything. No need to fuss."

Favor stepped forward. "We're investigating a possible burglary, ma'am."

Both Favor and Reggie's eyes were drawn to Polina's neck.

Reggie spoke first. "The necklace, Ms. Zelenka. Can you tell us where it is?"

Polina's hand rushed to her throat. Fear overtook her expression. "No, oh, no—"

Gracie knelt in front of her. "Don't panic. When you fainted, the Harry Winston guards got antsy. They insisted Simka give them the necklace. They locked it up, handed it off, and left."

Reggie punched in a number on his cell. "Code word? ... Good." He hung up and spoke to Favor and Ian. "All's secure. The guards and their prize are in the Air Tech van on their way to Winston's."

Polina let out a sigh. "Oh, thank goodness."

Seymour chuckled, "Simka tried to shoo the guards out while we were tending to you, but they would have none of it."

"My cousin can be a feisty one." She stretched to read the clock on her dressing table. "Is that the correct time? I hope she was able to make her flight."

Favor half-tipped his cap. "If you'll excuse us, ma'am. Though the necklace was the most obvious target, there are plenty of other items worth stealing on the premises."

While Seymour hovered over Polina, Gracie called to Ian. "Have a second?"

"For you, darlin'? Always."

She whispered. "Seymour and I are accompanying Polina to the after-party. If you're going to be around for a few more hours, could you give me a ride home after the party?" She peeked in at Seymour and Polina. "I owe him a favor. Alone time with the diva."

Ian nodded. "Gotcha. Text me when ya ready."

Seymour walked arm in arm with Polina through the crowded party. Food displayed like artwork filled long tables covered with silver table linens. Servers dressed in short black jackets, crisp white shirts, and bowties meandered through the throngs, offering all manner of drinks and hors d'oeuvres.

Grace looked like a hostess, flitting around the room, talking to everyone she met. How could she be excited and at ease at once in these surroundings? As for himself, he longed for a few quiet, no-fuss moments with Polina. In the two hours they had been there, she'd introduced him to more people than he had met his entire time in New York.

As if she could read his thoughts, Polina said, "There will be no quiz later, so forget about trying to remember everyone's name."

He admitted nothing but smiled. *What an understanding woman.*

When Ian and Gracie approached them, Gracie was wearing her coat.

Seymour was hasty in his assumption. "The party is over?"

Grace buttoned up. "No, but I've got an early start tomorrow, so Ian offered to give me a lift home. You don't mind, do you?"

Seymour surmised a plan had been hatched. "And if I did?"

"Then I would say you'd be silly to forego extra time with the guest of honor."

Polina chuckled. "You two run along then. Uri is only a call away."

Grace waved. "Thank you, Polina, for my new appreciation for the opera."

"You're welcome. And I'll be sure to call you the next time I have to decide on a gown."

Grace nearly screeched to a halt. "Will you? That will be so—"

Ian took her by the hand. "Come along, Gracie."

Minutes after they left, Polina said to Seymour, "Perhaps I can talk you into escaping, oops, I mean, *escorting* me home?" She scanned the room with its noisy cliques of people. "I don't think they'll miss us."

Talk me into it? Seymour chuckled inside. "I would not have it any other way. May I be so bold as to suggest we stop for a quiet cup of tea on the way?"

"Sounds marvelous. First, I need to go by my dressing room."

"You have had quite an evening. Do you feel strong enough to walk that distance?"

"Why? Are you afraid I'll faint again, and you'll have to carry me, Mr. Kaufman?"

"Oh no, I am not afraid at all." Seymour could feel the heat rising from his neck.

She threw her head back and laughed. "Now I've made you blush. I should be ashamed of myself ..." She paused."... but I'm not."

When they entered her dressing room, Polina disappeared behind an oversized screen to change. Seymour wondered if he should wait in the hall. He stood, sat, then stood again.

Before he could decide, she called out, "Have you been to Alimente's yet? The deli is a combination Yiddish-Moldovan-Romanian."

"No, I would remember."

"I didn't see you eat much at the party. I'm starving myself. You'll love the food, I promise." She came out in a rose-colored knit dress and pale gray sweater with pink pearl buttons.

Is there anything in which she does not look lovely?

Chapter Sixty

The night had grown cold. Gracie rubbed her hands together and stamped her feet to ward off frostbite. Her fancy opened-toed heels did not help. She welcomed Ian's warm arm around her as they waited for a cab.

"'Matchmaker, matchmaker,'" he sang.

She nudged him. "Some men need a little help. Seymour's one."

"He cleaned up good tonight, or was that all you?"

"Yes and no. He's the same sweet man, just more polished. A woman could do worse."

"Aye, speaking of looks, you turned quite a few heads yourself."

"Think so?"

"Know so. Mine was one of them. Favor, another."

"Favor?"

"Yes, you know, the handsome chief of security with the chiseled jaw and piercing dark eyes all the women swoon over."

"Well, I don't swoon, so you've got nothing to worry about."

"Who said I was worried?"

She didn't have an answer. "Here comes a taxi."

Once they reached her place, Ian asked, "Too tired for company?"

"I'm more wired than tired. Between the gala, Polina's fainting spell, the burglary, and the party—did they figure out what happened?"

Ian paid the cabbie and got out. "No one's sure there was a burglary. On a tip, the FBI arrested three international thieves, but that was a few days ago."

Gracie unlocked the door and headed for the stairs. "Nothing stolen then?"

"Thankfully, the necklace is back in the safe at Winston's. The security team and staff are going over the place now to see if anything's amiss."

They entered her apartment. Ian took his usual spot on the love seat.

"Back in a minute." Gracie headed to her bedroom. "Comfort is calling my name."

"And you leave me in this monkey suit?"

"Suits you, Quinn." She changed into jeans and a sweatshirt, then went to the kitchen and turned the kettle on. "Want some hot chocolate?"

"Sounds good."

After fixing two cups, she squirted a dollop of whipped cream on each. She set the tray on the ottoman, then plopped down next to him.

He took a sip. "Hmm, good. Dark chocolate?"

"Yup." She handed him a napkin. "You look better without a moustache."

He wiped his mouth, then pointed to an open journal, facedown, on the side table. "Have you taken up keepin' a diary?"

"That's one of Tempie's journals. Reading them helps me remember how special she was."

"She was that."

Gracie studied his sober profile. "Sometimes I forget how close you and Tempie had become. She loved her lunches with you."

"She was a sharp woman. Whenever I asked her opinion, she'd give it." He chuckled. "Actually, she'd give it even if I didn't ask."

"Now that sounds more like her." Gracie went to a bookmarked page in the journal. "Listen to what she wrote here."

> Some think I'm old, but I'm not. Years don't matter. All any of us have is today. What we do or don't do with it is what determines our age. Of course, my body may counsel, 'Within reason, Tempie,' but my mind argues, 'Reason' is but a kissing cousin to excuse.'

Ian folded his arms behind his head and smiled. "She had a way, did she not?"

Gracie turned the page. "Here's another one."

> Sometimes, I wonder if Benny knows. I value the student-mentor relationship we've had over the years. No sense ruining perfectly good humility—even if the student did grow up to be the world-famous Bennett Noble.

Gracie's jaw dropped, and she sat up straight. "Benny is Bennett Noble? I started reading the letters he wrote to Tempie, but I was too dullwitted to realize it was him."

"Didn't Tempie know he was the director you were working

with?"

"Of course, she did. But can't you hear her? 'I didn't tell you for your own good, dear.'"

He laughed. "That's exactly what she would've said. Between her journals and letters, this could be the start of a new PBS series. Are you going to tell Noble?"

"Tell?" She thought about the blue ribbon tied around the pack of letters. "No. Even better, I'll mail them to him."

He gave her an approving glance, then leaned over the journal. "What else does Tempie have to say?"

Gracie flipped over a few pages. "Here's one I haven't read."

> Watching two people I love dance about the truth and not see it is excruciating! Are they blind? Or pretending to be blind? Are they missing it or avoiding it? Are they scared or pretending not to be? When will my Gra—

Gracie stopped.

Ian sat up. "Hey, keep going, it was getting good."

"Nah, that's enough for tonight."

"Give it here. Who was Tempie writing about?"

"Nobody."

He fought her for the book and won. Still, Gracie kept grabbing at it. He dodged across the room and held it far above her head, then read where she'd left off. "'When will my Gracie and her Ian realize they're in love and get on with it? Life is too short to be that dumb.'"

Ian laughed while Gracie sulked back to the love seat. Tears threatened her composure. "Satisfied now?"

"Not really." Ian sat down beside her. "Tempie was wrong."

Gracie, dying inside, wiped at a tear with her sweatshirt sleeve.

Ian put his arm around her. "One of us has seen it for a long time. He's been waiting for the other one to open her big brown eyes."

Gracie searched his face. "Is it true? I'm in love with my best friend?" She tilted her head. "And just how long has this been going on, Mr. Quinn?"

"Not long enough." With a gentle touch, he raised her chin. "Now, may I kiss you?"

He didn't wait for her answer.

Chapter Sixty-One

Seymour eyed the restaurant as Uri pulled up in front of an unassuming eatery in Midtown Manhattan. Maps and posters of Romania, Moldova, and Israel decorated the windows. The menu was displayed on the door. A crooked Open sign hung above it.

This was Alimente's? Seymour was surprised. "Do you come here often?"

"Never, and I've been wanting to for years. Tonight is worthy of an adventure."

As they entered, the smell of pastrami wafted by, followed by fresh-baked rye bread. Of the dozen tables in the space, only half were occupied. Every table had a different covering made of white cotton, densely embroidered with colorful flowers and fruit. Lively folk music played in the background.

In an instant, Seymour was fourteen years old again back in Dobrogea. He studied the walls covered with framed autographed photos of people dressed in Eastern European garb.

Polina caught his eye. "This place is like a Moldovan Sardi's. You like?"

"I do." Seymour placed his hat on the seat beside him. "I am not sure what 'sardees' are, but it reminds me of home."

She giggled. "I thought it might. The stage crew eats lunch here all the time. They brag about it so much, I wanted to try it."

"Have you never accompanied them?"

"I fear they feel awkward around me. I do not fit in."

Not fit in? How could she think that?

Why not? You think the same thing about yourself, Seymour.

They found a table near the open kitchen.

Polina rested her folded arms on the table "So Dobrogea is the village where you lived as a boy?"

"Yes, until I was a young teen." Seymour stroked his beard, still finding it difficult to believe they were alone together. "I know you were mentored in Chisinau, but where did your family live?"

"My whole family—aunt, uncles, cousins included—lived in a tiny commune in Cunicea, about two hundred miles north of the capital. Lincoln Center is probably bigger than the whole place. Most of the family had never been to Chisinau when I was invited to go."

"Simka described it as a 'poor village in poorer country.'"

"Poor in money, rich in pride. I had to get out when I had the chance."

Seymour was surprised to hear Polina put it like that. "To escape was your only way to have a successful career?"

"Yes and no. Mainly, it was the only chance I had to help the rest of my family. That's why so many emigrate to America. Some even leave their spouses and children behind, and their families consider them heroes for doing so."

"Did your family think of you that way?"

"I had no husband or children, only my parents and extended family. I was blessed with a voice that gave me an excellent income. Helping them financially was my duty and honor. Later, when Vânât was able, he took over supporting his mother where I left off."

"Simka never mentioned it."

"Why would she? Helping each other is what families do."

"Perhaps I was too young to realize that when I came to the States."

"Your Uncle Jacob knew. Helping family is exactly what he did for you here."

Seymour mulled over her comment. "You are right." He reminded himself to call his uncle soon.

They talked easily over their comfort food until midnight. The more Seymour learned about Polina, the more he learned about himself.

We are not that different after all, are we Lord?

Chapter Sixty-Two

Midmorning, the day after the gala, the Chief sauntered to the Swiss International Air Lines counter at JFK with his passport and boarding pass in hand. He checked one piece of luggage but held onto his leather carry-on and herringbone cashmere topcoat. Going through customs and security was a breeze. Priority boarding allowed him to proceed directly to the aircraft.

After he stowed his things and settled into one of the first-class club chairs, a flight attendant approached him.

"How may I help you, sir?"

"What brands of Scotch do you carry?"

She recited their list.

"I'll have the MacCallan, neat, thank you."

The Scotch was smooth, soothing a lingering rough edge of concern. Twenty minutes later, lift-off was like silk. When the plane leveled at thirty thousand feet, he breathed freely.

Turning to the woman on his left, he said, "Caio, Mama. I hope your stay at the Crown Plaza was pleasant."

"Da, if you like sound of planes booming all night."

The Chief overlooked her complaint. "Everything went well? No complications?"

"What you think, Vânât? Did you forget I was one who taught you everything you know?"

"How could I? My sleight of hand will never be as slick as yours." At least that's what he always told her.

She wore pride on her face like others wore make-up. "Nu, but I could not do job without you as inside man." She cackled. "Best part for me was small spike to cousin's juice."

"How long did she stay out?"

"Long enough for much confusion."

He lowered his voice. "Where is it?"

She smirked and pulled out a black and red tapestry bag. Unzipping it, she revealed a pile of kids' costumes and accessories, all wrapped in cellophane, which he had purchased with Gracie. She pointed to one package and whispered, "Most valuable Cinderella necklace ever made. When we get to Moldova, we live like kings."

"That we will, Mama."

"Finally, that prima donna will pay for leaving me to marry such horrible man. Only two good days of marriage I had. Day you were born, and day he die."

The Chief had heard the complaint before, over and over. He hoped this act of revenge would ease the pain she'd suffered—thirty-three years with an abusive husband.

He mused about the secret kept between him and his father—the money Polina had wired them each month. Most of the funds went toward his private boarding school in England. His mother was told he'd won a scholarship. His father spent the balance on debauchery. He had threatened his son often. "If you tell that woman anything, I cut you off." Not a chance Vânât was willing to take—even for his mother.

She took an item wrapped in a dish towel out of the side pocket of her bag. "And this was meant for me. I watch my father carve every detail, waiting for birthday to come. Then he give to opera star cousin as go away gift."

"But now you have it, Mama."

His mother had eventually forgiven her father—but not Polina. She would say, "Papa's pride was at stake, and so was support from America—which she never sent. But *she* could have let me keep it."

He hoped having the treasured box would end her harping about it.

Changing the subject, he asked, "And how did you leave things with your friend, Seymour?"

"I sow big field of doubt. He thinks she is too good for him when it is other way around."

The Chief teased. "Is there a chance he might visit you in Moldova someday?" If only his mother could find a man, he'd even settle for a religious one.

"Nu. I had chance once. But when he finds out what I did," she sneered, "he and his precious God will never understand."

Working with his mother had stretched the Chief's patience. He never did like babysitting and vowed never to do it again. After this score, he wouldn't have to.

Good thing, since finding a worthwhile mark in Moldova was like fishing for tuna in the Dead Sea.

Chapter Sixty-Three

With her feelings for Ian outed by the entry in Tempie's journal, Gracie had tough choices to make. Once Ian finished fine-tuning the system he'd installed and training the security personnel on its intricacies, his time in New York would end. After years of being all wrapped in her dreams, being in love was new to her—and wouldn't be easy, especially since Ian's career goals were as strong as hers.

How could they grow their relationship hundreds of miles apart? Could she leave New York? Did she want to? How would she know what was right? Gracie needed answers. Would God supply them?

Plant yourself in a good church and grow. Her grandmother's advice stirred a hunger within her. She wanted to get to know God like Tempie and Seymour did. Maybe being in his house would help.

Gracie googled "good churches in Manhattan." Generic but to the point. At the top of the list, she was surprised to find a few of the churches she'd passed while hanging out with Harper on Broadway.

Would Ian go with her? Over the years, they'd had plenty of serious talks about God. She knew he was a believer. But church was never an option working every Sunday in the restaurant business. Then there were the other excuses she'd used—*I don't need to go to church to talk to God. I'm too busy. Don't feel like leaving the house. Besides, isn't Sunday supposed to be a day of rest?*

She texted Ian. "Hi." How could one tiny word be filled with so much emotion and so many questions?

He texted back. "Hi yourself."

She grinned and squiggled into the love seat like Leighton often did. "What are you doing this morning?"

"What did you have in mind?"

She took a deep breath then typed. "Church?"

"Aye! Tempie's dancin' in heaven!"

Her thumbs moved across the keys. "I think I found one."

"You're quick."

"God helped."

He texted. "Would you have me go with you?"

"If you want." She deleted that and typed. "I would. Meet me at Irving Plaza off Union Square at ten forty-five."

Gracie had attended Sunday services many times with her grandmother over the years. Tempie's congregation was populated by the demographics of old, really old, Cape Cod. This new church met in an old brick auditorium and was a microcosm of the city, filled with every generation and race.

The contemporary music and sound level were more than her grandmother would have ever accepted. The thirty-something minister in jeans and an untucked plaid shirt looked more like he worked in a hardware store. Yet his enthusiasm for Scripture was contagious. Gracie's faith awakened, and her hope swelled when Ian mentioned attending their midweek service.

Their plans for a quiet brunch after the service were sabotaged by a call from Reggie.

Ian kissed her. "I'm sorry. I'm Mr. Indispensable to your boss right now. And if I expect to move my business to New York soon, I'm going to need his recommendation to build my customer base."

Although her mouth was open, not a sound came out.

He removed a strand of hair caught in her lashes. "Yes, I would do that for you."

"You would?"

"Yes, because I am the perfect man."

She laughed. "Quinn, I know you well, remember?"

He opened his arms wide. "And yet you still want me. How grand is that?"

Gracie was basking in all things good when Harper called early the next morning.

"How do you feel about auditioning for a web-based miniseries this afternoon?" Harper talked fast. "Found it on Backstage.com."

"Depends. What're the details?"

"I'll read it. 'Web-based family series. G-rated. Auditions start Monday at three p.m. Stage 14, Greenpoint Ave., Brooklyn.' The roles are listed on their website."

Gracie was impressed with Harper's choice. "If it works out, I'll meet you there after I drop the kids off. And remind me to tell you my big news."

"What news?"

"When I see you." She snickered. The wait would drive Harper crazy.

On her way to the subway, Gracie called Seymour to find out how his post gala date had gone with Polina. "So, have anything to tell me about Saturday?"

He laughed. "I benefited greatly from your wiles. Polina and I had a full evening of shared history, good food, and interesting conversation. I am almost certain I was not alone in my enjoyment."

"Why are you so surprised?" She hopped onto the subway car and grabbed a handhold.

"Maybe not as surprised as inexperienced. Dating is unknown territory for me, but I find this particular terrain to my liking." He chuckled. "Do you know what Polina asked of me?"

"Not a clue."

"She wants me to teach her how to bowl! Me. Seymour Kaufman. Can you imagine?"

"Of course, I can." Gracie wanted to break out into a happy dance—but then she'd be one of those weird subway people she always talked about.

When she told him about Ian and her, his reaction was as positive as she'd hoped. "Praise God! He is a fine man."

"If that's not enough to celebrate, I'm on my way to an audition for a miniseries I feel good about."

"Perhaps it will be a double blessing. I pray God's peace will direct you."

Peace? I think he means wisdom.

Gracie told Harper about Ian—every wonderful detail.

Harper pressed her hands to her cheeks. "Oh, my! This can't be true."

"What are you trying to say?"

Harper chuckled. "We were wondering when you two would figure it out."

Gracie put her hands on her hips. "Who was wondering?"

"Uh, everyone."

Before Gracie could question her further, the assistant director began his spiel. He gave them the rehearsal and filming schedules. She was pleased they'd work easily with her nanny duties. He continued with the story synopsis and finished with a brief overview of each character and their parts.

This initial audition would be more of a read-through. Thankfully, the actors were given some time to go over their scenes. Gracie was impressed with the quality of the writing and the depth of the characters. Two principal roles were a good match for her type and skills.

While contemplating which to try out for, Seymour's chorus ran through her head. *Praise, God! He had a better plan for me!* Excitement ran full-on through her. Was this how Seymour had felt?

A few minutes later, the AD shouted, "Bellamy, Harper!"

Gracie gave her two thumbs-up, then went back to studying her potential scenes.

Out of nowhere, words from Tempie's journal popped into her head. "My Gracie has a gift with children. I only hope she gets to use it." *But I am using it as a nanny.* Gracie waved the doubt away.

Plenty of actors had started out in video and television and made it to Broadway or the big screen. She'd needed another chance, and here it was. Finally. And everything about this opportunity—the part, the story, the writing, the schedule—was right. Everything.

Then why did it feel wrong?

Stop it, Gracie. She blamed her anxiety on the audition-that-never-happened and the *Love and Waffles* fiasco. Then Miles's plea reverberated around her brain—*When we made people feel better, we felt better too. Why did we stop?*

Seymour. Tempie. Miles. What was God trying to tell her? Her stomach tightened. She had the urge to bolt. Something was missing. What was it?

Peace. I have none.

Gracie knew what she had to do.

Chapter Sixty-Four

Gracie took a few days before speaking with Reggie and Rachel about their seven-year-old's vision for a charitable foundation—not that Miles called it a *foundation*.

She drafted a mission statement, downloaded grant applications, outlined an informal business plan, created a budget and workable timeline, contacted local hospitals and social workers, and even started on a possible financial donors' list.

And she prayed—a lot. More than excited, Gracie was at peace.

Rachel and Reggie invited her to come down one evening after the children were in bed. They sat around the kitchen table over coffee while she showed them everything she'd put together.

Reggie refilled their cups. "Miles hasn't let go of the idea. We've been downplaying it so as not to get his hopes up."

Rachel read through Gracie's paperwork again. "You really think this will work?"

"I do. We're not starting some huge foundation. More of an afterschool and weekend project, which won't interfere with the children's studies. We control the time and place. He already loves to act, and Leighton can play one princess after another."

Rachel smiled. "She'd love that. And you'd be in charge?"

Gracie cleared her throat. "A-hem, we all know who'd really be in charge."

The three of them laughed.

"But I have a solution," Gracie said. "Miles can be Founder and Director, and I'll be his CFO. He has some good ideas—and not just good ideas for a child his age. He cares about these kids."

Rachel tilted her head. "How did this son of mine find the antidote for self-centeredness on center stage?"

"He's using his gifts." Gracie warmed her hands around her cup. "I promise, we'll start off slow and make it fun—for the cast and crew and the patients."

"He has to understand this is a commitment," Reggie said. "These kids being sick is bad enough without promising them a show and not following through."

"I know that, Daddy." Miles ran down the hall and skidded to a stop by his father's chair. "I won't quit, I won't."

Putting an arm around his son, Reggie asked, "How long have you been listening?"

"I couldn't sleep." Miles hiked up his super hero pajama bottoms. "Did we decide?"

Reggie nodded once to his wife, then hugged his son. "Yes. Our answer is yes."

Miles raised his arms and cheered. "Yes!"

Gracie gathered her papers. "Guess we need to hold our first staff meeting. Is Saturday good for you, Miles?"

"Is it, Mommy?"

Rachel checked her calendar. "All clear."

"Good." Miles paced back and forth. "I'll tell Zeke and Eli. Gracie, can you let Harper and Mr. Kaufman know? I don't have my own phone."

Gracie had a feeling it wouldn't be long before he did.

Rachel burst out laughing. "Make that CFO *and* his Executive Secretary."

Miles's brow puckered. "Gracie, I want to tell you something, but don't get mad."

"What is it?"

"Uh, I know Chase is your friend, and he bought all the costumes and stuff for last time, but I don't want to work with him."

"Son, what is it about Chase you don't like?" Reggie asked.

Miles shivered. "He makes me feel funny—not good funny."

Rachel deferred to Gracie. "Is this a matter to discuss at your staff meeting?"

Gracie could no longer discount Miles's feelings. "How you feel is always important enough to put on our agenda."

"One more thing," Miles said, "what's an *agenda* and how can I put it there?"

Gracie and Seymour had been summoned by Dan Favor to go over security video from the gala.

"This afternoon?" Gracie asked. "Well, Leighton has a play date, but I'll have Miles with me. Is that okay?"

"No problem. Reggie will be here too. Ms. Zelenka offered to show you the way over."

When they reached the security room, Favor, Reggie, and Ian were waiting for them. Ian jiggled his eyebrows and winked at her, making her feel all warm inside. They sat in the classroom chairs set in front of a row of monitors—Seymour next to Polina.

Favor removed his hat. "Watch the video. Maybe you'll recall someone who seemed out of place or made an impression on you. Viewing might be tedious, but we appreciate your time."

Gracie was confused. "If nothing was stolen, why are we looking?"

"The police think there may have been more professional thieves on the premises than we thought. This space is so big we still can't be sure nothing was taken." Favor nodded to Ian. "Give me three angles for now."

Ian ran early footage of the crowd outside the Met.

Gracie elbowed Seymour. "Hey, there we are."

Seymour squinted. "Where?"

Polina pointed to Seymour on the monitor. "Look at that handsome man."

Seymour's face turned the color of Polina's hot pink nail polish.

Reggie's cell rang. "Gotta take this, but keep going. I'll be back in a minute."

The soundless footage passed by. Favor was right. Viewing was tedious.

Until Miles jumped up and pointed. "There's Chase!"

"Chase in a tuxedo?" Gracie couldn't picture it. "Hardly."

Ian backed up the footage and froze the image from all three angles.

Polina leaned forward. "There's something about him. Can you zoom in?"

Ian did as she asked.

Miles chimed, "I told you it was him."

Gracie eyed Miles. "Why do you think he's Chase?"

"Hey, I remember that guy. He said something odd when I passed by." Favor tapped his forehead with the top of his fist. "What was it?"

"See." Miles put his finger on the image. "His white eyebrow like Zaide's."

Favor slapped his hat on his thigh. "Now I remember. He said 'Ciao.' Who says that anymore?"

Grace shook off her disbelief. "Chase does."

"Told you." Miles stood by Gracie. "Pro'bly, I didn't like him because he lied about spying on us."

Polina fidgeted with her collar. "That's odd. Simka's son Vânât was born with a birthmark on his brow like that. That could be his twin." She studied the monitor again. "But how could it be? He was with his aunt in Moldova." Polina wrung her hands.

Seymour covered her hands with his. "What is it?"

"There's more." Polina paused before she spoke. "When I checked Simka's room yesterday, all her belongings were gone except the clothes I bought her."

Gracie tried to ease Polina's concerns. "Perhaps she didn't feel right about taking them."

A tear trickled down Polina's cheek. "The manner in which she left them tells me plenty—torn to pieces in a heap on the closet floor. And the carved box her father gave me is missing too."

Seymour's eyes flashed like he'd made a discovery, then dimmed like he wasn't happy about it. "Oy. I may be somewhat rusty, but is not *Vânât* Romanian for *Chase*?"

Reggie returned before Polina answered.

"Daddy!" Miles yelled. "Chase was on TV!"

Gracie filled him in on the rest.

Reggie ruffled his son's unruly locks. "Nice work, son. Your intuition was right. Now, Mommy's waiting for you in the hall, but I'll see you when I get home, okay?"

Miles hugged him and left.

Reggie pulled up a chair and sat across from Polina. "That call was from the manager of Harry Winston's about the gala necklace."

Polina straightened. "Oh?"

"Perhaps you would like to fill us in, Ms. Zelenka?" Reggie said.

She hesitated. "What about the confidentiality agreement?"

"The agreement's been waived for the purpose of our investigation, but nothing will leave this room." Reggie addressed the others in the room. "Right?"

Everyone nodded.

"I was part of a conspiracy." Polina sighed. "Seymour, remember the awful rash I had the weeks before the gala?"

"What does that have to do with a conspiracy?"

"Well, I discovered I'm highly allergic to platinum. Every time I put that thing on, I broke out. The management at Winston's had a solution, but they swore me to secrecy because of the buzz about my wearing it."

Grace's forehead wrinkled. "But you *did* wear it."

"Not exactly." Polina tugged on her sleeves. "Years ago, when Harry Winston was still alive, one of his best jewelers—Oren, I think his name was—made a fabulous replica of the necklace. They use it at PR events, especially those where security is lean. That's the one I wore at the gala. No one was supposed to find out."

Reggie scratched his head. "Looks like we have a new kink in the story. When Winston's examined the piece the security guards returned, they discovered it wasn't the replica they'd lent you."

Polina tilted her head. "What do you mean?"

Gracie leaned in to get a better look at Reggie. "The necklace was the real one?"

"No," he said. "Another fake—only made with better quality materials."

Favor sat forward. "What kind of value are we talking here?"

Reggie counted on three fingers. "Real one, worth millions. New replica, crafted with higher quality materials, worth thousands. Fake one stolen—maybe a few hundred."

Favor laughed. "I take it Harry Winston's isn't that concerned about finding the thief."

Reggie grunted. "No, but we are. Someone got away with a theft—even if they took a loss."

Polina barely spoke above a whisper, "And my cousin and her son had a hand in it."

Chapter Sixty-Five

Bennett Noble's voicemail message was quite unexpected. "Noble here. I'll be at the Grove Street Starbucks in the West Village tomorrow night around eight. Meet me there?"

Meet for what? Gracie's feet were set on a new and narrow path. She didn't need any detours or distractions. Seeing him again would be nice, though. Maybe she could pick his brain about the foundation.

Noble stood when she arrived and gave her a hug. "Sit. Let's talk."

Talk about what? Now she was nervous.

"First, I had no idea Tempie was your grandmother until you sent me that stack of letters I wrote her over the years. I'm touched she kept them. Time and time again, she gave me some sage advice—and I used every bit of it."

"You never suspected she knew your full identity?"

"I should have." He tugged on his ear. "Your grandmother was a cagey one. Got me to do a lot of things I never wanted to do."

Gracie laughed. "I know what you mean."

After a pause, he became serious. "I asked you here for a reason, Grace. Would you consider playing Kat Hamilton in the next run of *Love and Waffles*?"

Gracie said a quick prayer and took a deep breath. "You make it hard for a girl to say no."

He raised his chin, staring at her from under his bushy eyebrows.

"But I'm afraid I have to. Remember *The Battle at Mount Sinai* production? We have plans for a small charitable foundation with a theater ministry for sick kids. We're working out the details."

He rested his arms on the table. "And you're committed to this venture?"

"I am."

"Are you certain?"

Why did he keep asking? "Quite."

He leaned back. "Good."

"Excuse me?"

"I heard about your foundation through the grapevine. Wanted to make sure you were committed." He reached into his pocket and pulled out an envelope. "I have a check for you, seed money for bothersome legal matters and miscellany."

Gracie was caught off guard. "Are you serious?"

"Of course," Noble said. "But I have one condition."

She didn't know if she'd like the condition. "And that is?"

"You name it the Temperance Camden Children's Foundation for the Arts."

Her hands covered her mouth, her eyes filled. "I don't know how to thank ... or what to say."

He handed her the envelope. "Yes would be suitable."

"Yes! I love the idea." Gracie's smile widened. "Now *I* have one condition."

Bennett frowned. "And that is?"

"As Tempie's granddaughter, can it be my turn to call on *you* for advice?"

He stuck out his hand. "We have a deal."

"Okay, my first question—what do you think about calling the cast and crew Tempie's Troupe?"

He slapped the table. "She would've loved it!"

Gracie caught a tear running down her cheek. "I think you're right."

Chapter Sixty-Six

Along the eastern bank of the Dniestr River, there is a small, wretched portion of Moldova called Transdniestr Moldovan Republic. Those who live and do business there pride themselves in all things illicit.

That is where the Chief and his mama went to fence their biggest take ever.

His mother introduced them to a hulk of a man behind the counter. "Simka Lonnit. This is son, Vânât." Still enclosed in the Cinderella cellophane, she proudly presented the masterpiece for his appraisal. "Handle with care," she barked, then whispered to her son. "Revenge is sweet, but money is sweeter."

They only had to wait minutes for the man to return. He grunted as he dropped the torn crinkled package on the counter. "Simka! Why do you bring junk to me?"

"What do you mean *junk*?" The Chief glared at his mother. "Mama, you said you made the switch."

"My own son questions me?" She pointed to hulk-man. "You are wrong. Examine again."

The dealer crossed his beefy, tattooed arms and growled. "You question Josif's appraisal?" Two large men emerged from the back room and stood on either side of him.

"No, no, we don't. Mama is upset, that's all. May I borrow your loupe, please?" The Chief examined the necklace for himself. "We apologize for wasting your time, Josif."

He pocketed the necklace, then took his sputtering mother by the shoulders and rotated her toward the door. "Mama, we need to go—now." He had to use his full strength to drag her out of the shop.

All the way home, she shook her fist and railed against Polina and the unscrupulous global underworld. "Someone must pay!"

Someone did pay—the Chief. His mother's anger and bitterness fueled a fire even he couldn't stamp out.

Two weeks later, the Chief—seated in coach—took a flight to Buenos Aires. Alone.

While the plane taxied to the runway, he checked his tablet for news. Two dumb faces grinned up at him—Ginger Hair and Cowboy Beaver—both holding checks. The headline read, "Hero Tipsters Collect $50 Grand Each."

Each?

About that time one of the brats behind him screamed, and the other one kicked the back of his seat.

Again.

Chapter Sixty-Seven

For Polina's first bowling lesson, Seymour found an alley with fewer neon lights and much less noise than the one he had taken Simka to in Brooklyn. One where they could actually hear the pins fall.

Testing the boundaries of fashion, he wore his Gransky's Gravediggers brown and orange bowling shirt and bright merlot Brunswick shoes. He counted on his new student's lack of pretension and sense of humor to be strong enough to take it.

He was pleased his affinity for clearing a seven-ten split had survived his hiatus from the sport. Not because of pride but because it gave Polina such joy. She jumped and clapped with his every success. Her efforts at knocking down pins would have been better if she had stood five feet from the pin deck. He wondered if she would want to return.

Polina sat to change out of her bowling shoes. "I didn't do very well, did I? My fingers kept slipping out of the holes. I might need more lessons."

If it meant spending time together, Seymour prayed she would throw one gutter ball after another. *Oh Lord, please forgive me. That was not kind.*

"Between your brises and your new theater group, will you have time?"

"I will make time." Seymour buttoned his coat.

"I keep forgetting to ask," she said, "does your group need costumes? I'm sure I could get the Met to donate some, maybe a few props too."

"They would do that?"

"When you have four or five different productions each week, many requiring hundreds of costumes, well, you do the math. And the Met prides itself on their commitment to the community, so I'm sure they'd be happy to give to a worthy cause …" She winked. "… especially if I ask them."

He was amused by her honesty.

When he reached for her rental shoes, she said, "Carrying a pair of shoes to the counter is easy." She grabbed hold of his hand. "What I need to work on is my *grip*."

Smiling, he wound his fingers through hers. "Perhaps we could do that together."

When their eyes locked, Seymour Kaufman prayed there was no key.

Chapter Sixty-Eight

Within six weeks of its first official season, Tempie's Troupe had finished its fourth performance with several more scheduled for the spring. Mount Sinai Children's Hospital was not only pleased to have them back, but they also recommended them to other children's hospitals and rehabilitation centers.

Gracie, Miles, and Harper had spent after school and weekend hours on outlining two new plays and reworking their basic production to fit the various audiences and facilities. They only had to change the title, rework a few scenes, and add more characters. Thanks to Rachel's connections, Polina's influence, and Bennett Noble's generous donation, they now had realistic scenery, lighting, a proper wardrobe, and regular musical accompaniment by Cedric Washington.

Gracie worked well with all levels of talent and no-talent. Though a challenge, she loved mentoring those God brought her way—both children and adults. If a person was healthy enough, willing to work for pennies, and had the heart to make sick kids feel better, their chances of getting chosen were excellent.

That afternoon's performance had been another blessing for everyone involved. With the patients tucked safely in their rooms and their guests long gone, Tempie's Troupe's makeshift stage was devoid of scenery, cast, and most of its crew. Gracie sat on the last trunk of props and smoothed her skirt.

Ian joined her, nudging her over. "A quarter for your thoughts?"

"A quarter?"

"Have you not heard of inflation?"

"I have." She rested her head on his shoulder. "Should I be worried?"

Ian put his arm around her. "Not a bit. The value of what you do for these children only increases."

"Think so?"

"Know so. Working with children the way you do is a gift. Hasn't anyone ever told you that?"

Gracie sighed, thinking of her grandmother's journal entry. "I think Tempie tried, but I was too star struck and obsessed with making it big as an actor."

"You're living in Manhattan, doing all the things you're gifted to do—writing, acting, working with children—and making a huge impact. I'd call that 'making it big.' Oh, and you haven't taken a selfie in over a week!"

"I'll have to fix that." Gracie put her cheek to his. "Say squeeze." Click! She snuggled into his warm arms and smiled.

Seymour was right, Lord. You had a better plan for me all along.

About the Author

Clarice G. James loves writing smart, fun, relatable contemporary women's fiction. Readers are likely to find a thread of romance, a sprinkling of humor, and/or an element of mystery throughout each story.

Manhattan Grace is her third novel. Her debut novel, *Double Header* (Mountainview Books LLC. December, 2015) was one of three winners in a Jerry Jenkins Operation First Novel contest. Her second novel, *Party of One*—a prequel to *Double Header*—was released in June, 2017, by Elk Lake Publishing, Inc.

Clarice says, "For a snapshot of my personality, keep reading."

- To me, the best part of *going* to the gym is *leaving.*
- If I ever invite you on a road trip, say no. I once got lost in a beach parking lot.

- My husband and I don't keep score in Scrabble. We're just happy we can spell.
- I'd rather shop for home goods than clothing any day.
- As a little girl, I used to soak all the family's toothbrushes in Lestoil.
- I love time alone with my grandchildren, so we can play make-believe without their parents spoiling our fun.
- My mouth kicks in before my brain because I have a sentence to compl-inish.

Clarice grew up on Cape Cod. For the last twelve years, she and her husband, David, have lived in Southern New Hampshire. Together, they have five children and ten grandchildren. She has been a grateful follower of Jesus Christ since 1980.

You can reach Clarice at cjames@claricejames.com or find her on Facebook at https://www.facebook.com/clarice.g.james. Or mail her at 3 Logan Court, Hudson, NH 03051. She'd love to hear from you.

Special Request: Now that you've read *Manhattan Grace*, Clarice would be so pleased if you'd write and post a review on www.amazon.com and www.goodreads.com. Thank you so much.

Other Books by Clarice G. James

Double Header (Mountainview Books, LLC. December, 2015): A rising Boston sports columnist fears losing the unblemished memories of her father when she learns she has a brother no one knew existed. In her search to identify this walking insult to his memory, she learns that God's playbook is less about *her* well-ordered plans and more about His.

Ask for *Double Header* at your local bookstore or go online to www.amazon.com or www.barnesandnoble.com. If you enjoyed the book, please write a review on www.amazon.com and www.goodreads.com. Thank you.

Party of One (Elk Lake Publishing, Inc. June, 2017): Risking her privacy, widow Annie McGee founds Party of One, a communal table for single diners, where she meets an electric mix of colorful characters who cause her to confront her fears, question her beliefs, doubt her self-assurance, and take another chance on love.

Ask for *Party of One* at your local bookstore or go online to www.amazon.com or www.barnesandnoble.com. If you enjoyed the book, please write a review on www.amazon.com and www.goodreads.com. Thank you.

Discussion Questions

(Includes spoilers!)

1. Can you relate to Gracie's assumptions about the path of her acting career? What "signs" and "coincidences" led her to make those assumptions?
2. Are you currently using your God-given gifts and talents in your work? Or are you still waiting in the wings off stage?
3. Have you ever assumed what the outcome of your efforts and education would be? Were you disappointed? Or were the results better than you had ever imagined?
4. Did you identify with Seymour's simple faith? Or did you think he was naïve?
5. Why do you think Seymour had such a grateful heart? Born with it? Nurtured?
6. Have you ever had a person, like Gracie's grandmother Tempie, who inspired you in your passions?
7. The Chief was a thief. What motivated him? Do you think he had a conscience or ever felt guilty?
8. Simka harbored bitterness against her cousin Polina for years. Why? What did Polina do to warrant such resentment?

9. Do you think Grace and Ian hid their feelings for one another? Or did those feelings develop over time?

10. Do you think Gracie flubbed her big chance at stardom? Or did she make the right choice?

11. What do you think happened to Simka and Vânât (the Chief) after the story's end?

12. What biblical themes or verses came to mind when you read this book?

Author Events

Meeting my readers and other aspiring writers at my various events is such a pleasure. Check my website https://claricejames.com/author-events to see where I'll be next.

If you or your group would like to host an author event, these types of venues are an ideal fit:

- **Book Clubs**: If you're in my area of the country and your book club selects one of my books, I can join you to discuss it—either on video chat or in person.
- **Bookstores**: I love to support small, locally-owned bookstores.
- **Cafés & Coffee Houses**: Chatting about books is always better over coffee.
- **Family-style Restaurants**: I'll be happy to set up a table in a private room, a corner, or the foyer.
- **Ladies Church Groups**: My books, *Party of One, Double Header,* and *Manhattan Grace* are written from a female perspective with women readers in mind. Themes include forgiveness, grief, loneliness, surrender, and discerning God's purpose for your life. I'd be pleased to speak on those topics.
- **Libraries**: Looking for an author event for your library? My author friends and I have done this before. (See Christian Author Round Table Talks below.)

- **Private Author-in-the-House Parties** (Invitation-Only): Author-in-the-House home parties (local to me) are fun and more personal. This venue gives readers and authors the chance to get to know one another better.

If you're in the New England area, I'd love to meet you at one of the interactive **Christian Author Round Table Talks** for new or pre-published writers. Attendees are encouraged to come armed with curiosity and questions for our panel of authors! Here are just some of the topics we cover:

- Step by step guide through the writing and publishing processes
- Finding the right kind of agent, editor, and publisher
- Things to do before you submit a manuscript to an agent or publisher
- What to include in a book proposal
- Pros of both self-publishing and traditional publishing

I'd love to hear from you. Email me at cjames@claricejames.com. Thank you.

Glossary of Foreign Words

Hebrew and Yiddish

- *azoy*: Is that so? Really?
- *aleikhem shalom* or *shalom aleikhem*: peace be upon you or unto you peace
- *bar mitzvah*: the religious initiation ceremony of a Jewish boy who has reached the age of 13 and is regarded as ready to observe religious precepts and eligible to take part in public worship
- *baruch ha-ba*: Blessed is he who comes in the name of the Lord.
- *bris*: the Jewish ceremony of circumcision
- *bubbe*: grandmother
- *chutzpah*: shameless audacity, boldness
- *ershter das ershter*: first things first
- *fershtay*: Do you understand?
- *gefilte fish*: a dish made from a poached mixture of ground deboned fish
- *hora*: a Romanian or Israeli dance in which the performers form a ring
- *kishke*: a beef intestine stuffed with a seasoned filling
- *latkes*: potato pancakes
- *mensch*: a person of integrity and honor

- *mitzvah*: a precept or commandment or a good deed done from a religious duty
- *mohel*: a Jew trained in the practice of brit milah, the "covenant of circumcision"
- *mazel tov*: a Jewish phrase expressing congratulations or wishing someone good luck
- *oy vey*: an interjection indicating dismay or grief
- *sandek*: person who has the honor of holding the eight-day-old baby during circumcision
- *shtick*: gimmick, style
- *seudate mitzvah*: an obligatory festive meal, usually referring to the celebratory meal following the fulfillment of a mitzvah (commandment), such as a bar mitzvah, a wedding, or a brit milah (ritual circumcision)
- *shalom*: hello, good-bye, peace
- *sheynem dank*: thank you very much
- *Yeshua*: Yeshua is the Hebrew name, and its English spelling is "Joshua." Iesous is the Greek transliteration of the Hebrew name, and its English spelling is "Jesus."
- *zaide*: grandfather
- *zhlub*: a coarse person; a boorish man; jerk, slob

Irish

- *amn't*: am not
- *eejit*: Irish and Scottish form of idiot.

Latin

- *nihil*: nothing

Moldovan and Romanian

- *ajuta-ma*: help me
- *borş de burechiuşe*: a soup native to Moldova, made with ravioli-like squares filled with mushrooms
- *colier*: necklace
- *coridor*: corridor, hallway
- *da*: yes
- *ghiveci*: Romanian vegetable stew
- *intra*: enter
- *mulţumiri*: thank you
- *pa pa*: bye bye
- *sarmale*: cabbage rolls
- *şi tu*: and you
- *smântână*: sour cream
- *un toast pentru familia şi noi prieteni*: A toast to family and new friends

Russian:

- *izvinite*: excuse me, sorry

Spanish

- *lo entiendes*: you understand
- *nada*: nothing
- *sí*: yes

References & Resources

(By genre, in order of appearance)

Bible: New King James Version. Copyright © 1982 by Thomas Nelson.

Ch 49: Psalms 16:8-11
Ch 49: Matthew 10:42
Ch 54: Matthew 6:28
Ch 55: 1 Peter 4:10

Books

Ch 1: *How the Grinch Stole Christmas*, Author Dr. Seuss, Random House Books for Young Readers, 1957

Movies

Ch 1: *Toy Story 2*. Directors John Lasseter, Ash Brandon, and Lee Unkrich, produced by Pixar Animation Studios and Walt Disney Pictures, 1999, Emeryville, CA

Ch 1: *The Ten Commandments*. Director Cecil B. de Mille, produced by Cecil B. de Mille Production and Paramount Pictures, 1956, Egypt, Mount Sinai, and the Sinai Peninsula.

Ch 1: *Frozen*. Directors Chris Buck and Jennifer Lee, produced by Peter Del Vecho, Walt Disney Pictures, Walt Disney Animation Studios, 2013, Burbank, CA

Ch 1: *Monsters, Inc.* Director Pete Docter, produced by Darla K. Anderson, Walt Disney Pictures, and Pixar Animation Studios, 2001, Burbank, CA

Ch 4: *Roman Holiday.* Director William Wyler, produced by William Wyler, Paramount Pictures, 1953, Hollywood, CA

Ch 4: *Breakfast at Tiffany's.* Director Blake Edwards, produced by Martin Jurow and Richard Shepherd, Paramount Pictures, 1961, Hollywood, CA

Ch 8: *Beauty and the Beast.* Directors Gary Trousdale and Kirk Wise, produced by Don Hahn, Walt Disney Pictures, Walt Disney Feature Animation, and Silver Screen Partners, 1991, Burbank, CA

Ch 44: *Men in Black.* Director Barry Sonnenfeld, produced by Walter F. Parkes and Laurie MacDonald, Amblin Entertainments, Parkes/MacDonald Productions, and Columbia Pictures, 1997, Universal City, CA

Ch 45: *Sabrina.* Director Billy Wilder, produced by Billy Wilder, Paramount Pictures, 1954, Hollywood, CA

Ch 47: *Guess Who's Coming to Dinner.* Director Stanley Kramer, produced by Stanley Kramer, Columbia Pictures, 1967, Hollywood, CA

Ch 49: *Holiday in Mexico.* Director George Sidney, produced by Metro-Goldwyn Mayer (MGM), 1946, Culver City, CA

Operas

Ch 21: *The Phantom of the Opera.* Composer Andrew Lloyd Webber, 1986

Ch 57: *Le nozze di Figaro* (*The Marriage of Figaro*). Composer Wolfgang Amadeus Mozart, 1786

Ch 57: *Rusalka.* Composer Antonin Dvořák, 1900

Ch 57: *Manon.* Composer Jules Massenet, 1882

Plays

Ch 1: *The Miracle Worker.* Playwright William Gibson, 1957

Ch 1: *Love and Waffles* is a fictitious title

Ch 1: *Pirates of the Maccabeans* is a fictitious title

Ch 4: *Powerless to Pump* is a fictitious title

Ch 8: *Little Black Lies* is a fictitious title

Ch 13: *Romeo and Juliet.* Playwright William Shakespeare, 1597

Ch 16: *Slick, Panacea,* and *Children of Duluth* are fictitious titles

Ch 17: *As You Like It.* Playwright William Shakespeare, 1599

Ch 17: *Bears Don't Cry* is a fictitious title

Ch 19: *Fiddler on the Roof.* Music by Jerry Bock, lyrics by Sheldon Harnick, and book by Joseph Stein, 1964

Ch 20: *Waiting for Godot.* Playwright Samuel Beckett, 1953

Ch 24: *The Battle at Mount Sinai* is a fictitious title

Ch 27: *The King and I.* Lyrics by Oscar Hammerstein II, music by Richard Rodgers, 1951

Ch 33: *Mile Marker 4* is a fictitious title

Ch 33: *Barefoot in the Park.* Playwright Neil Simon, 1963

Songs

Ch 19: "If I Were a Rich Man" from *Fiddler on the Roof.* Music by Jerry Bock, lyrics by Sheldon Harnick, book by Joseph Stein, 1964

Ch 27: "Marry You." Music and lyrics by Ari Levine, Bruno Mars, and Philip Lawrence, produced by Sony/ATV Music Publishing LLC, Warner/Chappell Music, Inc, Round Hill Music Big Loud Songs, BMG Rights Management US, LLC, 2010

Ch 49: "Good Night Sweetheart." Music and lyrics by Calvin Carter and James "Pookie" Hudson, 1953

Ch 57: "Matchmaker" from *Fiddler on the Roof.* Music by Jerry Bock, lyrics by Sheldon Harnick, book by Joseph Stein, 1964

Television Shows

Ch 1: *It's the Great Pumpkin, Charlie Brown.* Based on comic strip Peanuts by Charles Schultz. Directed by Bill Melendez, 1966

Ch 10: *Hear It Here First* is a fictitious title

Made in the USA
Columbia, SC
04 June 2018